MEET ME BY THE CLOCK

JO LOVETT

To Laura

Hope you enjoy and thank you for reading!

Jo xx

B
Boldwood

First published in Great Britain in 2025 by Boldwood Books Ltd.

Copyright © Jo Lovett, 2025

Cover Design by Head Design Ltd.

Cover Images: Shutterstock

The moral right of Jo Lovett to be identified as the author of this work has been asserted in accordance with the Copyright, Designs and Patents Act 1988.

All rights reserved. No part of this book may be reproduced in any form or by any electronic or mechanical means, including information storage and retrieval systems, without written permission from the author, except for the use of brief quotations in a book review. This book is a work of fiction and, except in the case of historical fact, any resemblance to actual persons, living or dead, is purely coincidental.

Every effort has been made to obtain the necessary permissions with reference to copyright material, both illustrative and quoted. We apologise for any omissions in this respect and will be pleased to make the appropriate acknowledgements in any future edition.

A CIP catalogue record for this book is available from the British Library.

Paperback ISBN 978-1-83656-117-0

Large Print ISBN 978-1-83656-116-3

Hardback ISBN 978-1-83656-115-6

Ebook ISBN 978-1-83656-118-7

Kindle ISBN 978-1-83656-119-4

Audio CD ISBN 978-1-83656-110-1

MP3 CD ISBN 978-1-83656-111-8

Digital audio download ISBN 978-1-83656-114-9

This book is printed on certified sustainable paper. Boldwood Books is dedicated to putting sustainability at the heart of our business. For more information please visit https://www.boldwoodbooks.com/about-us/sustainability/

Boldwood Books Ltd, 23 Bowerdean Street, London, SW6 3TN

www.boldwoodbooks.com

Za Sofyju

To Sophia

1

NADIA

In hindsight, Waterloo station wasn't the best place to choose to meet my blind date this evening.

I'm not sure why I didn't realise how rammed it would be; it's famously a very busy station, and a lot of people like to go out in town on sunny summer Saturdays. I hope Dougie (my date) and I are going to manage to spot each other amidst all the people swarming around.

My phone's buzzing away like nobody's business as I make my way over to our agreed meeting place – under the big station clock – at what I hope is the perfect speed to impress Dougie if he's watching. I don't want to be walking too fast (I don't want to look overkeen) or too slowly (I don't want to look nervous, although I *am* a bit nervous because I do not have the best track record with first dates). Maybe I should have worn a less bright dress and not told him what I'd be wearing, so I could have arrived a bit more anonymously; it feels weird going across the concourse like I'm on display.

Okay, no, it isn't weird. I am just walking across Waterloo station, like I often do, no biggie. I just happen to be on my seventh first date of the year (and it's still June) and the others have been *spectacular* disasters, but it's going to be absolutely fine.

My phone buzzes again, for what must be at least the twentieth time in the past ten minutes, and I stop for a moment to take it out of my bag, suddenly worried that it's Dougie himself, calling the date off.

No, it's fine, it's two chats: my work girlfriends about a midweek cinema trip; and my best friend, Gina. Gina, who is not an anxious person, has sent me eleven messages in the past fifteen minutes, all to the effect of: *Do not forget I can emergency-call you or call the police (not to be too OTT) if things get tricky – just message me.*

Hmm. I am now feeling a tiny bit anxious myself if I'm honest.

But, no, it *will* be fine. We're meeting in the middle of a busy station concourse and going for a drink at a busy local bar. All very safe. And I'm sure Dougie will be lovely. He's a friend of an acquaintance; of course he won't try anything dodgy. And if he isn't lovely, I can easily leave.

Also, I'm dressed for success, which is not to be sneezed at; it does actually work. I'm wearing my most flattering fit-and-flare dress, in a coral shade of red that I love, my favourite (incredibly comfortable) wedge heels and my swear-by scarlet lipstick.

Seventh time lucky. It's bound to be. Definitely.

* * *

As I get closer to the clock, I (obviously) begin to study the men already standing under it and those approaching it.

Dougie is Sammy-from-IT's flatmate. According to Sammy, Dougie is 'tall, average-build, blond and not bad-looking' and 'the perfect match' for me. I'm not *totally* convinced because Sammy does not actually really know me, and my initial reaction to his suggestion was no, certainly not. But then my colleague and very good friend Marisa pointed out that five out of my last six first dates have been via online dating (the other one was from an in-person speed-dating thing; I will *never* do that again) and persuaded me that maybe being set up by a mutual friend is the way forward (I'd definitely call Sammy more of an acquaintance than a friend but never mind).

I can't see any men of Dougie's description in the vicinity. There's a shorter blond man. There's a shorter man with very dark hair. And there's a tall man with mid-brown hair with his back to me. Hmm. I don't think any of these men are Dougie.

It's okay, though; it's still only two minutes past seven. He's probably just slightly late. Well, almost exactly on time, in fact, if he arrives soon. Sammy catches the Northern line to work, so I'm guessing that's how Dougie will be getting here, and no-one can ever predict exactly how long a Tube journey's going to take. He's probably just been delayed. Or maybe he's one of those people who's *always* slightly late. There's every chance that he's truly perfect for me and is in fact the future father of my adorable twin children and is rushing here now and we will reminisce in years to come about his cute-and-hardly-ever-annoying innate slight-lateness. Or alternatively... he's...

Oh! A woman right underneath the clock, a few feet ahead of me, has just screamed, 'You bastard,' at the man next to her. And now she's in floods of tears. He's shaking his head and looking pretty tearful himself. I'd guess they're a few years younger than my parents and they both look *stricken*.

It's horrible seeing two people so visibly upset and I whip my head away from them, hoping that I haven't been staring.

My eyes alight on two elderly women standing facing each

other, holding hands. They've both got moist eyes too, except their tears are accompanied by smiles and what sound like endearments. I'm smiling too, I realise, just looking at them. And possibly staring again.

Okay. I don't want to be voyeuristic; I don't want to intrude into either the sadness or the happiness of the personal moments of complete strangers. I'm going to stay here, a few feet away from the clock, so I'm not too close to either couple, and I'm going to look at the floor. Or maybe over at the Boots or the M&S food store I can see. Or maybe up towards the clock.

Hmm. The clock tells me that it is now eight minutes past seven.

I look around. There are no tall, blond men anywhere in sight.

The tall man with mid-brown hair who still has his back to me *could* perhaps at a push be described as vaguely blond, except his stance tells me that he's looking into the distance, so I'm guessing he's waiting for someone coming from one of the platforms in the opposite direction from where I came. Plus, he did do a slow three-sixty as I was approaching and if he'd been looking out for red he'd definitely have seen me. It really doesn't seem likely that he's Dougie.

I haven't yet been stood up on any of my dates but I do not have a good feeling about this.

I wonder how long I should wait. Also, given that Dougie is a friend of a friend, I feel that, if I leave on the assumption that he isn't going to turn up, it would be polite to let him know that I've gone. Just in case he does eventually make it.

But how should I word it?

Hi, it seems pretty obvious you've stood me up but I'm just letting you know that I'm going now, just on the off chance that you in fact got legitimately held up? No.

Hello, you arse, thanks a lot for standing me up? No.

Hi Dougie, I'm sure you had an excellent reason for not coming and I totally understand that, but I'm a busy woman so I'm off? Still no.

I really don't think he's coming.

I don't know Sammy well but I do know that he's very gossipy. I am really not looking forward to the whole office knowing that his flatmate stood me up. *After* he'd seen a photo of me and heard Sammy's description of me. And quite possibly seen me and then scarpered.

I think I'm going to message Dougie to say that I arrived (just in case he's seen me) but have had to leave due to a family emergency and I'm so sorry that I can't wait to apologise in person. Yes, that's perfect. I'm already cheering up, actually; I didn't really *want* to go on a blind date this evening if I'm honest.

After this, I think I'll give dating a rest for a bit. And then, when I'm ready to go again, I'm sure it will be eighth time lucky.

Okay. Just in case meeting Dougie *would* be seventh time lucky and he *has* been legitimately held up, and given that we were introduced by Sammy rather than a dating app, I'm going to give it until seven thirty before I leave. Just in case.

2

TOM

I know it's ridiculous but I'm beginning to worry slightly that Lola isn't going to turn up this evening. I mean, I know she is, because she's the one who instigated this and it was only three days ago when she messaged, and she was very precise about where she'd be coming from, where we should meet, everything. It's a little odd that she isn't here already, though.

Rationally, her train's probably delayed, British Rail being what it is.

What time is it, though? We definitely agreed to meet at seven. I'm surprised she hasn't messaged me to let me know she's running late.

I walk backwards to look up at the clock and, bugger... I've crashed into someone.

I hear a piercing scream (basically a very loud *Gaaaaah*) and get an impression of a lot of red clothing topped off by a lot of dark brown curly hair before I put my arm out and catch her (it turns out that the person I've nearly taken out is a medium-heighted woman).

'I'm so sorry,' I tell her. 'Should have looked where I was

going.' I'm surprised I didn't see her somehow in my peripheral vision; the dress she's wearing is *bright*.

'Oh, no, don't worry. It's easily done. Honestly.'

I hope she isn't just being polite. I have a nasty feeling that I might have crushed one of her feet beneath mine.

'Are you...' I begin to ask before I'm interrupted by an incredibly loud Tannoy announcement.

'What?' The woman frowns. I'm frowning too. 'What did they say? Lockdown? As in... what?'

'No bloody way,' screeches the middle-aged woman to my right, whose truly vicious argument I've been trying to ignore for the past few minutes. 'No way am I staying here with you,' she yells at the man she's been arguing with. 'That's life taking the piss one step too far.'

'I think you're going to have to stay, Carole,' the man tells her. 'We don't have to speak to each other.' He sounds quite hopeful.

'Too right I won't be speaking to you,' yells Carole. 'I'm going.'

The announcer informs us all again at very high volume through the Tannoy that we all need to stay exactly where we are for the time being and that all the station exits to the streets and Tube and Waterloo East mainline station have been closed.

I look around. The concourse is full of people – in ones and twos and larger groups – in various states of confusion, disbelief, irritation. Close to me, under the clock, there's the woman in red, Carole and her arguing partner, and two elderly women, who've been holding hands and beaming at each other since I got here.

The announcement starts again. No-one's really moving. It's actually quite hard to believe that this is happening but the gist of what they're saying seems to be that there's a suspected terrorist incident unfolding outside the station and that we're locked down inside. We must stay where we are for the time being until they've completed preliminary investigations and then it's possible that we will be asked to move.

'I don't want to worry you, but—' the woman in red's semi-whispering, like she even less wants to worry anyone else '—do you think they're telling us to stay exactly where we are because they think there could be a terrorist *inside* here with us?'

'Erm. No?' I reply cautiously, thinking *Fuck, maybe she's right. And oh my God, where's Lola? She must have been caught up in this.* And then I think, no, of course the woman isn't right. That would just be a monumental cock-up on the part of the police. They must have better information than that. I hope. 'No,' I state firmly. 'If there were a terrorist inside with us, they'd be moving us to shelter, wouldn't they, not leaving us here like sitting ducks.'

I say, 'Excuse me,' pull out my phone and try calling Lola. There's a ringtone, but she doesn't pick up, so I send her a quick message telling her that I'm already under the clock.

As I type, Carole screeches, 'Sitting ducks. Oh, God.'

Yep, I could probably have used a better expression.

'*Not* sitting ducks,' I say loudly. 'Very safe. Very, very safe.' I don't feel that anyone is going to benefit from Carole or anyone else getting too panicked. Obviously, I am myself panicking a little, about Lola, but, being rational, it would be incredibly unlucky for her to have been caught up in this and injured in any way. She's probably just somewhere on the other side of the concourse, or stuck on a train just outside the station. There are probably a million good reasons she hasn't picked up my message.

'Exactly,' agrees the woman in red. 'We're all going to be completely fine.' She waves her phone at us and then scrolls.

'Nothing on here. Social media, BBC News, nothing. If anyone had been injured so far there'd already be stuff about it online. We're going to be *fine*.'

'Really?' Carole's still operating at very high volume.

'Definitely,' the woman in red says. 'I mean, this is Waterloo station. They must have practised this loads of times. Obviously. All big stations must have done.'

'That is probably true,' concedes Carole.

'So we should all stay calm and do exactly what we're told,' says Carole's partner.

'Fuck off, Roger,' Carole tells him.

A muffled choking sound like a swallowed gasp of shocked laughter comes from the direction of the woman in red, and then to my admiration she steps into the breach and says to the rest of us, 'I think we might be stuck here together for a while. I'm Nadia.'

Carole and Roger stare at her.

The elderly women stare at her.

I take pity on her.

'I'm Tom,' I announce. 'I hope your foot's okay. I think I trod on it very hard just now.' She looked as though she might be hobbling.

'I mean, I'm pretty sure you broke my foot but other than that I'm okay.' She remains completely straight-faced for a moment, and then she grins at me. 'Joking. Totally fine. Honestly.'

'Ha.' I laugh politely. 'You got me there for a moment. I'm glad you're okay.'

'I'm Bea.' The taller of the two elderly women has released her companion and is holding her hand out, and Nadia and I both shake it.

After some hesitation, Roger shakes her hand too, and eventually so does Carole.

'And I'm Ruth,' the shorter elderly woman joins in. We shake hands with her too.

'Roger,' says Roger, and then he sticks his hand out, and Bea, Ruth, Nadia and I all politely pretend that we didn't already know his name.

And then Carole says, 'I'm Carole,' and we pretend again.

And then we all stare at each other for a few seconds, before Nadia says, 'Well this is a bit of a shock, isn't it.'

'It is, rather,' Bea agrees. And then, as though the words won't stay inside her, she says, 'I'm so sorry, I appreciate that this isn't exactly the best timing for a happy announcement and that we're all complete strangers, but I just have to tell someone: after decades of being apart for various reasons, Ruth and I have just got engaged.'

Ruth nods, beaming and looking a touch tearful, and they slide an arm each around the other's waist.

'Oh my goodness, that's wonderful news,' says Nadia. 'I'm so pleased for you. Congratulations.'

'Yes, huge congratulations,' I say.

There's a bit of a loud silence from where Roger and Carole are standing, both very rigid, about a metre apart from each other, and then Roger says, 'Great news. Congratulations,' and then Carole adds, 'How lovely.' Both of them sound very flat, but at a guess, they've just split up, possibly due to something Roger's done, going by the yelling Carole was doing before the loudspeaker announcement, and they probably aren't totally up for celebrating other people's news.

A few awkward seconds pass, and then Nadia says, 'I'm so happy for you. When did you first meet?'

I check my phone quickly as Bea says, '*Well*,' like she's about to start a long story.

There's no update on any news channel, and there's no reply from Lola. I try calling her again, and again she doesn't pick up.

'Are you alright?' Ruth asks me.

'Yes, no, I mean, yes. I was just checking on a... friend I was supposed to be meeting.'

'Oh, I'm so sorry,' Bea says quickly. 'I was being hugely insensitive. You must be very worried. I'm sure, though, that they're absolutely fine. What time were you supposed to be meeting?'

'Seven.'

We all, as one, look up at the clock. It's almost seven thirty now.

'They were probably held up by this incident,' Ruth says.

'Yeah.' I nod. Rationally, that is true. But why isn't Lola answering her phone?

'I'm *sure* they're alright,' Ruth says. 'Were you also...?' she probes delicately in Nadia's direction.

'Yes, but, you know, I...' Nadia looks round the circle that we've more or less formed ourselves into. 'It was a blind date. And I wasn't totally sure about it. And if I'm honest, I don't think he was going to turn up anyway. So really don't worry about me. And I'm really not worried about *him*; I'm sure he isn't involved in the incident. Well, I hope he isn't. No, I'm sure he isn't.'

We all mumble that we're sure Nadia's possible-blind-date is absolutely fine, especially since there's still no news of any casualties of any kind, while obviously not wanting to agree with her that – given how late he already was – he was probably not going to turn up, because it never makes anyone feel good to be stood up. It's odd, actually, because Nadia's very attractive-looking and on first meeting seems very nice, so why would a blind date not turn up? Saying that, people do get cold feet. And who knows how anyone comes across on a dating app or however they got in touch.

'Yeah, no, honestly, it's fine.' She clearly wishes we would all shut up, and fair enough. 'Bea, you were in the middle of telling us about how you and Ruth met.'

'Oh, yes, well, I'm not sure...'

'I'd love to hear the story,' Nadia says.

Roger and I agree that we would too. Carole seems to be having a bit of a silent strop, and who can blame her if this really is a break-up based on something Roger's done.

'Our relationship goes back nearly sixty years. We... Actually, maybe you should tell it, Ruth.' Bea looks lovingly at her.

I can't help wondering if this is kind of how Lola and I will be once we actually find each other tonight. Obviously, since we're thirty-five, we do not have a sixty-year relationship, but ten years of mutually thinking about each other on and off (and in my case experiencing a failed marriage during that time) and then getting back together – tonight – is pretty impressive.

'Let's *both* tell it.' There's something very endearing about Ruth. 'We first met at university when we were eighteen. And we became very close friends, but, well, speaking for myself, I'm not sure I even understood my feelings then. Things were very different in those days. And we both ended up in relationships with men.' She pauses and looks at Bea.

'Yes. And to give my husband his due,' Bea says, 'he was a good man and I did love him.'

'And neither of us can ever regret our marriages, because we both have children,' Ruth adds.

'Exactly,' Bea agrees. 'We obviously both love our children immensely. I have three daughters and Ruth has two sons. All in their forties now.'

'But, something was missing. Sexually. And we've found it.' Ruth does a *very* dirty laugh, which makes all the rest of us laugh, which is impressive, because I'm internally worrying about Lola every few seconds and Carole's still shooting homicidal looks at Roger pretty regularly.

'If it isn't too indelicate a question,' Nadia asks delicately, 'how *did* you find it?'

'You want the sexual *details*?' Ruth asks.

'No, no, no!' Nadia squeaks. 'I meant how did you find each other again?'

Bea sniggers and then says, 'We'd stayed in touch over the years and we ended up at the same barbecue recently, and talked late into the night. And then Ruth...'

'Thought to myself I've just turned seventy-six and I'd realised in recent years that I'm a lesbian and that Bea was the great love of my life and I just suddenly decided that I wanted to give it a shot.'

'So she told me.'

'And then we kissed. And it was wonderful.' Ruth's all misty-eyed and it *is* beautiful. And I can't stop thinking about Lola and hoping that she's alright.

'And then we both had family commitments and had to leave, and we agreed to meet here, this evening.'

'And when we got here...' Ruth pauses and looks up at Bea, and then they relink hands and squeeze.

'Ruth proposed. And I said yes.' Bea looks tearful in a happy way.

I congratulate them again and think about Lola as Nadia says, 'Oh, that's so, so wonderful. I'm so happy for you.'

Roger shifts around a bit where he's standing and then says, 'Good on you.'

Carole says, 'Congratulations.' And then she suddenly

changes the subject. 'Well, we're stuck here, aren't we. Why don't we do this too, Roger? Tell them our news?'

Roger shifts some more. 'I don't think...'

'Don't you? Oh, I do, actually.' Carole stands straighter and looks ahead of her as though she's addressing a large room of conference delegates. 'Roger and I got married twenty-eight years ago today. As in, today is our wedding anniversary. We arranged to meet here, under the clock, to go for a special dinner. Roger got here early. *And so did I.* From the opposite direction. Sad old loser that I am, I tiptoed up behind him to surprise him with a hug and a kiss. And it turned out that he was on the phone. Talking very sexually, shall we say. Would anyone like to guess who he was on the phone *to*?'

We all shake our heads mutely. This is awful but I don't have the words to halt it, and apparently the others don't either. And maybe Carole needs this, so maybe we shouldn't try to stop her, anyway.

'Roger, would you like to tell them?'

Roger mutters that he wouldn't and do we really need to do this.

'He was on the phone to my best friend,' Carole informs us, very loudly and very clearly. 'Such a cliché. Apparently they've been having an affair.'

Roger suddenly finds his voice. 'In my defence, you've been working very long hours and she was *there*.'

We all stare, wide-eyed, as Carole replies, 'I've been working hard to fund *our* lives. Remember how we had to have a nanny because you were too busy playing golf to look after our children? And shagging Samantha too, obviously.'

'Yes, well, I've said I'm sorry.'

'Oh well that's alright then.' There's a long, nasty, nasty pause, and then Carole suddenly bursts into huge, wracking sobs. Nadia and Ruth shake off their horror-struck musical-statue look and converge on her and hug her.

'You absolute tosser,' says Bea. There's something very powerful about swearing from someone of a generation that doesn't swear as much as subsequent generations do. Also, she isn't wrong. What an arse.

'In your defence?' joins in Nadia. 'Really?'

'My husband worked very long hours,' says Bea. 'And I hadn't been attracted to him for years. And I did not play away.'

'Well now I *do* still find Carole attractive.' Roger says it like he's paying her an actual compliment.

Carole lifts her head from Bea's shoulder to say, 'Oh, fuck off.'

'Carole, I'm so deeply sorry.' The words feel so inadequate but I want her to know how much I feel for her, how much any right-thinking person would.

'Er, solidarity?' Roger gives me a despising you're-letting-down-the-brethren look. I ignore him.

Ruth hugs Carole more tightly. 'Carole, would you prefer to continue to discuss this with Roger or perhaps stay here with us and ask him to take a few steps away?'

'Away.'

I look at Roger and indicate with my head that he might like to move a few steps to his left.

He shakes his head and pulls a small box out of his pocket. 'Carole, I bought you an anniversary present.' He opens it and tries to show it to her. 'Earrings, look.'

'Give them to Samantha,' Carole says, very quietly and quite magnificently.

Roger looks genuinely confused. 'But her ears aren't pierced.'

As the rest of us draw Carole away from him and turn our

backs, I see that Nadia has one arm round Carole's shoulders and her free hand clamped over her mouth and am pretty sure that, like me, she's almost laughing in shock at Roger's incredible behaviour but very aware that she cannot actually allow a laugh to escape.

'Carole, I am so deeply sorry,' says Ruth. 'We'd like to keep you company if we may. I promise we won't talk about our engagement again.'

'No, please do.' Carole sniffs. 'I'm happy for you. I'd like to be distracted by nice things before I think about sorting out the shit show that's my life. Divorce. I'll have to fucking pay him alimony, I'm guessing.'

'One of my sons is a divorce lawyer,' says Ruth. 'Ferocious, apparently. We'll get him involved.'

'Thank you.' Carole manages to smile a little. Then she physically shakes herself and says, 'Tell me more about your children.'

'Well.' Ruth launches into a description about the lawyer and her other son (a doctor) and the three other women listen to her, interjecting sometimes, while I surreptitiously check my phone to see if Lola's been in touch. Nope. Nothing.

There's still no real update on social media or the news outlets about what's going on here, either.

I try hard to focus on the conversation, which has now moved on to include stories from Carole and Bea about their adult children, rather than spiralling into extreme panic about Lola.

We met ten years ago at a party in a pub outside Waterloo and just had an incredible connection. Nothing happened between us because I was about to move to New York for an amazing work opportunity and Lola was in a relationship (it turned out). She told me at the end of the evening, on our way into the station, that she was actually twelve weeks pregnant, and for that reason didn't want to leave her partner, which I obviously totally understood.

We did swap numbers and made one of those straight-out-of-a-corny-film agreements – which you don't think real people would ever make – that if we were both single in ten years' time we'd meet here at Waterloo under the clock tonight, on the longest night of the year, ten years on.

I actually deleted her number a couple of days after that meeting because I just felt grubby thinking about someone who had a partner and was having a baby with him, and put her out of my mind, and managed not to think about her much after that, other than on the occasions I walked past the pub where we'd met.

And then, three days ago, I got a text from her asking if I was still single. I *am* officially single, as of about nine months ago. And apparently so is she now.

And so we agreed to meet. And if I'm honest, I've been *really* excited about it.

And it seems inconceivable that she would contact me out of the blue, send all the messages she sent, and then not turn up.

And for that reason, worry is clawing away at me now.

Nadia breaks into my thoughts. 'Honestly, Tom, I'm sure your friend is okay. British Rail being what it is, they were probably just delayed, and then got caught up in all of this.'

'No replies to any of my messages, though?'

'There are *so* many rational explanations for that,' Nadia says. 'Lost the phone. Stuck in an underground station somewhere due to all of this. Out of data. To name but three.' She has the air of a woman who could name about fifty possible explanations but has suddenly realised that it might seem insensitive to turn my worry into a guessing game.

'Yes, there are,' says Ruth firmly. 'Why don't you tell us about your friend? If you'd like to? Please don't feel you *have* to, of course.'

And then I find myself doing exactly what Bea and Ruth and Carole did: I find myself seduced into that splurge-your-secrets-to-strangers-who-have-just-become-your-new-best-friends thing.

'Her name is Lola,' I begin.

3

NADIA

As Tom fills us in on his very romantic ten-year wait for Lola, I can't decide whether I'm worried that something bad *has* happened to her (that would be such terrible timing for them both) or whether, yes, she's just stuck underground due to all of this (although she would already have been several minutes late before the alert happened) or whether, maybe, she got cold feet. We're heading towards quarter to eight now, and you would really think that she could have got in touch with him if she wanted to.

Maybe I'm just being negative, though, because of Dougie's blatant no-show.

I wonder, actually, whether I should let him know that I'm okay.

I murmur an apology and pull out my phone to send a message to him, but then realise that, no, if he's nowhere near the station because he never came at all (highly likely), it's far too embarrassing. And if he's nearby, he'll know that there's no panic going on and everyone seems fine and that nothing bad will have happened to me.

Yeah, no, I'm not sending him a message.

'She's tall and slim, with long, straight, blonde hair, and very beautiful, but most of all funny, kind and amazing company, just an all-round wonderful person,' Tom's saying.

Our chorus of *Aw* is interrupted by an announcement over the loudspeaker.

'False alarm?' Ruth says, when it's finished. 'All free to go?'

'Except, any excuse for a train delay, so we won't be *able* to leave.' Roger has reappeared.

Carole has been looking almost cheery, but she immediately tenses.

'Roger. Please leave us,' says Bea.

'Don't come back to the house tonight,' Carole says.

'Well, where am I going to stay?'

'Samantha's?' Carole suggests sarkily.

Roger begins to speak and Carole says, 'No. Enough.'

'Could I make a suggestion?' Bea asks. 'Perhaps, while all the train delays die down, the five of us could go somewhere together? Continue talking, Carole? About whatever you like. You might perhaps even like to stay with one of us tonight? We could go somewhere local, Tom, in case you make contact with Lola.'

'I'd like that,' Carole says decisively.

'I would too.' I mean it. I instinctively really like this little group of people and somehow it feels as though we've formed a bond. I'd love to talk more to them. Plus, I am of course all dressed up and I'd rather not have nowhere to go.

'That would be great, actually.' Tom shoves his phone back in his pocket, clearly still not having received any kind of response from Lola. Presumably he's very worried and would like to continue to be distracted.

'There's an excellent tapas place a few minutes away. We

could go there?' Ruth suggests. 'Our treat if anyone's hungry; we'd love to have dinner with you.'

'We would. And I *love* the sound of "our" and "we",' says Bea.

'Me too.' Ruth smiles at her and, honestly, it's gorgeous.

I glance at Tom and see that he can't help smiling at the sight of them, just like I can't. I really hope he gets *his* happy ending this evening.

'That sounds perfect, thank you,' Carole says.

Roger's eyes swivel between the five of us a few times, and then he just turns round and shuffles away.

The rest of us (after realising that, amidst all the drama, none of us had reassured loved ones who might have heard that there was an issue at Waterloo, and shooting off a few messages to say that we're okay) join the large crowd of people heading out of the station.

There's already this sense between us – well, I feel it, and I *think* the others do too – that we've become a little group. It feels similar to that thing you see on a reality show where there's an initial group that arrive and bond really fast and then if anyone else gets introduced to the group, even only a few hours later, it's like they're interlopers. I think we've bonded very quickly, just like that.

We're jostled a lot and make sure we stay together; we match our pace to Ruth's (she's apparently had a knee operation fairly recently and isn't back to her top walking speed yet); we laugh together about a couple of small incidents on the way out; and, honestly, it doesn't feel a stretch to say that I've made four unlikely new friends under the clock this evening.

About fifteen minutes later, we're seated at a table towards the back of the tapas place. There's a man on a little platform halfway up the back wall playing a guitar, the air's buzzing with chat, tantalising smells are wafting their way over to us from neighbouring tables, Tom's phone has reception so he doesn't have to worry that he'll miss a call from Lola, and even Carole's smile looks less forced now.

Basically, it's looking like a *way* better evening for me than a blind date would have been.

'Do you all drink?' asks Bea. 'I'd love to order a bottle of champagne to celebrate our news. If that's alright, Carole. I don't want to be insensitive.'

'Okay, let's get this out immediately,' says Carole. 'You're lovely people. I'm very lucky to have met you this evening, because I *needed* – need – some loveliness around me right now. I'm happy for you. I want to be distracted. Please don't feel that you're being insensitive towards me. You aren't. I'd love to help you celebrate. In fact, if I may, I'll celebrate on my own behalf too. It's the start of a new life for me, one that I hadn't expected, but if I'm honest, there are downsides to living with Roger.'

We all nod, because, well, yes. Roger and downsides. Not difficult to imagine.

And then Ruth orders the champagne and some tap water, and we all start looking at the menu.

Tom glances at his phone – there's been no reply to the message he sent to Lola telling her in great detail where we are – and I quickly check mine too.

Obviously, there's no word from Dougie.

'Are you worried too?' Ruth asks me.

'No.' I take a lovely big, long sip of the champagne the waiter's just poured for us and as it goes down feel myself warm inside. And then (it *cannot* be because of just one sip of champagne; it must be the strange bonding thing we've had going on), I find myself doing what the others have all done, and splurging my thoughts.

'Basically, this evening I was supposed to be meeting a blind date, as I mentioned. I have a terrible record with blind dates and meeting people from apps. *Terrible*. They always go very badly. So I had actually decided to stop doing them, and wait for love if and when it hits. Except it never does, and I *would* like to meet someone. So when a colleague said that his flatmate would be perfect for me, and I'd be perfect for *him*, I was too easily persuaded into agreeing to meet this evening. And the flatmate clearly either didn't turn up at all, or he did and saw me and scarpered.'

'Logically—' Tom takes a piece of bread '—he did not turn up, see you and leave, because he couldn't have seen you before you saw him. So he obviously just decided not to turn up and didn't let you know. So he's obviously a rude arse and you've had a lucky escape and it's no reflection whatsoever on you.'

'Hmm.' I consider this for a moment. 'But it *feels* like a reflection. Maybe the way my colleague described me put him off.'

'I mean.' Tom's phone pings and his eyes slide to it and then back to me. Clearly not Lola. 'No. That just isn't likely. The most likely thing is that he got blind-date cold feet, as in he didn't want to go on a blind date at all. A lot of people don't. I've never been on one.'

'*Really*?' I am *so* envious. I would *love* never to have been on one. And never to go on one again. (I need to develop better willpower.) 'But how do you meet people? Do dating apps work for you?'

'No, I've always just kind of met people in real life. Uni. Work. Barbecues. The usual. Apart from the odd weird one.'

'Okay, I have two comments on that.' I dip some bread in olive oil. 'One. Based on my friends and me I really didn't think there was a usual place to meet. And two: what was your weirdest one ever?'

'That's a good question.'

We both pause to join the others in thanking the server as he fills the table with plates of enticing tapas.

'Weird meets?' I prompt when we've finished exclaiming with the others over how extremely delicious everything looks.

'I once met someone while we were both vomiting from food poisoning, in adjacent toilet cubicles, and then dated her for six months.' Tom takes a spoonful of patatas bravas.

I nod, satisfied. 'Definitely weird. You must have *really* liked each other if you were attracted despite the vomiting and the misery.'

'Yeah, no, the funny thing is – not really. I think we *thought* we'd bonded because we were so miserable and no-one else had been through that with us but as time went on it became apparent that you can't build a relationship on mutual gastrointestinal issues.'

I laugh. 'This is making me feel better about my own disastrous love life. Give me some more.'

'Let me think.' Tom hands me a plate of ham and cheese croquettes. My mouth waters just from the smell of them. 'Okay. Not to big up my own weird dating experience but this is a good one. Car crash. Both of us equally at fault. We reversed into each other.'

'No, no, no.' I shake my head sorrowfully. 'Clearly you don't read or watch enough romcoms to know that that's a huge cliché. In fiction it happens *all* the time. Actually, I say it happens all the time; that is not in fact true. It *used* to happen all the time. It's gone out of fashion recently; I'm guessing because it got overused.'

'I see.' Tom narrows his eyes. 'I didn't realise you were so judgemental. Fine. I *assure* you that I have better ones than that, that you will *not* be able to say were clichés.'

I laugh again and savour a garlicky prawn as Tom thinks for

a moment, before he begins to tell me some more of his frankly ridiculous stories.

'You did *what*?' asks Carole as Tom's description of beginning to date a woman he met landing in a cow pat after diving over a wall to escape a stampeding herd of cows (that were not in fact stampeding) falls in a lull in the other three's conversation.

Soon they've joined in and have begun to swap their weirdest first-meets too.

'Honestly,' I say eventually, wiping actual tears from under my eyes after a truly stunning story from Ruth involving going to the wrong wedding. 'Why don't I have any insane meet stories? Are these all *true*?'

Apparently they are.

'Did you refer to some disastrous first dates, though?' asks Tom, like he's trying to comfort me about my lack of weird first-meets.

'Well, I mean, yes, obviously. Billions.'

'How many exactly?' asks Bea.

'Tonight's no-show was the seventh bad first date this year. A combination of being set up by friends and a dating app.'

'My goodness.' Carole's fully joining in with all the conversation now, and she's *great*. Roger is not just a philandering arse, he's an idiot. He *will* be worse off without her, I'm sure. 'What was wrong with all the others? Did you go for any second dates?'

We've moved on from the slightly awkward *if-you-feel-happy-to-share* qualifiers on all our questions now, like we've reached proper friendship level already. I genuinely feel like I'm sitting at a table with a group of close girlfriends (okay, Tom's a man, but he's so easy to talk to he could genuinely be an actual female friend).

'Okay. So. Number one. His actual *first line* to me was: "I've never met a girl with hair like yours who wasn't *hot* in bed". I walked out.'

I begin to tick them off on my fingers.

'Number two. I liked him. I thought we were getting on well. We *were* getting on well. Then he showed me a photo of his last girlfriend and I discovered it was a colleague of mine. Who had told us all a couple of weeks before that she'd dumped her boyfriend because his sexual fetishes were too weird for her.

'Number three. We got as far as a kiss and it was *bad*. The first one missed. His lips landed on my cheek and mine were kind of fish-like kissing air. Then we made contact and there was *no* chemistry. And kissing is weird when you've realised that you don't *want* to be kissing that person.'

Beas nods a lot. 'Tell me about it.'

Ruth nods too.

'Number four?' Carole asks.

'Hang on.' I think back. 'Oh, yes. We were meeting in a bar and I got there before him. I'd told him I'd be wearing a green top. He arrived and went straight up to a woman in a pink top, with a huge smile on his face. When we established that I was his blind date, not her, his face fell several feet, and then he spent ages telling me that he was colour blind and that was why he got pink and green confused. Totally missing the point that I could not spend an evening with someone who had *beamed* at another woman and looked like he was going to cry when he realised that *I* was his date.'

'He was an idiot,' states Tom.

'Aww, thank you.' I almost believe him. He's very good at that, I've already realised: making people feel better.

'Number five?' asks Ruth.

'Your bog-standard recently divorced man who wanted to

tell me all about the ex. I was free therapy, basically. Even freer when at the end of the evening I said that I was so sorry but I wasn't sure it had worked and that I didn't think we should necessarily meet again, and he walked straight out without paying his half of the bill.'

'*That*,' Carole says, 'is classic Roger-style behaviour.'

'Tosser,' we all chorus, because that's where we're up to now on the Roger situation: every so often, Carole throws in a comment about him and we all agree that he's a tosser.

'Number six?' asks Bea.

'Another classic,' I say. 'Because I am an idiot. We had what seemed like a lovely evening together in a restaurant and then I went to the loo but turned back because I hadn't picked up my bag and wanted to reapply my lipstick, and he was making a quick call to his wife to say he was late at a client dinner and might have to stay in a hotel overnight.'

'Tosser,' the others say automatically.

'Oh dear.' Ruth leans over and squeezes my hand briefly. 'I don't think dating strangers is working for you.'

'That's an understatement.'

'I'm not going to be dating for a *long* time,' Carole says. 'You're welcome to join me.'

'Thank you,' I say. 'I think I should.'

'Love will find you when you least expect it.' Bea smiles at me and then at Ruth, and I swallow at the gorgeousness of their evident happiness.

I see Tom check his phone again.

'Still nothing,' he says when he sees me looking.

'She *is* okay, I'm sure of it,' I say.

Tom's face falls a little and I realise that I've kind of said the wrong thing. In that he clearly doesn't want to think that anything bad's happened to her, but also he doesn't want to think that there's no good reason she hasn't turned up. And we know now that the whole bomb scare was just a scare and no-one at all was injured (thank goodness).

'What I mean,' I amend, 'is that there was clearly a good reason that she hasn't come this evening.' I'd *like* to point out that he is apparently excellent at meeting people in weird ways, so if this doesn't work out he'll probably meet someone again soon, except I don't think he'd like to hear that, because obviously he's been waiting for Lola for ten years. In fact, maybe the reason that none of the rest of his relationships worked out in that time was that he subconsciously didn't want them to because of Lola. 'You *will* see her soon.'

He perks up. 'Think so?'

'Definitely.' If I'm honest, I wouldn't *totally* put money on it.

4

TOM

I really cannot understand why Nadia assuring me that everything's going to be okay genuinely does make me believe it will be (I mean, how would she know?), but it does.

Maybe it's just because I very much want her reassurances to be true.

The conversation moves on from first dates to the guitar player above us and Spanish and Latin American music (Bea used to be a music teacher it turns out and her knowledge is fascinating), through food anecdotes, to how many pets we've all had, and I realise that all four of the others are nice. Just very, very nice.

If you'd told me a few hours ago that Lola wouldn't turn up and I'd find myself at a restaurant table with this on-the-face-of-it mismatched assortment of women, I'd have been astonished. But here I am. And, despite my burgeoning worry that I – like Nadia – have been stood up this evening, or – even worse – that something's happened to Lola, I'm enjoying myself.

Eventually, with reluctance, we acknowledge that we are the

last people in the restaurant and that we really ought to leave and let the staff finish tidying up and go home.

Carole's been looking a lot perkier, but suddenly she's drooping again.

'Carole, you really can't go home on your own tonight,' Bea says. 'You must come and stay with us.'

'Oh no. I can't intrude. You literally got engaged this evening.'

'No. We insist,' Ruth says.

'Yes, we do.' Bea's voice has turned steely and suddenly I'm imagining her having an unruly class of children with no interest in music under extremely firm control. 'Also, you must all three of you come to our wedding as guests of honour.'

'Oh, wow, thank you.' Nadia beams. 'I'd love to.'

Carole and I smile too and thank them.

Carole capitulates on the staying-over on condition that she treat them to a taxi back to Ruth's North London home. An empty black cab passes us very soon, and once the three of them are inside it, Nadia and I head off back to Waterloo together, as fast as we can, heads down, because the heavens opened while we were inside and the rain's immense.

'Where do you live?' I ask as we reach the shelter of the station.

'In a shoebox in Wimbledon. What about you?'

'Near Clapham Junction, also in a shoebox. Same train line.'

'Look.' Nadia points up at the big departures board. 'There's one in three minutes. We should run.'

We make a dash for the platform and hurl ourselves into the first carriage.

'Oh my goodness.' She puts her bag down on the seat next to her and gives herself a little shake. 'That rain was unbelievable. As was everything else that happened this evening.'

'What, you don't usually get locked down at Waterloo in a false alarm and then wind up at a restaurant with four strangers, two of whom have just got engaged five decades after they first met and one of whom has just split up with her husband on their wedding anniversary?'

She eye-rolls me. 'Well, obviously I do that all the time. But only on work nights, not at the weekend.'

'Oh I *see*. Seriously, though, yes, it has indeed been a very unusual evening.'

'It's an odd contrast,' Nadia muses. 'Between Bea and Ruth's gorgeous love story – thank goodness they have finally got together – and Carole's nightmare.'

'Yeah.' I look through the grimy windows as the train gathers speed and the illuminated station platforms disappear behind us.

'It kind of makes you think.'

'Yeah,' I repeat. Selfishly thinking about myself first, I'm really hoping to go down the gorgeous love story path rather than the nightmare one. And I hope the same for Nadia, obviously.

'It's inspirational, really. Both their stories.'

'That is true.' I feel like I can't say *Yeah* a third time. Also, it *is* true. 'Yes. Makes you think doesn't it. Like – we should take some life lessons from it.' I do *not* want to wait until I'm in my seventies like Bea and Ruth to get together with Lola. Maybe I should just send her a message right now telling her how much I love her – how much I always have. I haven't used the L-word since she got back in touch three days ago; I wanted to wait until I saw her. Usually it isn't a word I'd use easily, but it's ten years since we first met; that's a long time, long enough to know.

Nadia's nodding. 'Yep. Almost like we should make some resolutions on the back of it.'

I nod, because weirdly (I am not a resolution person), I agree.

'I love a resolution,' she says. 'But they've got to be for a good reason, and also you have to start them on a memorable date. Calendar date, not got-stood-up-yet-again kind of date. Today's a good date.'

'Is it?' I'm confused if I'm honest. 'A random twenty-something date in June?'

'The longest day of the year?'

'Oh, right.' We're interrupted by both our phones vibrating at once.

I obviously look immediately at mine.

It isn't Lola, it's Ruth – posting in the chat ('The Waterloo Five') she set up for the five of us before we left the restaurant – that she hopes we're both dry and safely on trains. We assure her that we are and then we all gush about our evening together (quite a long chat even though Nadia and I are sitting next to each other and the three others are in the same cab), before Nadia finishes it with a three-heart-emoji message.

I think back to what we were talking about and then ask, 'So... the longest day of the year?'

'Yes. Normally I just go for New Year's and birthday resolutions. And occasionally the first of the month. But I'm thinking the longest day of the year and also the date of Bea and Ruth's engagement is a great place to start.'

'Do your resolutions usually work?'

She screws up her face, which makes me laugh. 'Sometimes they do. Sometimes they spectacularly do not. But I think I'm better off with them. My life disintegrates fast into total chaos if I don't make lists and plans.'

'Fair enough. So what's your resolution going to be now?'

'To stop making so many mistakes.'

I raise my eyebrows.

'In my love life,' she elaborates.

'How, though? Don't you want a resolution to be more specific than that?'

'Yes, I'm going to have to think about that. I need some rules. Like don't go on any blind dates at all going forward.'

'Maybe not a blanket no-blind-date rule, though? What if someone who knows you really well and has your best interests at heart thinks they know the perfect person for you? And they're right? You don't want to miss out. Although obviously you don't *need* a partner. No-one needs a partner.'

'I kind of do want a partner, though. But that does make sense; obviously having no partner is far better than being with the wrong person.' Nadia folds her arms across her chest and tilts her head to one side, before unfolding her arms. Almost like she was thinking and wanted to block the world out while she did it. 'Maybe I've been trying too hard. Maybe I just need to be open-minded full stop, as in not *reject* possible dates, but also not seek them out actively. No more dating sites or blind dates, or accepting people who ask me out just because I want to believe that once I've got to know them a bit better I'll actually find them attractive.'

'So how will that work in practice?' I ask.

'I think I'm just going to let it happen. Or not. Like I'm not going to go on any more dating apps. And I'm not going to accept dates unless I'm *sure*. But also I won't swear off men. I'll be wise basically. I'll do it the old-fashioned way. And I will *not* let myself panic if I haven't met anyone soon.'

'Very wise.'

'I mean.' She twinkles at me. 'Obviously I *will* panic because if I'm honest it's been kind of a *thing* recently. Looking for someone. I'm thirty-three and a lot of my friends have settled down, and at the beginning of this year I just started trying really hard to meet someone. Which, I now realise, is a very bad idea.'

'*Maybe*,' I suggest, 'set a timeline during which you are not allowed to panic about it.'

'That's a very good idea,' she approves. 'I'm going to go six months. I'll re-evaluate in the New Year. A proper swearing-off men dating detox for the next six months until the first of January, and after that it will have to happen organically, I won't be going out looking for love.'

'Nice.'

She grins at me and then says, 'Okay, you. What's your resolution?'

'Lola. I'm going to find her and check she's okay and I'm going to tell her I love her.' It is *weird* that I'm telling Nadia this because it's deeply personal. But at the same time, it seems entirely natural to talk about it with her, I suppose because of the evening we've just shared. 'I feel like she might have had second thoughts about meeting up again after such a long time and maybe if I'd put all my cards on the table it might have made a difference. I don't want to have any regrets.'

'Yes, regrets are awful. I think that's a very good plan.'

We exchange smiles and then I glance outside and see that we're going through Queenstown Road, Battersea, and that the next station will be Clapham Junction.

As I say, 'Next stop's me,' my phone vibrates yet again. You really don't realise how often you get some kind of message or notification until you're anxiously waiting to hear from someone, and I almost don't pick it up because I'm just feeling pathetic now every time I flip it over and see that, no, obviously it is not from Lola because time has established that I will not be hearing from her this evening.

And then I *do* look at it.

And oh my God it *is* a message from Lola.

It takes me way longer than usual to open the message, and the whole time I'm fumbling with my phone my heart's thudding so loudly inside my ribcage that I'm surprised Nadia doesn't comment in concern.

'From Lola,' I tell Nadia as I focus on my phone.

Finally I have the message open. It's a short one:

> I'm so sorry.

I want to tell Nadia. It would feel weird not to. It's like she, Bea, Ruth and Carole have all lived with me through this evening's hope and anticipation morphing to misery and resignation. But I can't actually get the words out, so instead I show her the screen.

'Oh, Tom. Oh, no.' Nadia's eyes are suddenly glistening.

'Yeah.' I'm almost tearful myself, and I can't remember the last time I actually cried. 'Should I reply?'

The doors beep and we both look over.

'I'll stay on.' I don't want to get off until I've worked out what to say to Lola. 'I can turn round at Wimbledon and come back.'

Nadia nods. 'I feel like you *should* reply. In the same way that you regret not having told her you love her, you'd regret not answering.'

'Very true.' I'm already typing.

> Is everything okay?

Her reply comes through immediately.

> Not really but also yes. So... kind of.

I show the screen to Nadia and then stare at it.

I really don't know what to say to that.

'That's kind of confusing and I'm guessing you aren't sure what to say but I feel like you should reply quickly,' Nadia says, 'in case she goes offline again and you're left wondering.'

'Good point.' I begin to type quickly. I just write my immediate thoughts out because I'm panicking, and then I send the message as fast as I can.

> I hope that means that overall you're more okay than not... Could we maybe rearrange our meeting?

I wish I could have asked why she didn't turn up but it I couldn't think of a good way of wording it.

Her reply comes equally quickly.

> Maybe...

I suddenly panic more. I need to say it. So I do.

> I love you.

I have no shame; I show it to Nadia straight after sending it.

We both sit and stare at the screen. Lola's read it. She begins to write. And then she stops. And starts again. And then stops.

And stays stopped.

The doors beep and Nadia says, 'This is my stop.'

'Oh, okay.' I stand up too and we both get off. It's still pissing it down – it's one of those evenings where you're quite surprised there's any rain left in the sky – and we both get fairly drenched in the smallish gap between the train and the awning that extends along the platform.

Once we're back in the dry, I look at my phone again.

And there's nothing. And Lola is no longer online.

So to summarise the situation, she stood me up, then told me that she was more or less okay and *might* meet me, and in that moment I lost my mind (hindsight is a beautiful thing that has kicked in pretty quickly) and told her I loved her, and she... has ghosted me.

Stunning.

5

NADIA

'I'm so sorry.' I hate seeing people sad, especially kind people, and from what I've seen of him this evening Tom is very kind. Not just in being polite and charming to us all over our unexpected dinner, but little things, like he was very quick to turn the conversation whenever Carole seemed miserable again, and he was much more tolerant than a lot of people would be to a server when she spilt definitely-oily-and-staining tomato sauce on his quite-new-and-not-cheap-looking leather shoes. So, yes, properly kind, I think.

He's also clearly pretty miserable. He's tall and solid and looks like he's mid-thirties, and he's one of those just-the-right-side-of-handsome-but-not-too-handsome people who are often very confident socially (and he was indeed unselfconscious and chatty-but-not-too-chatty when we all met) but right now he looks like a little boy who's had his last Haribo snaffled by an adult he trusted, just as he was popping it into his mouth. Bewildered, heading towards very hurt.

'Yeah, no.' He shakes his head. 'It is what it is. Not meant to be, I guess. Although...'

I wait. I feel as though he has thoughts he's going to have to work through. I certainly would in his position.

'Did that seem weird to you? Her wording?' he asks.

'A little,' I say cautiously, 'but I don't actually know her of course.'

'Yeah.' He looks back at his phone and rereads the messages, before looking up and staring ahead of him with the hurt-following-Haribo-theft look on his face again.

I feel he shouldn't be alone now, so I don't want to leave him. Although maybe he has a housemate who he's close to who he'd like to talk to.

'Do you live alone?' I ask.

'Yes?' His voice is inflected as though it's an odd question.

'I just...' I'm choosing my words carefully because I don't want to imply that things are so bad that he shouldn't be alone, but, also, surely he'd be better off with someone to talk to. 'I thought you might want to talk things through more. Let's go and get a drink?'

Tom nods. 'Yeah, actually, that would be great. Thank you. If you're sure you aren't in a rush to get home.'

'No, all good, but shall we go now?' It's been colder than I expected this evening, since the rain started, and this platform is a bit of a wind tunnel, and I'd *love* to be standing somewhere warmer. Actually, I'd love to be *sitting* somewhere warmer. I check my watch. 'Oh. The pubs will all be closed. A wine bar?' I look at his tight smile and miserable eyes and try to think of a quiet, non-party-like wine bar in the vicinity, and fail. 'Or a coffee at mine? My flat's a seven-and-a-half-minute brisk walk away.'

Tom manages a little laugh. 'Not to be too precise.' He hesitates. 'Are you sure? It's quite late already and I'm not at my best.'

I nod. 'Absolutely. Really. I'd hate to think of you going home and being miserable by yourself.'

'Yes, please, then. Thank you.'

And just like that, he's coming back to my flat with me for a coffee, and it feels completely natural because somehow this evening I genuinely feel as though I made four new proper friends, and of those friends Tom is the closest in age to me.

I'm not even *that* horrified about what I've just remembered is the big tip I left my living room in, because good friends do not judge you on temporary messiness. Although I should probably warn him.

As we walk along the platform, I say, 'I would like to mention that I was in a very big rush when I went out and as you know I was on my way to a blind date and I wanted to look my best, so I might have the entire contents of my wardrobe strewn across the flat.'

Tom laughs and says, 'Noted.'

We barely speak once we emerge from the station, because the rain's so heavy now that it drowns out all other sounds, even the road traffic; we just concentrate on hurrying to my flat.

We go at my fastest pace (a jog/speed-walk combination that Tom keeps up with effortlessly, although, to be fair to me, his legs are a lot longer than mine, plus I'm in my wedges) and smash my usual seven and a half minutes.

When we get there, we burst through the main door into the building and stand in the hall dripping.

I'm finding it difficult not to snigger, even though it isn't very sensitive to Tom's misery, because the way raindrops are making their way down his ears and falling from his lobes is very comical.

I'm obviously looking ridiculous too, because, despite Lola, Tom's actually looking as though his own lips are twitching.

We just stand there dripping for a few moments, before I realise that I should do something about the water and say, 'Okay, my flat's on the first floor,' and head for the stairs.

When we get inside my front door, which opens straight into my open-plan kitchen-living room, I leave my sodden shoes on the doormat (I *really* hope they're going to recover from the water because I *love* them) and Tom stands on the mat next to them, trying to avoid dripping onto the floor. I'm grateful for that, because I'm very protective of my floorboards; my friend Gina and I lovingly (and incredibly unenjoyably) sanded them with a rented machine last year when I moved in, and then varnished them and nearly asphyxiated ourselves, and I'm not at all keen (and neither is Gina) to have to redo them.

A couple of minutes later, I'm in a dry top and jeans, and Tom's wearing an old T-shirt of my brother's that I found at the back of my wardrobe, we've both towel-dried our hair and I have the kettle on.

I turn round from getting mugs out of a cupboard and catch Tom checking his phone again.

'Anything else?' I ask.

He shakes his head mutely, and then a few seconds later says, 'I should have asked her why she didn't show up this evening.'

'You could still ask?'

He shakes his head again. 'I feel like that could sound accusatory. If we're going to speak again, I don't feel like I can begin with that kind of question.'

'Yep, you're right.' I pause and sip my still-too-hot coffee, ow. 'I'm so, so sorry again that this has happened. I don't think you should be annoyed with yourself for not having asked that question, though; she might not have replied to it, because she *could* have volunteered the information, and it's kind of obvious that a lot of people in your position would want to know, and maybe she would have volunteered it if she was happy to say?'

'True.' He takes the steaming mug of coffee I hold out for him and wraps his hands around it. 'Thank you. That's good. Funny how cold you can get in the rain, even on a warmish evening.'

'Yes, like your actual bones feel damp.'

'Exactly. It's refreshing, though, after the heat we've had. Looking on the bright side.' He makes a face (which, to my admiration, does nothing to diminish his handsomeness; I'm pretty sure most people would look like gargoyles if they did that) and then continues. 'I think I'm going to have to look on the bright side about Lola.'

'You know what. There *will* be a bright side.' I'm trying hard to think of genuine positives. 'Maybe now wasn't exactly the right time. Maybe it *will* happen – I mean, I'm sure there's every chance it will – but just today, this week, this month, maybe this year is wrong. And when it does happen it will be perfect. *And* —' I'm warming up now; I'm *sure* I can think of *loads* of cheering-up things to say '—as you pointed out to me, no-one should *need* to be in a relationship.'

'I did say that,' he agrees. 'Was I talking total crap, though, just to cheer you up?'

'Er what?' I frown at him. '*Were* you?'

'I don't know.' He does a face-scrunch *sorry*. 'I think I might have been.'

Yep, he totally was, I realise. Hmm. Yes. I've been carried along for the past hour or so on a tide of Tom's convincing bullshit about not wanting a partner, but, actually, I *do* want someone. This is not about me, though. And also, wanting is not needing.

'No,' I state. 'We do not *need* partners. No-one does. You

would *like* a partner. So would I. You're deeply disappointed this evening because you thought you were going to reconnect with a woman you fell in love with at first sight ten years ago and have always believed was the one for you. And I'm, well, just generally disappointed in love. But we definitely do not actually *need* partners.' I'm warming to my theme. 'Think about all the amazing, *happy*, successful single people there are. Elderly and middle-aged ones, not just young ones. They have other meaningful relationships. I mean, what's so different about a romantic relationship from a non-romantic friendship?'

'Sex,' Tom points out.

'That's just a detail,' I tell him. 'Sex is *not* the be-all and end-all. I mean, obviously good sex is amazing, but, you know, maybe the way forward is meaningless hook-ups to satisfy the sex thing and then great, meaningful, deeply satisfying non-romantic friendships.'

'Really?'

'Absolutely,' I lie. I personally do not like meaningless hook-ups. I've found that out the hard way and have established that I would much rather have *no* sex. Although I do *like* sex, a lot, in the right context.

'You're looking wistful; you're *totally* lying.'

'Yes, okay, fine, I *was* lying a *bit*, because meaningless hook-ups are not actually for me. But also, I wasn't. Lots of people do like them. And also, most people – most people I know, anyway – go through dry phases. And they are totally, completely fine with that, usually. Like the vast majority of people would surely rather be single than with the wrong person. And if you're single and you *don't* like meaningless hook-ups, you're going to be sex-free.' I want to wind this strand of conversation up now, because Gina keeps popping into my head; she's very vocally into sex toys for her own personal use, no need for a partner, and I don't enjoy her monologues on the topic, and I don't want to start a similar conversation now. I don't need more than one friend in my life who likes to have long (or indeed any) discussions about masturbation. 'Anyway, basically, good sex is obviously a lovely added extra, but equally obviously your average person *can* perfectly happily live without it.'

'True,' Tom concedes.

I press my advantage. 'So, basically, what we're saying—' I don't think this is too much of a stretch '—is that the main benefit of a good romantic relationship is in fact emotional. And you can get emotional support from friends. And you can have fun with friends. And if you need a plus-one for events you can take a friend.' I close my eyes for a moment remembering the time I plus-oned Gina to my grandmother's eighty-fifth birthday party.

'Thinking about a bad plus-one experience?'

'Just my friend Gina at a family barbecue. She ended up talking about masturbation with *my uncle*.'

Tom's eyes widen. 'Wow.'

'Yeah.'

We sit in silence for a couple of beats before I remember that I'm supposed to be helping him achieve a happier state of mind.

'You're going to be fine,' I continue. 'Your friends will help you. *We*, your new Waterloo friends, will help you.'

It's just occurred to me – kind of lucidly, as opposed to being at the back of my mind – that Tom does not in fact know Lola at all really; they messaged after they first met, but in person he's spent precisely one two-hour-long evening with her, ever, and that was ten years ago. Who *knows* whether in practice they would actually like each other now as friends? Obviously they might be in lust with each other but I know from bitter experience (I have *so* much bitter dating experience) that there's only so far mutual lust will carry you in a relationship.

I open my mouth to point out that for all he knows she's an axe murderer or a bigamist or just really not very nice or not someone ten-years-older Tom-of-today gets on with that well, and then close it again. He is *clearly* not ready to hear that yet; what was I thinking?

Also, everyone knows that it's a very bad idea for friends to criticise each other's partners or exes unless they are definitely, completely, no-going-back exes forever. It's terrible for a friendship when Friend A has heavily criticised Friend B's ex when the split turns out only to have been temporary. (Yep, also bitter experience – with my friend Samrita and her now husband – we did get over it but it took a while.)

So I go in a different conversational direction.

'I think we need to amend our resolutions.' I stand up and go over to my desk in the corner of the room and return with a brand-new notebook and a pen (I love stationery).

'We're going to write them down?'

'Can it hurt?'

'Very fair point; it can't.' Tom takes a big slurp of coffee.

'Exactly. And it's scientifically proven that if you write stuff down you're more likely to stick to it.'

'Really?' He raises one eyebrow.

'Definitely. And even more so if you write it *with* someone, so you're accountable to each other.'

'Yes, now that definitely *is* true.'

'Exactly. Okay. So.' I open the book and twiddle the pen while I think. 'Where did we get to?'

'You're going to stop trying to find love; you're just going to let it creep up on you so if it happens it happens, and if it doesn't, all good? So you're going to stop going on dating apps full stop, and you won't automatically say yes to blind dates but you also won't be entirely closed-minded to them, I think you said? But basically no dating, for at least six months.'

'Yes. All correct. My dating detox.' I note all of that down, sorting it into bullet points. 'Okay, now you.'

Oh. Tom's resolution was to find Lola, check she's okay and tell her he loves her. But since then we've had the no-reply to his I-love-you.

'Erm.' I feel like it would be better if I wait for him to suggest things because my mind is completely good-idea-free.

'Yes. Me. Well. Yeah. I'd like to find Lola somehow, see her in person, tell her in person that I love her and see what happens.'

I nod. I'm feeling very uneasy on his behalf because it could obviously all end horribly. But I can see that he needs to do this. Everyone needs closure sometimes and ten years is an unusually long time.

'Okay.' I click my pen on and start writing. 'There. Done.'

Tom nods.

I look at the page. 'Actually, not really done.'

'We aren't?'

'No. I've just written what we want to achieve, but not *how* we're going to achieve it. We need a way forward. Something more concrete than just "let things happen but not for six months" in my case and "look for Lola to check she's okay and say *I love you*".'

'Kind of difficult to make fully concrete plans sometimes, though?'

'Okay.' I twiddle the pen again. 'Maybe that isn't exactly what I mean. Maybe it's that I don't like what I've written for either of us. It isn't positive enough. Like, I feel we need to be taking some kind of affirmative action. Okay, yours *is* positive action. But as we said before, it shouldn't be the be-all and end-all.'

'So you're saying...?' Tom looks a bit confused.

'That we need to resolve to prove to ourselves that neither of us *needs* a partner. As in, we do not *need* romance, because we have good friends.' I write that down.

'That's still very wishy-washy, though. Shouldn't it be something more specific?'

I smile at Tom, pleased that he's finally entering properly into this.

'You're right. Okay. Here we go.' I click the pen on again with a flourish. 'Basically, what do we need from a romantic partner? Other than sex. For everything else, we're going to prove to ourselves that we're totally fine – *more* than totally fine – with our platonic friends.'

'Fun, emotional support, a plus-one,' Tom reels off.

I write them all down.

'So have we made a plan?' Tom asks.

'Yes. We're going to do everything we just said.' I close the notebook with a satisfying snap.

'*How* are we going to do it, though?'

'It'll come to us,' I say airily.

'Good, then,' Tom says.

'I don't like your tone.' I frown at him. 'You sound doubtful.' Hmm. I reopen the notebook and look at what I've written.

And no. These are not the kind of resolutions that should be written down. This is not a 'go for a 3k run every Sunday and Wednesday, eat max one extra-large bag of Tyrrell's crinkly ready-salted once a fortnight and only one chocolate bar a week' reminder that I wouldn't really mind anyone seeing. This reads like an article in a teenage magazine from pre TikTok days and I'd be mortified for pretty much anyone to see it.

I'm mortified that *Tom's* seen it, and he's part of it.

'Yeah, no. We don't need to have this written down. We just need to *agree* it and hold each other accountable.' I pull the page from its ring-spine and scrunch it into a small ball before taking it over to my recycling bin.

'Agreed,' Tom says as I close the bin. 'For sanity we both need a plan and we need next steps but, yeah, not in writing.'

'Thinking about next steps, do you know Lola's surname?' I ask delicately as I sit back down.

'Well, would you believe it, it's Smith. It would be so much easier if it were a more unusual name. And yes, sadly I've googled and there are quite a few Lola Smiths including a very talented young footballer, it seems, but I couldn't find her at all. I'm guessing she doesn't do social media and isn't on LinkedIn.'

I wonder how often it truly isn't possible to find someone online. Surely not that often. Although if you only have a name to go by and there's no description of them on their work website and they don't do social media, maybe it isn't surprising. Also, maybe Tom doesn't have full details.

'It could be that Lola's short for something,' I suggest. 'If it's an abbreviation it might make it even harder to find her.' I finish the last of my coffee and look at Tom's already-empty mug. 'Another one?' I stand up as he nods a *yes please*.

We end up googling and social media searching all sorts of names including variations on and longer versions of Lola all the way through our second cups of coffee.

We get nowhere.

'I'm so sorry,' I tell Tom as he places his empty cup down. 'Another one?'

'You sure I'm not outstaying my welcome?' He looks over at where my kitchen clock's showing that it's heading towards 1 a.m.

'Absolutely.' I'd feel terrible if he went home looking as miserable as he does right now. We need to talk about something more positive than fruitless online searches for Lola.

Once I've placed refilled, steaming mugs on the table, I sit back down and say, 'You know, from my perspective anyway, there are *so* many good reasons to be single. As in, there are *active* upsides to not having a partner.'

'Yes, there definitely are. I mean, I'm single now, and until Lola got in touch I was completely happy about it.'

'Exactly.' I'm going to get the conversation away from Lola and onto less mournful topics if it kills me. 'You can spread out across the whole bed.' I ignore an annoying little thought that I *like* having a cuddle in bed with the right person. That whole limbs-tangled-in-the-morning thing is lovely. 'On a work night in particular, you just want a really good night's sleep.'

'True. And you can get up and go to bed when you want to. And eat what you want when you want. Exercise as much or as little as you like.'

Hooray, we're finally off the Lola topic.

'Watch what you want on TV,' I add.

'The list could go on,' Tom says.

'Exactly.'

'She's never going to reply, is she?' he asks as I'm trying to think of another positive.

Oh. Okay. Yep, obviously it's going to take more than a silly list of fake positives about being single to distract him. Understandably.

I focus on his question. 'I'm not sure.' My gut says *no*, but does he want to hear that?

'I don't think she is.' He checks his phone again and then turns it face down. 'Distract me. Tell me what you're doing tomorrow.'

'Erm. Well. Due to his no-show, I *won't* be thinking about the terrible date I had tonight with Dougie, which is a plus. I'm going to get up late and go for brunch and then a walk with my old schoolfriend Holly who lives round the corner and then I'm going to my parents' for dinner where my mother will light-heartedly except also very seriously grill me about my love life and I will grit my teeth and think how mortified she would be if she knew that I'd been stood up last night.' Oh. *Whoops*. That wasn't very cheery. 'And I will be *pleased* that I'm single,' I add carefully.

Tom laughs. A lot.

'What?' I pat my face. Do I have food hanging off it or something?

'Sorry.' He is literally holding his sides.

I start to laugh too, entirely because Tom is laughing.

Eventually we both stop.

'Sorry,' he says again. 'It was just suddenly *so* funny the way you've been trying *so* hard to convince me that honestly it's *fine*, in fact better than fine, it's *desirable* to be stood up by the woman you've thought about for years and years because actually who in their right minds wants romance, and then the *first* thing you said about your actual life was basically that your mother is going to nag you about not having a partner and you aren't going to enjoy it.'

'Well. I can't believe that I've been laughing just because you were laughing when the premise of your amusement was actually wrong.' I pick up my pen from where it's still sitting on top of my notebook and point it at him triumphantly. 'It is not that I want a partner, it's that I don't enjoy my *mother* wanting me to have a partner. That is an entirely different thing. All I need is for my mother to think I'm with someone and I'm sorted. And then in a few years' time for her to think I have children and again I'll be sorted.'

'Well, that shouldn't be a problem. You just need to get yourself a fake partner and fake kids.'

'Oh yes, easy. If I'm honest...' It's like all the caffeine I've had this evening is acting like a truth drug on me; I really don't usually confide this much in people. 'Sometimes I wonder whether I should ask Gina to be my fake girlfriend. But then I think that would be really complicated because my mum's main stated reason for wanting to me to have a partner is that she'd like to be a grandmother so then I'd either have to lie about having a third-party male friend sperm donor, or I'd have to research fertility treatment, and then I'd have to tell proper lies rather than vaguely saying I was planning to try in due course.'

'Wow.' Tom's tone is awed. 'You've actually thought seriously about this, haven't you?'

'Nope, not at all,' I lie.

'Why not ask a male friend?'

'I don't have any single male friends I know well enough. My guy friends from uni and work are all partnered up now. When I think about it, the whole plus-one thing is one of the biggest reasons I've been on so many first dates. It would make life *so* much easier to have someone to take to weddings, family barbecues, work things where you're going to see an ex...'

'Yes, tell me about it. I've been single for nine months now and that is *definitely* one of the worst things. Especially once you hit thirty-five, as I did in April. You should hear *my* mother on the subject of biological clocks – in her words they tick for men too, not just women.'

We sit for a moment in silence, kind of mutually eye-rolling at the shitness of being nagged about singledom, and then Tom suddenly sits up straight.

'I have an idea,' he almost yells. 'We can plus-one *each other*. Say we're in the early stages of a relationship, nothing serious, so no-one's asking us when-are-the-babies-coming questions. It doesn't seem like we have any friends in common, so no-one will be able to catch us out.'

'Oh my God,' I say, awed. 'You're a *genius*.'

'I know.' He does a preening pout and a shoulder waggle, which makes me laugh. 'So... let's do it?' He sticks his hand out and I shake it with no hesitation.

And there we go. We're fake-plus-one partners. Which I think is the best dating decision I've made for years.

6

TOM

I leave Nadia's shortly after our plus-one agreement (which was either pure genius or an incredibly stupid suggestion; I'm not sure which), because it's quarter past two in the morning and Nadia's hidden a yawn more than a couple of times, and she's already gone massively above and beyond this evening for someone who only a few hours ago was a complete stranger.

'Thank you again,' I say as she opens her front door. 'I'm genuinely feeling quite cheery, which is astonishing.' I make a big effort and don't actually say Lola's name out loud; I'm aware that I might have sounded somewhat broken-record-like this evening.

'I really hope that's true,' Nadia says.

'I mean, of course it is,' I say as jovially as I can. 'Because we have our plus-one problems sorted.'

'We do indeed.' She grins at me and I grin back (Nadia's smiles are infectious) and then we share a quick hug before I step outside her flat and she says, 'Goodnight,' and closes the door behind me and clinks some locks.

* * *

I decide to splash out on an Uber because I don't think there's an easy night bus route from Nadia's to mine, and also I've had a shit evening.

A Prius arrives very quickly and I hop inside and we begin to drive along empty main roads at way over the speed limit.

As I stare out of the car windows at street-light-illuminated rain, I realise that the evening hasn't all been shit. Yes, the Lola thing has been gut-wrenchingly awful, but meeting Bea, Ruth, Carole and Nadia and forming our little group is the kind of experience that happens very rarely and really does restore your belief in the inherent *decency* of people. I really do think we'll probably stay in touch. And the fake-plus-one thing: I mean, given that I will almost certainly *not* be getting back together with Lola after all, and, having been reminded of Lola, am unlikely to want to date anyone else any time soon, it could be like a genuine gift from heaven to avoid are-you-dating questions. And I'm sure that Nadia will understand if I have to pull out of our agreement if Lola and I do get back together.

Yeah, Lola and I are clearly *not* going to get back together. I know that. It's really difficult not to hope, though.

I'm home way more quickly than I should have been, due to the driver's speeding (I point out to him when I get out that it's dangerous to drive that fast on residential roads and realise from the look in his eye that he'll be giving me a one-star passenger rating), and go straight to bed, because I'm very tired.

* * *

I cannot sleep. It's 3.45 a.m. and I am wide, wide awake. Too much caffeine. And too many circular thoughts about Lola. It's weird. I'm not usually a big thinker like this, I usually just get on with things, but apparently tonight I can't.

I never have insomnia. Unsurprisingly, it's as shit as everyone unfortunate enough to suffer with it regularly says it is.

I ask the internet what to do. The internet has a lot of advice.

I turn my pillow over to the cool side. Doesn't work. I feel very drowsy for a minute and then think about how I will *not* be sharing a pillow with Lola and suddenly I'm wide awake.

I get up and walk round the room. Doesn't work in the slightest. It makes me feel less drowsy.

I get up and go to the kitchen and have a glass of water. Now I'm even wider awake. Who knew that water was a stimulant. (I Google and the internet tells me that it isn't unless you were dehydrated before you drank it. Maybe I was.)

I make a list of things I'm worried about. Lola. Monday lunchtime's tricky work meeting. The leak in my bathroom. Feeling like shit for the next couple of days because of being up all night tonight.

At least it's Sunday and I have nothing on today. Thank goodness my parents' extended family barbecue has been postponed until next Sunday because of the extreme rain this weekend.

The thought of the barbecue reminds me of Lola again because, if I'm honest, before they postponed it I think I might have been imagining taking her there with me. I am really not going to be amused by the chat there will be about how I am now the *only* one of my siblings and cousins still not married for life. I can literally hear my Aunt Laura going 'tick, tock, Tom,' and then cackling with laughter.

I wonder if Nadia's free next Sunday. We *could* kick off the plus-one thing right now.

On the spur of the moment, I send her a message asking her.

And then I...

* * *

Yeah, thankfully I went to sleep.

Also thankfully, I didn't set an alarm, so I actually get six hours' sleep in before I wake up, very disorientated because I basically never have a lie-in.

The first thing I do (pathetically) is reach for my phone and check for a response from Lola. I can see that she's been active online in the past half hour (and I know that she saw my message last night) but there's nothing. Which shouldn't be a surprise, but gives me a sinking, life-is-just-*boring* feeling all over again.

I haven't heard back from Nadia but I'm sure I will. She's one of those people who you sense from the off are reliable.

Okay, I'm not going to wallow. I'm going to go to the gym and then message my mate Dom to see if he wants to go for a couple of beers later. It would be ridiculous to let this Lola thing get to me too much. I hadn't even thought about her for a while before she texted last week.

I am not going to think about her any more.

I think about her the second I get out of the shower when I check my phone for the message she has of course not sent. It's becoming a *ridiculous* compulsion.

I don't let myself look at my phone until after I finish in the gym.

Lola has obviously not messaged.

Bea has, though. She's reiterating her invitation to us all to their wedding, which will be very soon. That makes me smile.

And Nadia has replied. It turns out she's one of those people who sends a stream of messages rather than one long one. Also, she likes a capitalised emphasis.

> Morning (just). I had a big lie-in. I could NOT get to sleep after all that coffee – did you sleep??

> And are you okay?

> I would very happily be your plus-one next Sunday

> I have a plus-one question for you: work summer drinks – I don't want to go for long but I would LOVE to go and take someone for an hour to show Sammy (the blind date setter-upper) and Dougie (the blind date no-shower) that I am NOT the biggest loser they have ever met

> And on the subject of Dougie OMG

> I've had a message from him via Sammy via my friend Marisa (or the other way round, not sure which way that should be written) and HONESTLY

> He totally WOULD have shown up (he says) BUT he hooked up with someone else that afternoon and was 'too busy having sex' to remember to message me to let me know he wouldn't be showing up and also he didn't think it would be 'tactful' to the woman he was having sex with to message another one even if just to pre-date dump her. WHAT A LOVELY MAN

I'm laughing as I type my reply.

> Yep, I also had a caffeine no-sleep issue, which internet tips were no help with whatsoever; decaf next time I have four cups after midnight. I'm actually okay, thank you. And thank you so much about the barbecue next Sunday. I'll send details. Absolutely about your summer drinks – what's the date, though? If I'm busy I'm sure I can switch things round so that we can pop in for an hour. And Dougie – what a tit. No other word.

I see the beginnings of another stream of consciousness, which I already know I'm going to love.

> Glad you're okay
>
> Thank you about the drinks!!
>
> They're this Thursday, 6 p.m. until late
>
> Er, I have to warn you that there's a theme
>
> Although actually as an anonymous plus-one I'm sure you don't have to stick to it
>
> And then maybe I won't either

I wait but that's it. Now I'm intrigued. I have to ask.

> What is that theme?

> Well.
>
> My boss is a big cartoon fan (kids films only, any era)
>
> And so
>
> We – all adults, mainly over thirty – have to dress up as a cartoon character, with a penalty if we go boring

I'm laughing again.

> I can do any time Thursday from about seven onwards and I do have to admit that I own a Tom (as in Jerry) costume.

Thank you thank you thank you about Thursday

On the costume: without being rude I think Michael (boss) would classify Tom and Jerry as boring. His example of the MOST well known we're allowed to go is Hades from Hercules

> Sorry WHO? Very hard work to find?? Let's go very unambitious on the costume and you can blame me. What if we say we're going on somewhere smart afterwards?

Perfect – you're a genius

I stumble through the rest of Sunday tired and kind of morose about Lola (I despise myself for how often I check for messages from her and, obviously, find nothing), but really not as miserable as I might have been, for which I have to thank my old friends (I go for a pint with a couple of my best friends) but also my new Waterloo friends. Nadia, obviously, and also the others; Bea and Ruth send some follow-up messages about their wedding – they're planning to set a date tomorrow once venue offices are open – and Carole messages to thank us all for our support and to confirm that she's booted Roger out, and it's genuinely nice to hear from them.

It's a busy week for me at work – I'm a deputy head in a big comprehensive, which involves very few dull days – which makes it easier for me not to think about Lola and her no-show *too* much (okay, if I'm honest I do think about it more than I would like but I do manage to obsess less as the week goes on, helped by busyness and some excellent motivational messages from Nadia, which just make me laugh).

Before I know it, we've arrived at Thursday.

We've agreed to meet under the Waterloo clock again. I'm slightly delayed and sprint across the concourse once I'm free of the heaving escalators emerging from the Tube, because I really don't want Nadia to think she's been stood up twice in five days.

I can see her looking in the opposite direction from me and call, 'Nadia, hi,' from a few metres away.

She spins round, nearly knocking a man carrying a tiny dog flying, says, 'Sorry, sorry,' to him and then, with a huge smile, says to me, 'Thank you *so* much for doing this for me.'

'Hey, no, my pleasure.'

We exchange a hug and then Nadia says, 'That way,' pointing at the main exit.

'Sorry I'm a bit late,' I say as we begin to move in the direction that leads to the South Bank. 'I was helping out with an after-school swimming club that we do at one of the local pools, because one of the sports teachers is on parental leave this week, and two kids pushed two others in fully clothed, which led to a lot of unforeseen hassle.' There was one point during our tapas dinner with the others where Carole asked us about our jobs, so I know that Nadia works in accountancy (and doesn't love it) and I know that she knows what I do.

'How fully clothed were they?' asks Nadia, sounding awed.

'Shoes, bags, the works. They shouldn't have been next to the pool like that in the first place. But they were. They both had phones on them, which are probably ruined. One of those situations where a kid does something that affords them a few seconds of gratification and causes a lot of adults a *huge* amount of admin to sort it out.'

'It probably caused them more than a few seconds' gratification,' Nadia says. 'Looking on the bright side.'

'True. Especially when one of the lifeguards lost it and called them effing little shits. Which, if I'm honest, was the high point of my working day too, because clearly I cannot say that to them, but it did sum up the situation perfectly.'

Nadia laughs. 'Well. In the circumstances I'm amazed that you made it to meet me pretty much on time.'

I resist the temptation to hug her in gratitude that she's so understanding and remind myself that I should *not* conflate all women (*any* women, or people, in fact) and that just because my ex-wife used to go *mad* if I was late back from a school thing (a common occurrence in an expect-the-unexpected job), it doesn't mean other people will.

Instead, I say, 'Obviously it's disappointing that I didn't have time to don my Tom costume.'

'Well fortunately,' Nadia says, 'I brought you something to wear.'

'You did?' I'm not *big* into fancy dress if I'm honest.

'I went simple. Just to show willing for Michael, who really is quite a mean boss.' She opens the large bag she has over her shoulder and pulls out two bunny headbands. 'Bugs Bunny,' she tells me. 'Obviously not as niche as Hades from *Hercules*, but it's a small effort. Hopefully there'll be a critical mass of people not joining in. But just in case...'

'Good thinking. Everyone should carry bunny ear headbands in their bag to cover all eventualities. So, is there anything I should know before we go in? Do we need to have a story that we have to get straight?'

'Well, basically Sammy has the emotional maturity of a toddler and has spent the entire week sniggering about me getting stood up on Saturday night. I've just been smiling and telling him that honestly it was the best thing that could have happened to me. My lovely colleague Marisa, whose maturity level is similar to his but who is an amazing friend, has been taking positive action like putting salt in his coffee and chewing gum on his chair. I'm thinking that sticking to the truth is always the best thing, so we should maybe just say we met at Waterloo station on Saturday during a false bomb alarm and it's *really* early days but we're enjoying each other's company.'

'That's the perfect story,' I approve. 'Then if we don't know stuff about each other, all good.'

'Exactly.'

I actually cannot understand why Nadia has such bad dating luck. Objectively, she's very attractive – pretty face, tanned skin, great hair – and she's also lovely, as demonstrated by the fact that she's now delicately asking me about Lola and how I'm feeling.

'Yeah, no, no reply, and I'm trying to ignore the whole thing. I think I'd still like to look for her – see her in person, get closure – but not right now.'

'Makes sense,' she tells me. 'It *will* be okay.' And weirdly, I feel like she's right, and I feel a little better.

* * *

The work do is in a café on the South Bank; Nadia's boss Michael has rented out the whole of the upstairs.

'The food will be shit.' Nadia hands me my Bugs Bunny ears as we traipse up the stairs behind a Minnie Mouse, a Donald Duck and a Cinderella. (Clearly no-one heeded the boss's request that the characters be niche.) 'But I hear that the views are great.'

When we enter, we're almost immediately surrounded by people who Nadia clearly knows well.

Nadia introduces me as Tom, with no explanation, and from the way her eyes are dancing and she looks as though she's about to giggle I can see that she's enjoying being mysterious. I'm enjoying it too if I'm honest. I'm saying, 'Hi, I'm Tom,' and shaking hands and offering no explanation whatsoever about myself, and it's genuinely good entertainment watching the who-*is*-he pantomime unfold.

Nadia manoeuvres us slightly further into the room, and I quickly realise why: my hand is shaken by a tall, thin man, who's dressed in a very sharp brown, checked suit and pointy shoes, with no concession whatsoever made to the Disney theme (unless he's a cinematic villain I haven't heard of), and Nadia introduces us.

'Tom, this is Sammy.'

'Hey. Tommmm,' he says. I do not like his smirk. 'I'm guessing you're Nadia's brother.'

'*Brother*!' I feign exaggerated horror. 'Do I *look* like her brother?'

'Housemate?' Sammy asks, his eyes going between the two of us like he's watching a table tennis match. 'University friend?'

'Nope,' I say. 'We're...' I look at Nadia, smile fondly in her direction, and then let my smile drop as I return my gaze to Sammy. 'It's early days. We don't want to label things yet.'

I don't know where that sentence came from but I'm pretty proud of myself.

I think Nadia's impressed by my innovation too, because she grins at me before saying soulfully to Sammy, 'That's right. Early days.'

'Early days of what?'

I do not appreciate his scoff. I'd *like* to swear at him, but these are Nadia's work drinks and I'm here to make her life better, not worse, so I say, 'Of our relationship?' like he's really stupid. And then I put my arm round Nadia's shoulders and she puts her arm round my waist, and I smile soppily down at her while keeping an eye on Sammy in my periphery, and say, 'Shall we go and find some food?'

'Good idea.'

'Great to meet you, Sammy,' I say and draw Nadia away from him.

'OMG,' she whispers as we go. 'That was *perfect*. He's such a *snake*.'

'He really bloody is,' I agree.

We wander over to a corner before removing our arms from each other so we can grab some of the many canapés being circulated on platters.

They look delicious.

They do not taste delicious.

'You weren't wrong about the food,' I tell Nadia after I swallow a strange gelatinous thing as quickly as I can.

She nods and points at her mouth and chews a lot.

'You have to swallow,' I tell her.

'Can't.'

I look round and grab a couple of napkins from a table to my right.

'Thank you,' she says, having discreetly removed the chewy thing and then hidden her napkin-wrapped mouthful under some cutlery on an unused plate on the same table. 'I don't know what I was thinking. *Never* eat anything at these events. Michael uses the same outside caterer every time, and anyone with any common sense learns their lesson the first time.'

'Easily forgotten when you've just had a run-in with Sammy.' I take a large sip of the glass of wine a waiter just handed to me, and then grimace. 'Whoa. That's a cross between Marmite and vinegar.'

'Whoops, sorry. I should have mentioned: only drink water at these events. And always have a big sandwich beforehand. I can't believe I forgot about that. What if we leave here in the next half hour and I buy you dinner to thank you for your truly awe-inspiring acting for Sammy?'

As I'm about to say that would be great but she isn't paying, and suggest grabbing us both some water now – I really need to clear the horrible taste in my mouth and I imagine Nadia does too – I'm interrupted by Nadia's friend Marisa, who I was introduced to as soon as we arrived.

'I hope you're enjoying the delicious food and wine, Tom,' she says.

'I've sampled it and I was awestruck,' I reply.

Marisa (who is dressed as Jessica Rabbit) spares a moment to smile, before continuing with, 'So what do you do? Workwise?'

'I'm a teacher.'

'And you and Nadia met at Waterloo on Saturday evening?'

'Yep.'

'And you're... single?'

'Yep.' I'm trying not to laugh at the interrogation.

'So it's lovely that you came this evening.'

I nod very seriously. 'It's certainly an evening to remember.'

'Although we're going to have to leave soon, I think,' Nadia says.

'Nooooo. What about the dancing at the end?' Marisa says. 'You have to stay.'

'We have another... thing... to go to,' I say. I feel that a whole evening could be a *lot* of pretending that might catch one or both of us out. I'm sure we can manage that in due course, but maybe we should work our way up to it.

'Yes, a thing,' Nadia says.

'So, Tom, where do you live?' Marisa isn't letting go of the interrogation.

'Clapham.' I feel as though this is a very strange conversation. I don't think I'm usually a mono-syllabist. 'In a flat,' I elaborate. 'On my own.' Okay, no, also weird.

'Meeting at Waterloo the way you did is such a gorgeous meet-cute,' Marisa says.

'Meet-cute?' I ask.

'It's a romcom term,' Nadia supplies. 'Marisa and I love a romcom.'

'What's your favourite kind of film?' Marisa asks sternly, which makes me laugh out loud. I love that she's such a caring friend to Nadia (if a little scarily intense).

Nadia's looking at me very enquiringly too. Apparently I need to answer the question seriously.

'I don't really have strong film preferences. But if I had to choose I'd maybe go for one of those drama-documentaries. Or a war film. As in a historical one.'

'Good,' Marisa approves. Nadia nods too.

'What would have been a bad answer?' I ask.

'I mean.' Nadia looks at me as though I'm mad. 'The obvious. Extreme violence.'

'Or a weirdly babyish love of kids' films.' Marisa is not tolerant apparently. 'And a lot of porn.'

'No-one would really admit that, would they?' I point out.

Marisa narrows her eyes. '*Do* you watch porn? I can allow a certain amount, but we need to know that no actors were abused during the making of it. And beyond a certain point it's too much.'

I find myself saying, 'I do not,' which, frankly, feels like too much information.

Nadia's shaking her head. '*Marisa*. Outrageous. Tom can watch as much porn as he likes. Or not. I mean, it's nothing to do with us.'

'Well, it's something to do with *you*.' Marisa opens her mouth to say more and Nadia puts her hands over her ears.

'No. Honestly, no.' She looks at me. I'm just laughing. 'Tom and I have known each other for five days.'

'You should get to know each other better,' Marisa tells us. 'Porn habits are one of the first things any couple should talk about.'

'On that note,' I suggest, 'shall we go to that dinner and talk on the way?'

'Good idea.' Nadia hugs Marisa and says she'll see her tomorrow, and then we begin to make our way towards the exit, with Marisa yelling at our backs not to forget what we need to be talking about.

As we exit, a *lot* of people we didn't encounter on our way in are interested to meet me. Apparently Nadia and her unfortunate dating history are very well known in her office.

We field all the many questions that we're asked (they're all on similar themes: where did we meet; how did we meet; exactly how long ago), agree that it's lovely to see me at the drinks, agree also that we put even less effort into the cartoon theme than everyone else did, and then, thankfully, the music is turned up high and no-one can hear anyone else speak and we're able to slide out of the door.

'Well,' says Nadia when our ears have stopped ringing. 'Thank you. That was *very* good. No-one's going to nag me about dating for ages. This fake-plus-one thing is genius.'

She's right. It is.

7

NADIA

'What's your favourite food?' I ask as we wander along the South Bank away from the drinks.

'You're sounding like Marisa.'

'That is true. But I'm not actually interrogating you; I want to buy you dinner to thank you for this evening.'

'You're going to do me a big return favour on Sunday, plus even without that what are friends for, and therefore I cannot allow you to pay for me, but dinner would be great if you have time.'

He has a point, I realise. If we carry on with this, it'll get silly if whoever gets helped out plus-one-wise buys the other dinner each time. 'Okay. Fair point. We'll go halves. But you have to choose where we go. That's only fair.'

'Only if you have a right of veto.'

'I will accept that right of veto,' I say generously, 'because there are one or two things that I *hate*.'

'I didn't have you pegged as a fussy easter.' Tom sounds slightly disapproving, like people should just not *be* fussy.

'Not fussy. Just discerning. Mainly, I just really don't like peas.'

'Oh, okay, well, all good, because I don't know any pea restaurants.'

* * *

Fifteen minutes later, we're seated in a pub that Tom says he's been to a few times before. It's next door to a very nice-looking but reasonably priced Italian restaurant with someone playing the piano in the corner that I would have *loved* to go to.

To be fair, the pub has a wooden floor, velvet chairs that are both comfortable and clean, and lots of traditional features, and it's busy but not rammed, so everyone has a seat, and there's a hum of conversation but you can totally hear yourself speak. So it's very nice.

However. High on the wall to the right of the very attractive olde-worlde fireplace is an enormous TV screen with a football match showing on it and a large proportion of the pub's clientele are not speaking, their attention fixed on the match.

Tom bears all the marks of a man who'd really like to be focusing his entire attention on the match too and might if he's honest have chosen this pub *because* of the match. Which, obviously, is understandable if watching it is what he'd been planning to do this evening rather than go to my work drinks. But being with someone who's more interested in a TV screen than you does make for limited conversation. Which is why, after a few disastrous sports-watching-related dates, I now always swipe on by when confronted with anyone who describes themselves straight off as a football or rugby fan.

I wonder for a moment how Tom would describe himself. I think he'd go a bit sarcastic, do one of those descriptions where he pulls out three very random and niche facts about himself and makes you laugh. So you could get sucked unsuspectingly into spending an evening with him only to discover he's blatantly a huge football fan. (I'm not thinking at *all* about the time I was on a second date with someone who was so fixated on Formula One – I am so not into watching cars go round in circles and people possibly die in terrible crashes – that it took him fifty-seven minutes after I had told him I was leaving and walked out to message me to ask if I was okay and where I was.)

It's fine, though, because Tom and I are not *actually* dating and he's just done me a massive favour, so his football fannery does not matter to me.

'Sorry.' He shifts his chair infinitesimally away from the direction of the screen. 'Just wanted to keep an eye on what's going on. It's a friendly but it's interesting to see England's form before the Euros start.'

'Absolutely,' I say politely.

'You aren't a football fan?' He's clearly trying to pretend that he doesn't have an eye on the screen, but he really does.

'No, not really. Well, not at all actually.' It's so refreshing not to have to pretend when talking to a man I don't know that well. On a date, I'd be (pathetically, I now realise) saying that I *quite* liked it and then I'd be up a conversational creek when asked what team I support or expected to have knowledge about the intricacies of the offside rule. 'I don't know anything about it at all and it's never appealed.' *So* refreshing.

Tom laughs and says, 'Whoops. This pub was quite a selfish choice then, sorry. Although. What? *How* can football not appeal? It's an amazing game. What sport *do* you like? What's your favourite sport? Oh.' He mock-panic eye-swivels and says, 'I just heard myself and that sounded *way* too hypocritically interrogatory following our conversations earlier.'

I laugh and say, 'I'm going to allow it unless you go full Marisa and veer towards questions about porn-watching.'

He laughs. 'Noted. I will try really, really hard not to ask anything of that nature.' He pulls his eyes away from the screen again and says, 'So what *is* your favourite sport?'

'Tennis,' I say firmly. 'Which is genuinely an amazing game.' A lot of football fans have zero interest in tennis, I've noticed. 'Wimbledon final or a football match?'

'Football every time.'

I tsk. 'Honestly.' I take one of the menus from between the salt and pepper pots in the middle of the table. 'There's loads of football and Wimbledon's only once a year.'

'In my defence—' Tom puts his beer glass down and takes a menu too '—I've been a huge football fan – specifically Arsenal and England – since my early teens, initially because I wanted to fit in with my school friends and then because I just fell in love with the game. I like playing too. I'm in a five-a-side team that plays, badly, in a local league, and I love it. A great release from the rest of life.'

I nod. Fair enough. There are not many people who don't need a release from life. In fact, I should admire Tom for the fact he can still be interested in football after his big Lola disappointment at the weekend.

Tom looks up from his menu. 'I'm guessing you won't be ordering the pea risotto or the broad bean and garden pea salad. Looks like it's pea season.'

I laugh. 'Yes, June's a bad month for me to eat out.'

'Kind of interesting to find out what your fake-other-half-for-the-evening's going to choose?' Tom says after a minute.

'Totally,' I agree. It's strange having a fairly intense evening with someone the way we did on Saturday and feeling that you've got to know them quite well but also basically knowing absolutely nothing at all about them.

'Easy choice for me.' Tom puts his menu down. 'Pie and chips.' He glances up at the screen, which makes me realise that he very politely has not in fact looked at it for at least a couple of minutes. 'With mushy peas on the side,' he adds with relish. 'You have to go classic pub food in a pub.'

'Hmm,' I say.

'You planning to go non-classic?'

'Kind of.'

I order linguine with prawns and chilli oil.

'Not classic,' Tom says after the server leaves us. 'Don't say I didn't warn you.'

While we're waiting for the food, we order a second glass of rosé (me) and a pint (Tom). It's no surprise to me that our drinks tastes are different, because it's fast becoming apparent that we have *nothing* in common.

'Wild camping?' I repeat in horror when Tom asks if I like it. 'As in with no campsite or loos or showers or electricity or anything? No. Definitely not.'

'But there's the beauty of waking up in the morning surrounded entirely by nature and absolutely nothing else,' Tom says.

I shake my head. 'I don't mind a hike. And I said I'll go glamping this summer for a long weekend with my brother and his wife and kids, and I'm genuinely looking forward to it, but I have no interest in being without a proper loo and running water for that length of time.'

'Salsa dancing?' Tom says a few minutes later, sounding aghast, when I mention how much I like it. 'Certainly not for me. *Please* don't tell me that you're going to need a plus-one for a salsa evening.'

'Well, now you mention it... Next Friday...'

His eyes swivel and then he laughs when I say, 'Joking.'

There's a roar from a lot of people around us, and Tom looks over at the screen.

'Yessss,' he yells when he realises what's happened.

He looks back at me, clearly having had to force himself not to continue looking at the screen, and I say, 'That is *very* polite of you but you have to watch the replay.'

He breaks into a wide grin, and says, 'Yeah, I do.'

I watch it too and have to admit it was a very good goal.

The two teams are now one all, and there are only ten minutes left of the game.

'So it's a friendly? Is it important at all?' I ask.

'Kind of.' Tom then – half an eye on the screen again – explains about preparation for the Euros and group stages and how England have been playing recently under their new manager and some other things that I immediately forget.

'Let's watch the rest of it,' I say.

'Sure?' He quirks an eyebrow. 'I mean, it isn't tennis.'

'I'll try really hard to deal with it,' I tell him.

It's surprisingly tense. Most of the people in the pub are rooting for England, and they *deserve* to win if they've been playing like this the whole time, because they've definitely had way more possession than the other side.

When a man with a very curly blond mullet sneaks a goal in for England just past the post ninety seconds before the final whistle, and the pub erupts, I'm yelling just as much as everyone else. We basically carry on cheering until the game's fully over. It's hard to remember that it was just a friendly.

'My *word*,' Tom says when we've all quietened down (I think most people must have quite sore throats by now), 'I've had a good effect on you. You were *enjoying* that.'

'I accept that I did, in the moment, enjoy it. But ten minutes is not ninety minutes. And it was an international. And there was a good atmosphere around us.'

'Have you been to an actual match in person?'

I shake my head.

'You're going to have to come to one with me. If you want to dislike football, fair enough, but you've got to have something to base your hatred on. So far, from where I'm standing, you never watch it, and on the rare occasions that you *do*, you like it.'

'Hmm.' I take the last two sips of my wine. 'Maybe. In the right weather.'

'I'll do my best. Another one?'

I look at both our empty glasses and then at my watch. 'I'm tempted, but it's nearly ten thirty and it's a work night. And you sound *really* busy with work so I feel like we should go home.'

'You must be busy too?' Tom asks as we stand up.

'Well, yes and no. As an accountant, I have a lot of stuff to do but nobody's going to die or fail their GCSEs if I oversleep one morning.'

'Firstly, just in case you mean that seriously, all jobs make the world go round and I cannot describe how much of my job involves pointless admin now. And secondly, er, wouldn't Mean Michael go *mad* if you were late?'

'The key is to have a loyal friend tell him you're extremely ill but nonetheless working from home because you're so devoted to the job.'

Tom nods, like he's impressed. 'Nice.'

As we amble in the direction of the station, I say, 'Thank you again for earlier. It was *so* cool when you met Sammy.'

'I know. This plus-one thing is actually very low maintenance: high net return for minimal outlay. I've been thinking: I just have to show up to your work things every so often for literally half an hour at a time, still doing the "taking it slowly" thing, and everyone will be convinced. It could go on for years. Definitely for the whole of your dating detox.'

'Yes. It's perfect. *And*, because it isn't real, we can just stop when we like.'

Tom nods. 'What you're trying to say is that I'm a genius.'

'You actually are,' I agree. 'When we were with Marisa at the drinks, I was trying to work out whether I felt guilty. Like, I probably should have done, because she's a very good friend, but also, sometimes you just really, really want people to stop trying to interfere in your love life. Or lack of. And maybe she *would* be upset if she knew, but hopefully she'd just understand that I have been *over* Sammy and his snideness this week, and also that I don't want to hurt her feelings by telling her that I really want her to stop trying to find dates for me, but I do.'

'Precisely.' Tom grabs my elbow and jay-walks us across the road (which makes me squeak; I always very anally wait for the green man). 'I don't want to hurt my family but they'll never find out. And it isn't really a lie. Lots of people take friends as plus-ones to events. People are just assuming there's something between us because we've only just met and we're of different genders.'

'You're so right.' I beam at him. 'We aren't doing a bad thing at all.'

We get on the same train again, and bicker amicably again about what sports we do and don't enjoy watching until Tom gets off at Clapham Junction after extracting a promise from me that I'll text him when I get home so he doesn't worry about me.

Once he's gone, I check my phone for messages and, yes, there are *loads*.

They're mainly from Marisa saying that she really liked Tom and how pleased she is for me and how *nice* he was and how maybe we can double date now (she's going out with this absolute dick called Jeremy and no we cannot obviously – Tom's going to have to be fictitiously very busy), but there are several others from work girlfriends and Sammy (how did he even get my number?) saying that Tom's *hot* and I am *punching* (thank you, Sammy). And another one pops in from Marisa saying that she's sorry, sorry, sorry about giving Sammy my number in a moment of weakness because he kept shoving Hugo spritzes at her and she kept drinking them, and I am certainly not punching, it's *Tom* who is punching.

I think about Tom and decide that he definitely is what a lot of people would call a catch but there *is* the football downside to him. And his love of pies. And the fact that he would walk straight on by that lovely-looking Italian restaurant in favour of the pub. And his taste in films.

Definitely not my type in real life, however nice, funny and good-looking he might be.

In fake-plus-one life, though, he's *exactly* my type. Everyone at work completely bought the me-and-Tom thing. It's perfect.

* * *

I'm still extremely pleased about our fake relationship when Tom and I meet at Waterloo on Sunday to go to his parents' house at the northernmost end of the Northern Line.

Hopefully it will work as perfectly for Tom as it has for me so far.

He messaged while we were on our separate trains to say that his mum literally this *morning* slipped in a little, 'Your cousin Jack's bringing his new girlfriend. He's only twenty-seven and already looks as though he's likely to settle down soon,' comment when she phoned him to check – for what Tom said was about the tenth time – that he was going this afternoon. He said he thinks she must be planning to try out a fancy new recipe or something because he never pulls out of family things and she never usually checks up on him.

He also said that everyone's going to get a surprise when they see me because on both occasions he's tried to tell his mum that he's bringing someone she's bulldozed (his word) on through with some chat of her own and he hasn't had the opportunity, so he's decided to give her a nice surprise. Plus, he didn't want to introduce me as an actual girlfriend, so he thought it would be best just to say when he gets there that he's brought a new friend and waffle a few words about how we met very recently and it's early days in our friendship, nice and ambiguous so that no-one's really deceiving anyone.

'Nice dress,' Tom says, one eye on me and one eye on the hordes of people swirling round us as we make our way towards the Tube entrance.

'Thank you.' I'm proud of my choice of clothing today. If you're going to do something, do it properly. What would a very new, early-days-but-things-look-promising girlfriend wear to meet her boyfriend's parents at an afternoon barbecue? She'd wear her prettiest summery flowery dress and bring a nice bag. I spent quite a long time trying to work out whether the new girlfriend would dress it down with trainers or go a bit more formal, and decided in the end to go for strappy but flat gold sandals, because I'm never quite sure what the older generation think of trainers, and Tom said his grandmother and her sister, his great-aunt, are going to be there, and I wouldn't want to be disrespectful.

Tom is wearing trainers, and these aren't my most comfortable footwear ever, so I'm regretting my shoe choice, but never mind. This isn't about me, this is about Tom getting a break from people nagging him while he's getting over his Lola disappointment.

I ask him about Lola once we're seated on the Tube.

'I'm still not sure whether I should let sleeping dogs lie or maybe look for her just to check she's okay. But, on balance, if she got cold feet, I'm not sure how appropriate it would be to try to find her; I certainly shouldn't try to meet her in person if she doesn't want to. I might send her another message in a couple of weeks' time, just saying I hope she's okay.'

'I think that sounds very wise,' I say. It definitely sounded like a high-risk strategy finding her in person and telling her he loved her. That *could* be great but rationally it seemed more likely it would be a complete disaster.

* * *

When we arrive at Totteridge and Whetstone Tube station, I'm surprised to see that it's now three thirty; it's taken us about forty minutes from Waterloo. It's a *long* way from Central London.

Tom tells me that his parents' house is a ten-minute walk.

I look at him with narrowed eyes. 'At your speed?' I check.

'No, at the speed of a galloping horse or a snail. Yes, at a person's speed.'

I shake my head. '*Your* speed is not my speed.' I don't think he's fully aware of that because each time we've walked anywhere I've basically been trotting to keep up with him, but I can't do that in these supremely uncomfortable shoes. I bought them at the end of last summer in a sale, and they were not a good buy it turns out. 'I need to put some plasters on my toes and heels.' Fortunately I've come prepared for any eventuality; I have many things, including plasters, in my tote.

With me plastered up, we begin the walk.

At my speed.

A couple of minutes in, Tom said, 'I'm guessing that we're going at your pace now? And that's why you said my speed is not yours?'

'Yep.'

To change the subject away from my slow walking, I say, 'So tell me about your family.'

'It's large. Noisy, fun, nice. They're great. It's just that the older generation's little obsession with me settling down and having kids is sometimes not what I want. My brother Jake has three kids, aged five, three and one, and my sister Libby has twins aged four, and three of my cousins, all similar age to us, also have young kids, and my mum can't help letting slip from time to time her conviction that I need to have kids imminently or everyone will be missing out because there'll be a big age gap.'

I'm not totally sure what to say because I don't want to criticise Tom's mum to him, obviously, but I do think it's very silly for families to say things like that. What if he doesn't want kids, or can't have them for some reason, or who knows what. Plus, there have to be pros and cons to different age gaps, surely.

I settle for saying, 'Weird how, even though of course it's lovely, sometimes people really caring about you and wanting the best for you can be slightly suffocating.'

'It's exactly that.'

* * *

For the rest of the walk Tom tells me stories from his (misspent) youth based on what we're walking past at the time, until we turn into a leafy road with a small number of extremely large houses, and he tells me we've pretty much arrived.

Halfway along the road, we stop at the iron gates of a quite extraordinarily wide house, and Tom presses the buzzer on a keypad to the side, saying, 'This is us.'

Moments later, the gate slides sideways and we walk through into the gigantic drive, where there are literally seven cars parked (I count them twice), with space for several more, without anyone having to be even the tiniest bit careful with their manoeuvring. It's basically the size of a small actual car park.

The house itself is stone and has more windows across the front than I can count at first sight.

'I can hear everyone out in the garden,' Tom says, directing me diagonally across the drive towards the corner of the house.

When we get to the corner (it takes an appreciable length of time to walk over there), we go through a very pretty archway framed in rose trees and I see lawn. Lots and lots and lots of lawn. It feels like acres. Over to our left, there are dozens of people, adults plus several little kids, all talking and laughing. Straight ahead of us, basically tucked away in the right-hand corner of the garden, there's a tennis court. In the far left corner, which is *really* far away, there's a swimming pool surrounded by a fence and a gate.

'This is very nice,' I say. I think of my three-bed-plus-loft-conversion-semi childhood home in New Malden and wonder whether Tom grew up here. And whether it's nice living in such an *enormous* house; wouldn't it be a little un-cosy? You could all spread out and never really even see each other. Obviously the garden's absolutely stunning, though. You could have *so* much fun in it.

'Yeah, we're lucky with this garden. Come and meet everyone.'

'Best fake-new-girlfriend foot forward,' I say.

As we get closer to the group, I see that there's quite a white colour scheme going on with the way everyone's dressed, and congratulate myself on the lucky chance that I chose the dress I'm wearing – pale cream with little yellow flowers – rather than the sky-blue alternative I'd been considering.

Maybe Tom forgot to tell me about the colour theme. Maybe he didn't know. It's only really the women who are doing it; the men are mainly dressed similarly to Tom, who's wearing a white T-shirt but blue shorts, more of a half-arsed white theme.

As we get even closer, I note to my surprise that a lot of the women aren't just in white, they're in *tennis*-style whites, as in white skorts and tops, or tennis dresses. The men look quite tennissy too, I realise, scanning the group with my eyes.

Maybe there's a tennis-dress theme to this party that Tom forgot to tell me about.

A woman with silvery-blonde hair and a very good tan of the type fair people can only have in June if they spend a lot of the year in sunnier places or a *lot* of time outside in not much clothing, and who has extremely toned legs (much more toned than mine even though she has to be nearly twice my age) hurtles towards us, arms outstretched, calling, 'Tom!'

'Mum!' He envelops her in an enthusiastic hug, before saying, 'Apologies, I should have introduced you immediately.' He releases his mother and says, 'Mum, this is Nadia, a new, um, my new, um, friend.'

I'm impressed. He sounds exactly like you *would* do if you had a very new girlfriend who you didn't yet want to label as such.

'Nadia.' His mum puts her hand out and I move forward and shake it. 'How do you do?'

'Very well, thank you. It's lovely to meet you.' I give her my best wide-but-polite smile, and she does smile back, although her smile's tighter than mine. I'm pretty sure I read once that the royals disliked Kate Middleton for saying she was pleased to meet them instead of How-do-you-do-ing them, but luckily I'm never going to have to impress this woman for real.

'Sorry we're a bit late,' Tom says. 'Terrible journey.'

I blink. We had an *excellent* journey. And we were both about five minutes earlier than the time he'd suggested we meet at Waterloo. And when we made general chit-chat about what we'd been doing earlier in the day he said he'd been to the gym and then just chilled. Which leads me to suspect that he hadn't wanted to arrive any earlier.

'Don't worry, darling. But we should probably play your first matches sooner rather than later. You and Nadia can partner each other; we can jig things around. You can get changed inside, Nadia.'

'Changed?' I query. Are they... maybe... wearing tennis kit because... we're all supposed to be *playing* tennis? I can't play tennis with *serious* tennis players. I do like playing, in an occasional, really not very good way, but not *properly*. 'Do you mean to play tennis?'

Tom and his mum both look at me as though I'm a little mad and as one say, 'Yes?'

'I don't have any tennis kit with me,' I tell them. Why *would* I have tennis kit with me? When I thought I'd covered any eventuality I'd thought of things like plasters, an umbrella, a cardigan, an emergency cereal bar and a pair of scissors. I did not have sports covered.

'Oh.' Tom's mum stares at me for a moment, but not as much as Tom's staring at me.

'I really thought I'd mentioned it,' he says.

I think back. I've had a busy couple of days; maybe I wasn't paying enough attention. Oh.

'I think you referred to "a couple of games", and in my head I interpreted that as board games,' I explain.

'Board games.' Tom's mother stares at me as though I've just told her I was expecting to play *naked* games.

I nod and smile and say, 'Yep, a misunderstanding. Anyway, not to worry, I'm very happy to watch you all.' More than happy, actually. I do love watching tennis, any standard, not just Grand Slams, and I would *way* prefer to watch than play, because clearly several of the family take tennis quite seriously. No-one owns an actual adult tennis dress if they can't play.

'No, no, we wouldn't hear of it. You can borrow some kit.'

'Oh, that's very kind,' I say, sure that I won't really be playing tennis this afternoon with these people. 'But I don't have any trainers with me and I can't play in these. Honestly, I'm *really* happy to watch. I do love watching tennis.'

'She does love watching tennis,' Tom agrees. 'We had a conversation about tennis-watching the other evening while we were watching the England match.'

'I can find you some shoes,' Tom's mum tells me.

And then she marches me off towards where a terrace merges seamlessly into an enormous kitchen, which is a slightly odd mix of farmhouse units and an expanse of modern, shiny-tiled floor so huge that it brings Heathrow Terminal 5 to mind. And also makes me wonder how long it would take to clean.

Back to the essentials, I do not want to play tennis this afternoon.

But never mind, all in a good cause, and how bad can it be?

8

TOM

I don't know what I was thinking when I suggested this fake-plus-one thing. It's a stupid idea.

I'm effectively lying to my family. I mean, I didn't explicitly say that Nadia's my girlfriend, but that's clearly what they all think. That is what I very obviously implied.

And now Mum's taken Nadia inside and is going to make sure she gets into tennis kit, like it or not (I'm guessing not, and I'm also guessing that Mum will literally manhandle her into the kit if she objects), and then we're going to play tennis together and Nadia clearly does not want to do that. And then we're going to chat to my whole, entire family over the barbecue and I will eventually extract us but by that time we will have been tacitly lying to them for many hours.

And then there will be questions in the future. Which will be no less annoying than previous questions, just different. They'll be of the 'when are you moving in together and trying for babies; the clock's ticking' genre rather than the 'when are you ever going to start a new serious relationship; the clock's ticking' type.

And then if they like Nadia they'll be disappointed if they hear that we drifted apart.

And if they don't like her, well, that would probably be quite a good thing.

But realistically they *will* like her, because even though she clearly has quite different tastes in Sunday activities from my family, I think it would be really difficult to spend time with her and *not* like her. She has a very sunny personality. Like, my mum was looking quite frosty just now, and then she melted (as far as she does); she almost smiled at Nadia.

This feels like a mess, entirely of my own creation. I'm such an idiot.

I'm almost tempted to own up right now. I'm really not enjoying the guilt.

'You've ruined all Mum's plans.' My brother Jake is grinning next to me. 'She was going to invite the new neighbours to pop in later *with their daughter* who Mum was definitely planning to set you up with.'

'Wow.' That would explain why she checked so many times that I was definitely coming this afternoon.

'Yeah. Guessing she won't be calling them now.'

'Wow,' I repeat, not sure how to deal with that information. Should I now be pleased that I brought Nadia or feel even worse about the implicit lying?

I can see Nadia in the kitchen standing talking to Mum.

Oh God. I think Mum's grilling her about something. Her moral compass? Her background? Does she want babies and if so how many and how soon? Who knows? It can't be good, though.

I'm going in.

'Hey.' I walk a little too grenade-like fast into the kitchen and slightly skid to a halt. Mum and Nadia both stare at me.

'Hey,' I repeat.

Mum smiles at me, kind of fondly, which alarms me.

'What are we talking about?' My fake chirpiness is utterly ridiculous, making me sound like an awkward sitcom character.

'Jam,' Nadia says.

I raise my eyebrows.

'I'm just describing my mixed berry compote recipe to Nadia,' Mum elaborates.

Well there you go. Jam recipe sharing. I did not expect that.

'Great.' I look between them and decide they're looking dangerously chummy and that I will not be leaving them to it.

'Let me write it down for you.' Mum turns to get paper and pen from a drawer, and I shake my head slightly at Nadia as she smiles at me blandly.

Once the recipe's been written down and handed over, Nadia places it carefully into a pocket inside the large gold bag she's carrying, which I had assumed contained tennis kit, and then Mum says, 'I'll be back in a couple of minutes; I'm just going to go and find some things for you.'

I decide that we definitely shouldn't be talking about anything we don't want anyone to overhear because you never know who might pop up at any moment, so I leap straight into conversation with: 'Do you like cooking? Or baking? Or jam-making?'

'Yes. Especially baking, which is clearly not very healthy when you live alone, so I take a lot of cakes and biscuits into work for my colleagues.' Nadia's answer is as stilted as my question was.

'I have a colleague like that. The head of Biology. She's very popular, especially on Mondays. She's in her fifties and has four children and the youngest has just gone to uni. She says she's always baked on Sundays and can't stop but now she doesn't have enough people in the house to eat all her baked goods so we have to perform that service for her. She does this insanely good chocolate fudge cake. Also a ginger and pineapple one.'

Nadia nods enthusiastically, clearly as happy as I am that we've got some proper chat going now. 'Ginger and pineapple. That's such a good combo. I'm going to try it. That empty nest thing must be so hard. It's almost enough to put you off having babies in the first place.'

'Nothing should put you off having babies,' declares my mother. She's popped back up from nowhere and sends a hideously embarrassing wink in my direction, which I can only describe as roguish.

I laugh, because I would absolutely have to cry otherwise.

Nadia's laughing too, looking a lot less uncomfortable than I feel, and that would be because this is not her mother who we're having a baby conversation with while pretending to be dating.

'Tom, why don't you come with us to help Nadia get changed,' my oblivious mother continues.

Now Nadia isn't looking so comfortable, understandably. She has her mouth open and her eyes raised, and behind Mum's back is mouthing *eek* at me.

I mouth back that I will obviously turn my back, because I'm not sure what else to do, in that I can't really refuse to go, and then we both traipse after Mum to a spare bedroom (there are quite a few now that my siblings and I have fully moved out).

Fortunately, it's en-suite, so Nadia can get changed in there with the door closed, which I point out in a whisper as soon as the bedroom door's closed behind Mum.

'Good idea.' Nadia whisks herself and the tennis kit into the bathroom and locks the door behind her with a very emphatic click.

'Oh my *God*,' she says loudly a couple of minutes later. There are muffled sounds and then she repeats, 'Oh my God.' She opens the door and peeks round it. 'Okay. I don't totally know what to do about this. I don't actually mind about your family because I don't know them at all but I do know you and I have to beg you either to go and tell your mum that I have food poisoning or promise me that you will not look at me at *all*. If you do look at me you'll have to banish all memory of anything you see and never refer to it again.'

'We *could* do food poisoning.' Or a terrible headache. Any illness would do. Now she's mentioned it, I feel like that would be an *excellent* idea. I would very much like to put an end to this stupid situation as soon as possible.

'I would *love* not to wear this outfit.' Nadia still has her whole body hidden behind the door. 'But I think it might be rude to your parents because it would be really obvious that the food poisoning and changing for tennis were linked and I think your mum might be offended, and the whole point of this – I think – was to keep your family happy?'

She's right; I don't want to upset anyone. I mean, any more than they'll be upset in future when Nadia and I 'split up'. We should stay for tennis and the barbecue and then leave and then I'll tell my family in a few weeks' time that we've split up and that I'm not going to date again for a while. And there's a silver lining: that *would* get them off my back a little. They did hold off for a while after my ex-wife and I split up.

'Yeah, I think you're right,' I say.

'Dammit.' She's still just a door with a tilted talking head. She doesn't strike me as particularly vain or histrionic, so I'm wondering how bad the tennis kit *is*.

'Are you... ready to go?' I check.

'You know, I wouldn't mind *not* going for a while?'

'Um. Okay.' I'd stood up when the door opened but now I sit back down on the bed.

Nadia closes the door again and then quite a long time later – I think a good couple of minutes – says, 'Okay, I'm actually going to come out now.'

'Great.' I look up as the door opens, and then just stare.

Nadia screws her face up and says, 'So what do you think?' She does a slowish three-sixty for me and I stare some more.

'Tom?'

'Um. Crikey.'

'Exactly.'

'Um.' I'm trying so hard not to laugh it's almost physically painful.

'What do you think is the worst bit?' Nadia asks, very conversationally.

My answer is instantaneous. 'The frilly pants, no question.' My mother has supplied her with a very short dress, which does not cover the frilly tennis pants that I vaguely remember women wearing for tennis when I was a child. They aren't unflattering, in fact weirdly quite the opposite, but they do look very, very peculiar. The dress is very tight and surprisingly low-cut for a tennis dress. 'Also, the... Yep.' No, I cannot refer out loud to her cleavage. Also, I tell myself sternly, I really should not be noticing it at all. She is my *fake* girlfriend. It's hard *not* to notice it, though.

Nadia cranes over her shoulder to look at her bottom and then looks down at herself.

Then she sees herself for the first time in the floor-length mirror in the corner of the room.

'My. Goodness,' she says after a moment. She stares at

herself again and suddenly laughs. 'Fuck it. Let's do it. I don't know them. It does not matter.'

'Are you sure?' I ask. 'We *could* go down the food-poisoning route.'

'Nope, I'm fine, I'm doing it. Unless you don't want me to?'

'Well, I...'

We stare at each other for a minute, and then my mother calls from downstairs. 'I don't want to interrupt you but just to let you know that you're on court next.'

We do this weird thing where we both do a little nod at the same time, and then I holler, 'Coming,' and off we go downstairs.

I try very, very hard not to find any humour in the way that as Nadia walks the dress rides up so that more and more of the frills are on show. The pants kind of remind me of some white chickens my grandparents had when I was little. Absolutely not what Nadia would want to hear right now.

* * *

When we get to the kitchen, Mum's eyes widen and she clamps her lips together for a second, before saying, 'Excellent. The shoes are just here.'

'The shoes are quite... large,' Nadia says when she puts her first foot in. She looks up at us from where she's crouched on the floor. I don't have any words. Apparently nor does Mum (unusual). After a couple of moments, Nadia breaks the silence. 'Better for a shoe to be too big than too small.'

Then, as I nod, she stands up, pulls her dress down as far as it will go, and sets off across the garden towards the tennis court.

I jog a few paces to catch her up and then say, 'Are you sure you're okay with this?'

'Totally. I'm already looking forward to the excellent anecdote this is going to become.'

'Erm, good?'

Nadia laughs. 'Honestly, yes. One more thing I need to mention, by the way, is that I really cannot play tennis.'

'Just flash your frills. They'll laugh so much they won't be able to hit the ball.'

***

Our opponents are my cousin Josh and his husband Jameel. Josh is pretty good; I know that.

'Just so you know,' Nadia says cheerfully as she shakes hands with them, 'I can't play at all. You won't enjoy the match unless you're terrible too.'

'Don't worry.' Jameel does a very pro-looking practice swing. 'I haven't played for a couple of years.'

'Oh, cool. That's cheered me up.' Nadia doesn't seem to have clocked how good his swing is.

It becomes obvious on the second point of the first game (after Josh aced Nadia on the first point) that Jameel must have been bordering on Wimbledon-qualifying levels before he stopped if this is how he plays after two years out.

At the end of the first game, we switch ends (Mum's a stickler for taking matches very seriously).

'I would *love* to be able to play tennis like you,' Nadia tells Jameel.

'Ha, thanks. I might have spent a bit too much time on a court and not enough time in the classroom when I was a kid.'

'Time very, very well spent,' Nadia says admiringly, and he grins.

We lose the set six love and Nadia laughs all the way

through, which makes the rest of us laugh too. When it finishes, the four of us walk off court (well, three of us walk and Nadia limps), and then Josh, Jameel and I accept strawberry- and cucumber-decorated Pimm's from my mother, while Nadia says she'd love a drink but that she *has* to go and get changed first. We all look at her and, as one, nod, because, yes, it's clear that any sane person would be a lot happier out of that tennis dress and the frilly pants and into some more normal clothing.

She returns about five minutes later, walking barefoot across the lawn, and Josh suggests we all go and sit under a tree to cool down. Josh and I are six weeks apart in age and his parents' house is only about a mile away, and we have a lot in common, interests and personality wise, so he's always been a very good friend as well as my cousin.

Jameel seems to have fallen under Nadia's spell when she congratulated him on his tennis and then he showed her how to do some basic strokes and she totally failed to get it but laughed and laughed about it.

'I'd *love* to learn to skate,' Josh is now saying, 'and I'm pretty sure Jameel would too. Why don't the four of us go sometime?'

And, honestly, it feels even worse than the lie we're presenting to my mum. It's *normal* to lie a little bit to your mother; lots of people do, for everyone's sake. I mean, okay, they don't lie about their fake date, but equally there's definitely, at certain times in your life, a lot of economising with the truth to your parents, to protect their sensibilities. But I've never lied to Josh, or he to me. I mean, I was the first person he told when he came out. And here I am sitting under a tree with him and his husband in my parents' garden with a random woman I've known for eight days pretending that she's my new girlfriend.

I do not feel good about myself.

'Definitely,' I say.

'So we haven't asked yet how you two met,' Jameel says.

'Erm.' I'm slightly speechless.

'There was a false alarm bomb scare at Waterloo last Saturday and we got stuck together for hours under the clock on the concourse, and we just got chatting,' Nadia supplies. 'And ended up going for dinner afterwards with the others who were also under the clock, and talked some more.'

'Oh, wow, so it's *very* early days,' Josh says.

'Yeah, you get to know each other surprisingly fast in that kind of situation,' Nadia continues. I'm very grateful to her; I don't want to say anything because I don't want to feel like an even bigger liar than I already am.

'Such a romantic way to meet,' Jameel says. 'That clock's going to be *your* place.'

Josh nods.

This is terrible. They're getting *invested* in me and Nadia as a couple.

Thankfully, Nadia says, 'Ha, yes, the clock. We're a walking cliché. So tell me about *you* two; how did *you* meet?'

'Even more of a cliché,' Jameel says. 'Injury-free minor car crash. Which was his fault. But he still believes it was my fault.'

Reminded of our conversation in the tapas place about meeting someone in a car crash, I instinctively look at Nadia, who's smiling at me, her thoughts clearly having gone in the same direction.

'I need to hear the full details,' she tells Jameel, laughing, and then she continues to question him, keeping the conversation firmly on them and not us.

As Nadia and Jameel chat, Josh leans close to me and says, 'You alright?'

I hesitate, wishing I could just confess, and then realise that I can't. It would be ridiculously awkward and ruin the day for everyone. I just need to chalk this up to life experience. Do not do fake dating; it's stupid and farcical and rude to your family and friends. And I should fake split up with Nadia and move on.

'Yeah, all good,' I say. 'Just suddenly *really* thirsty for some water.' We've been drinking Pimm's since we finished playing tennis. 'Let me go and get us a jug and glasses.' And I jump up and practically sprint across the garden towards the kitchen.

When I get back, the three of them are deep in a really serious conversation about why the ice cream section is near the start of supermarkets because it makes it even more likely for it to have melted by the time you get home. That's a very good question, actually, I realise.

We're all discussing whether it makes more sense to put chocolate or cheese near the tills, bearing in mind the necessity for cheese to be refrigerated (Nadia is very much a cheese woman it seems), when Mum calls Josh and Jameel over for their next match (yes, we are having rounds; family tennis tournaments are serious business for my mother).

'You have a very nice family,' Nadia tells me. 'Friends as well as relatives. And they all care about you a lot.'

I nod. She's right. I should probably be more appreciative. Sometimes you can take the best things in your life for granted. And you shouldn't. And, also, you shouldn't lie to them. And if you do lie to them in a totally gratuitous, utterly ridiculous way, as I am doing, you should probably not make yourself feel better by owning up; you should probably slide out of the lie as quickly and as gracefully as you can without ever upsetting your relatives by telling them you did such a bad thing, and then learn from your mistake and never do it again.

So I lean back on my elbows and say, 'Yeah, I'm lucky. Can't really imagine my life without them and I should probably just be grateful that they – Mum in particular – care enough to hassle me about my "life plans" as she calls them.'

We're under the biggest tree in the garden and it's a hot afternoon, plus I haven't seen my family as much as usual recently because I've been very busy at work with A-level and GCSE exam season, school trips, the usual summer busyness, so my relatives are keen to catch up with me and even keener to meet Nadia, so gradually everyone who isn't still being forced by my mother to play tennis comes over and joins us.

It's really nice, one of those family get-togethers where you just feel deeply, contentedly relaxed amongst people you've known your whole life whose company you enjoy and who you know have your back.

Except, also, it isn't, because Nadia fits in *really* well with them, humour-wise, conversation-wise, everything-wise; no-one's talking to her only because they feel they *have* to because of me, she just slots right in, as though there was a little hole in our family group waiting to be filled by her.

And that is clearly *awful*.

I am awful.

I'm lying to the most important people in my world.

I'm an idiot.

'You okay?' Libby, my sister, asks me.

'Yeah, sorry, just a bit tired.' I realise I've been staring into the distance, immersed in my guilty feelings.

Which is so stupid, because as I've already decided, this is *fine*; it was just a stupid idea, and I just won't do it again, end of. It will be *fine*.

I pull my attention back and focus on Libby and the others; I'm going to stop thinking and get on with enjoying their company.

***

Forty-five minutes later, the tennis tournament is done and we've all clapped Josh and Jameel (who played better and better the stronger his opposition got until he eventually admitted that he literally *did* qualify for Wimbledon as a junior player).

My father and his two brothers have been basically pretty much ignoring everyone else the whole time since we arrived because they've been extremely focused on the incredibly important task of getting my dad's barbecue exactly right.

'Food's up,' he yells, and we all stand up to begin to make our way over to him.

Mum materialises at Nadia's side and says, 'Let me introduce you to my husband now he has some attention to spare.' She indicates to me imperiously with her head that I should follow them and ushers Nadia in Dad's direction. 'Jim, this is Nadia.'

Dad squints at her and says, 'Hello, Nadia.'

'Tom's new girlfriend,' Mum tells him.

I manage not to wince and instead paste a smile on my face.

'Hello,' Nadia says. 'Thank you so much for having me. The food looks and smells amazing.'

Dad preens a little. 'If I say it myself, barbecuing is very much my forte and you should try a bit of everything.'

We all laugh and then, acutely uncomfortable about my deception, I say, 'That steak looks amazing. Nadia, what would you like?' hoping to avoid any more chat.

'A bit of everything, please.'

'Good choice.' Dad's beaming at her. 'Where did you two meet?'

Nadia trots out the Waterloo story, pretty much my entire family overhear, and we all agree that under the clock will indeed become our special place.

Once we've done that, it's actually all good; I concentrate on the (very good) food and drink and the conversation and, yep, it's great.

It's even good when, after we finish eating, my mother suggests that we all take advantage of the warm evening and late sunset and go for a dip in the pool, and Nadia says she doesn't have a costume, and Mum obviously says not to worry she can borrow one, and Nadia, less obviously, says, extremely firmly, that she is fine thank you and will watch, and Mum, even less obviously, just says of course, she should do as she likes.

Because, as Josh and Jameel observed, Nadia really does fit very well into my family.

Which definitely does make the lie worse.

9

NADIA

What a very strange experience, I think, as Tom and I finally begin the walk across the lawn to leave his parents' house.

His family are lovely. I liked them a lot. And I have been here under false pretences. Weird. Misrepresenting your friendship to someone's devoted family is very different from misrepresenting it to your annoying colleagues, some of whom definitely don't have your best interests at heart.

I kind of want to say something about it to Tom – the whole nasty-taste-in-your-mouth-about-lying-to-nice-people thing. But... I'm not sure what to say. Because, while for two people who've only known each other for eight days we've got to know each other quite well, we also *have* only known each other for eight days.

Also, right now, I have a big immediate problem, which is going to start to cause me serious short-term problems as soon as we get off this lawn: I have *really* bad blisters from the tennis shoes.

We get to the edge of the lawn and I stop.

Tom carries on walking for a few paces and then turns round.

He looks at where I'm holding my sandals dangling from my left hand and after a moment asks, 'Should you put your shoes on?'

'I should have mentioned it before we left, sorry.' The thing is, I didn't want to take Tom away from the others for a private conversation, and I also didn't want to upset his mother by saying in front of her that she's basically maimed me for the rest of the day. 'I can't wear them. I got blisters from the tennis shoes and the front straps of my sandals cut exactly across them and when I tried to put them on before, it was searing agony. And that is not an exaggeration.'

'Plasters?'

'Searing agony *with* plasters.'

'Erm.' He stares at me. 'It's a long way to walk in searing agony. And it's also a long way to walk barefoot.'

I nod.

'Piggyback,' Tom declares a second later.

I shake my head. 'That is not practical.'

'I've given piggybacks to large men over extended distances. I can definitely carry you to the station.'

'Okay, I can see that you might be able to. But it's too undignified.'

'What is both practical *and* dignified, though?'

'Not sure. I feel like there *must* be options. Like borrowing a pair of flip-flops. But I didn't want to mention it in front of your mum because I didn't want to make her feel bad about the blisters.'

'Flip-flops are a brilliant idea. Back in a minute.' Tom's already striding back along the side of the house.

I sit down on the grass to wait. It's quite nice being here by myself actually, a nice rest from the weirdness of all the pretending.

'No flip-flops, would you believe it,' Tom says quite a few minutes later, his deep voice coming round the corner before he does. 'So we have two options. I know which one I think's better.'

'What are the options? Oh!' I see that he's pulling a mid-sized child's fairly ancient scooter, clearly from the early days of ubiquitous scootering, because it has quite a strange shape and three wheels, but is far taller than you would expect a three-wheeled toddler-style scooter to be. 'Yep, that could maybe work.' No, it bloody could not actually. 'But my other foot would still be bare and on the pavement.'

'Both feet on the scooter and I pull you. And then a piggy-back up and down steps.'

'Really?' No. 'What's the other option?'

'Libby and her husband Marc are actually driving to Marc's parents' house in Surrey this evening, and they're happy to go through London and drop us on the way.'

I think about that one for a second. That's a really long time with Tom's sister, and she seemed quite keen to question me during the barbecue. Plus, we've done a lot of tacit lying already to a lot of people that Tom's close to and I know how I feel about that: not good.

'What do you think about that?' I ask.

'Probably wouldn't *choose* to do it if we had other options. What about an Uber?'

I shake my head. 'That would cost *so* much. I mean you could practically pay someone to create an AI fake girlfriend for you for that kind of money.'

'Scooter then?'

'*Surely* there's a better solution.' I'm not three years old. I can't be pulled around on a scooter. We could bump into my neighbours at the end of the journey; far too embarrassing. I wrack my brain, before suddenly shouting, 'Wellies!' I can't believe I didn't think of them before. 'Maybe a size too big padded out with tissues.'

'Of *course*.' Tom looks pretty relieved; his face has broken into a wide smile. 'What size?'

'I'm a five, so I think maybe a six if you can find any? Or a seven?'

Off he goes, and I sit myself down again, a lot happier now.

* * *

About ten minutes later we're on our way, me with my feet wedged into pink and navy polka dot (I quite like the design, not joking), size-eight wellingtons with tissues wedged all round the front of my feet.

It is not comfortable.

By the end of the road I slightly want to cry.

By the end of the next road I want to swear.

By the mini roundabout a couple of hundred metres later I do start swearing.

'Should we go back?' Tom asks.

'Are we about halfway to the station?'

'Yes.'

'Might as well carry on then.'

And on we go with me going, 'One, two, three, *fuck*, one, two, three, *fuuuuuck*.' Swearing does help. It's scientifically proven. It doesn't help enough, though. It's really fecking painful. It's also a bit disgusting; too much information but the wellies are making my feet sweat and I feel like the tissues are shredding and balling so they've gone into hard but irregular little bits so the effect is a foot-surround of gravel rather than the cotton wool that I was aiming for.

When we get to the station, there are steps. I stupidly take the first step as though it's just a regular, easy, human undertaking.

It is excruciating agony because it pushes my blisters against the gravelly tissues and the rigid boot upper. There is really not a lot of give in these wellies.

I hover on the second step from the top and perform an incredible feat and do not howl in pain, I just do a little *ouch* and cling onto the handrail and wait for the pain to subside to a level where I can think about *anything* else.

'You okay?' asks Tom from the bottom of the steps.

Such a stupid question. I am incredibly un-okay.

'Yes, fine,' I say, in a pretty normal voice, actually.

I wait a few more seconds and then I decide to go for it. I turn my foot sideways and take a second step down.

No. Ow, ow, ow, ow, ow. That is *not* the way forward. That is terrible agony.

'Are you *sure* you're okay?' Tom asks.

'I think I'm just going to have to make a couple of adjustments to the wellies. I need to take them off and get the tissues out.' How am I going to sit down, though? I feel like I can't do that without more serious pain. And I'll be in the way of everyone going in and out.

'Maybe do it down here?' Tom clearly has no idea whatsoever of the incredible and impossible challenge that getting down the steps would entail.

'I can't get down there. I can't do another step like this. It's too painful.' I'm aware that I sound ridiculous but there are nine more steps to go and honestly I don't think Hercules had bigger challenges than that. And I am not Hercules.

'Okay, simple solution: what about if I carry you down these few steps and then you can sort your boots out here.'

I say, 'Thank you,' miserably, because, yes, that is a good plan, but, no, I don't want to be an adult carried down some steps by another adult because that's quite weird.

Tom blithely double-steps his way back up, apparently completely taking his unblistered feet for granted, and swings me up into his arms.

And it's so weird. He has me cradled, his left arm under my thighs and knees, his right round my waist. It would be kind of boyfriend-girlfriendy, except I'm clutching my bag to my chest and staring straight ahead at the tiled wall opposite like a very proper Victorian spinster.

I'm incredibly aware of how wide and solid his chest is and how hard and capable his arms are and of where he's touching me. I glance towards his face and nearly gasp out loud when I realise how very close it is to my head. His jaw is so perfectly square. And, oh God, there's something very, very intimate-seeming about being this close to his Adam's apple.

We reach the bottom and Tom just stands there for a moment, holding me, while I continue clutching my bag and dividing my gaze between the wall and his profile.

Then he does a very big swallow, and I nearly squeak out loud at the sight of his Adam's apple moving, and then he says, his voice a little croaky, 'Will it hurt if I put you back on your feet?'

My feet! I had literally forgotten about them.

'I think it might,' I say. 'Maybe I can lean forward and pull one off and then stand on that foot.'

'The floor's very grimy, though?'

'That is true.'

We just stay there, with him holding me, for another few – very long – seconds, and then I say, 'There's a bench!'

'Oh, yes, excellent, yes.' And Tom strides over to it and sets me down on it as though I'm a hot potato. He then sits down too, at more than arm's length distance from me.

'Thank you.' I should *not* be thinking about how weirdly good it felt to be held by him and how weirdly bereft I feel now that I'm no longer in his arms, and will obviously never be again, because he is deeply in love with Lola and I am on my man detox.

I can't actually believe that I haven't really registered before how incredibly attractive he is. I mean, I *have*, because you can't not notice his handsomeness and niceness. But, also, I just haven't been thinking about him like that. Because of Lola. And because I just don't meet men like that, randomly – I meet them on apps or blind dates through friends. And also, we have literally nothing in common. Nothing. Our families are very different. He is a football fan (on my 'never in a million years would I date' list), he likes *playing* tennis, he has terrible taste in films. He eats pie and mushy peas *by choice*. And the entire premise of our situation is that we are absolutely *not* dating for real.

I need to ignore this weird attraction that's suddenly come over me and concentrate on sorting my feet out and getting home.

'Okay,' I say, in as normal an I'm-in-no-way-suddenly-massively-sexually-attracted-to-you voice as I can produce. 'I'm going to take the first one off.'

And I have to say: if there's one thing that can take your mind off sudden sexual attraction, fast, it's incredible foot pain.

It is not enjoyable pulling the boot off.

'Eeoow.' I'm quite appalled by my *own* foot. I hope Tom isn't looking at it. I check sideways. Oh, he is.

It's *grim*. The plasters must have peeled up at the edges and got stuck to the tissues. There's redness and damp rawness and bits of flappy skin, and there are tissues stuck to the damp bits.

'Wow.' Tom is jaw-dropped. 'That looks *so* painful.'

'It is,' I confirm. I pull all the bits of tissue off my foot (owwwww) and then Tom shakes the boot out into a bin for me.

'How are you going to put it back on, though? And actually walk? How can you do that?'

'I'm thinking new plasters and no tissues.' Good job I have a whole new pack of plasters in my bag.

I take my other boot off (that foot's even worse) and then, after I've wiggled my feet for a bit in blessed relief that they're free of the agony, I replaster them, very carefully, and then bite the bullet and put my feet back in.

And then I walk with a kind of shuffling slide, and lift each leg with my hands under my knee when it comes to steps, and like that I proceed in a peculiar and very slow but fairly manageable way.

* * *

I cannot describe how relieved I am when we are finally sitting on the train and pulling out of the station.

'How are we going to manage at Waterloo?' Tom asks.

'Problem for the future.' I'm leaning back, my eyes closed, just *adoring* my seat and the weight off my feet.

'I owe you big.' He doesn't sound that convincing, actually.

I open one eye. 'How... do you think this afternoon went?'

'Um, well,' Tom says. 'They loved you. I could see confetti in my mother's eyes.'

I really want to ask him if he feels guilty about it but I can't work out how to phrase it because clearly if he *doesn't* it would sound as though I were judging him. And – just like all they've seen is a snapshot of me and they're making assumptions based on that, that Tom and I are a couple – all I've seen is a snapshot of them, and maybe if I hadn't been there they'd have been a complete nightmare. So maybe Tom *does* think it was good that we hoodwinked them.

I don't think either of us wants to talk about this right now.

'I'm just going to check my messages,' I say. 'In case there's anything urgent.'

I have no urgent messages.

Tom checks his too.

And then we sit there, next to each other, and it's a little weird, because we've *been* a couple all day, not in a PDA way, but very much in a social way, and now we're just two fake daters sitting awkwardly next to each other at the beginning of a remarkably long Tube ride.

'Want to play the best phone game ever?' Tom asks eventually, over the rattle of the train as we go into a tunnel. 'It's called Brawl Stars.'

'Porn stars?' I'm a bit shocked that a teacher would play a game with that name.

'Brawl stars,' he shouts. 'One of my colleagues got me into it after he confiscated phones from Year 8 kids playing it at morning break. He'd been watching them over their shoulders for a few minutes and managed to get addicted to it in that time. And now he's dragging me down with him.'

'*Oh*. Yes. Definitely. I'm very happy to be dragged down too.' That's a very good idea. I download it and he's right, it's really good, and it's a lot of fun going up against each other.

'This is why kids get so addicted to games on their phones,' I say several stops later.

'No shit,' Tom says.

And then we get back to it.

* * *

When we get to Waterloo, I resume my slow slide-shuffle, and it's okay. Not entirely un-painful, but entirely manageable. I can do steps, up and down, and everything.

'Can I take you back to yours in a taxi?' Tom offers.

'I'm honestly fine, thank you very much.' I really just want to get home now, by myself. Tom's great company but it all felt a bit weird back there.

'Are you really sure?'

'Yes, really definitely.'

'Okay,' he says. 'Let's at least get on the same train and I can help you. I can come back to Wimbledon with you?'

'No, honestly. I'm completely fine.'

He looks unconvinced, so I say, 'I might actually meet a friend at the station when I get back, so I genuinely will be alright.'

'Okay, if you're absolutely certain.'

'I am.' This conversation's getting silly. 'Let's play one more round of Brawl Stars while we have time.'

* * *

'So this is me,' Tom says as we approach Clapham Junction. 'If you're still sure you don't need any help.'

'Totally. Thank you.' I give him a big, I-am-absolutely-fine smile.

'Okay, well, thank you very much for today. Incredibly above and beyond. I owe you.'

He stands up and we have a slightly awkward moment,

because how *do* you say goodbye after a day like today; should there be hugging or cheek-kissing?

In the end he leans down for a quick air kiss and then he turns and goes. And I am simultaneously weirdly bereft and relieved.

* * *

When I eventually get inside my flat, after very slow slide-shuffling and a crawl up the stairs inside my building, I pull the boots off and then lie on the sofa, enjoying the fact that my feet are finally free.

I stare at the ceiling, really not sure what to think about the day. It's as though Tom and I have committed a crime together, that we share a big guilty secret now. I kind of feel as though the easiest thing now would be to never see each other again. Fake dating should obviously remain in fiction; in real life you just can't do it.

I heave myself off the sofa and go over to the kitchen area. I need a cup of tea.

Oh my *goodness* the joy of not having to wear anything on my feet.

As I flick the kettle on it's like something flicks in the decision-making part of my mind too. We should stop the fake dating now. It did work well with my colleagues, but I don't want to carry on lying to Marisa. And I can't believe Tom really wants to carry on lying to his family.

As I take the first slurp of my tea, a message comes in from him.

> Thank you so much. The frilly pants and the blisters were far beyond the call of duty. How are your feet now? Do you have flip-flops? Will they work?

> I have very happy feet now that I'm back home and shoe-free, and it was no problem. You have a lovely family

Who we lied to. Not great. I kind of want to just say goodbye forever now. But there's Bea and Ruth's wedding. And Tom's just sent another message.

> Gonna need to collect my mum's wellies from you

> Oh yes! Maybe at the wedding?

> Good idea. Goodnight then and thank you again

Yep, I think we have to stop fake dating.

10

TOM

Bea and Ruth have really pulled some speedy wedding planning out of the bag and today is their big day.

I don't like to think of when I got married (the whole thing was a huge mistake – in a nutshell, my wife and I got married too quickly, and had absolutely nothing in common, and one day after getting home early from a school trip during which most of the kids came down with food poisoning, I found her in bed with someone else – and our divorce came through on the second anniversary of the wedding) but I do know from that and all other weddings I've heard about that big ones usually take many months, if not years, to organise.

But not, apparently, if you're determined and are in your seventies and feel that time is of the essence and (in Bea's words) happen to have a younger brother who's a vicar and who can fit you in three weeks on Tuesday.

I've had a few conversations with Nadia since the barbecue (I obviously had to ask after her feet, and she thanked me for the plasters and flip-flops that I sent her because I couldn't not send her something after a day like that and those seemed the only obvious gifts) but I've kind of withdrawn a little and so has she.

I'm not sure why she doesn't seem so keen to chat; it could be anything from being busy at work to having succumbed to her dating app addiction (or actually having met someone in real life) to hating me due to the blisters and frilly pants.

I do know why I don't want to chat so much: that day was just too odd. I didn't enjoy lying to my whole family; it made me feel quite grubby, and it made me feel as though Nadia and I share a dirty secret. And I suppose no-one really wants to spend time with someone with whom they share grubbiness. I don't, anyway, I've discovered.

Also, my family loved her. Definitely. I know them and they did. For example, while they didn't say so, it was clear from the off that none of them liked my ex-wife. (They were right not to.) In contrast I could just tell that they *did* like Nadia. And rightly so; from what I've seen she *is* nice and likeable.

Anyway, it isn't just that they loved her that's the problem, it's the fact that me taking her *did* work in that for the first time for a long time there's been no speculation or hinting or anything from a single member of my family. And I think that that's because they all hope that I have finally recovered from my marriage debacle and they don't want to jinx it by saying anything.

And that makes me feel awful, far worse than I've been feeling with all the men-have-biological-clocks-too chat. That was just kind of irritating (and obviously rooted in them having my best interests at heart). This feels deceitful and horrible.

Also. And this is a big thing. Nadia and I have absolutely nothing in common (other than an immediate addiction to Brawl Stars) and she is just not someone I would ever date (I'm not doing the nothing-in-common thing again after what happened with my ex-wife). Plus, I still have feelings for Lola, which need to be resolved, and Nadia's been in a dating mess and is very much in need of her man detox. Nonetheless, something odd happened on the day of the barbecue.

I think I veered too much down the method acting route. Or the sun got to me. Or the Pimm's. Or the far-too-tight-and-too-short-and-ridiculously-low-cut dress and the frilly pants coupled with Nadia's – objectively – lovely figure. And her crazy hair and glorious smile.

But basically, yep, I was finding her very physically attractive. And she's obviously easy company.

And then when I carried her down the steps at the station, I just... Well, I don't know. But she fitted very well into my arms. Very well. I mean, I can literally still conjure up that feeling of having her softness held against me, the way her hair smelt.

And it felt as though I was kind of cheating on Lola just by feeling that. In that I told Lola I loved her and we left it at that. I mean, clearly, *clearly*, she does not also love me. But I suppose I feel that I need to say *er anyway goodbye, I'm done* before starting something with someone else.

And I will not be starting something with someone with whom I have nothing in common. Nadia and I have nothing in common. So I am *not* in any way doing the wrong thing if I spend time with her. But, weirdly, I *felt* as though I was in that moment.

Anyway, all to say, we've been chatting much more sporadically and fairly minimally.

* * *

We've both been active on our Waterloo Five group chat, though. I know from it that Nadia and Carole are both working from 'home' today (i.e. on their train journeys and during any pauses in the wedding), Nadia because she doesn't have much annual leave left and Carole because she's very senior and very busy. I'm lucky, because my school summer holidays have just started, and while I do have work to do over the next few weeks, I can have a break today and just enjoy the day.

The wedding's in a church in a village just outside Basingstoke, and the reception's in a nearby country hotel.

Having not exchanged messages with Nadia for several days, I didn't really want to restart our chat by asking about travel, but in the end decided that I should, because it seemed pretty likely that we'd be on the same train out of Waterloo, and it wouldn't be great for things to be actively awkward between us, like we're trying to avoid each other.

So I messaged her and, yes, we are booked onto the same train, and here I am at Waterloo on the concourse under the clock waiting to meet her.

I see her exit the barriers at the far right side of the station and begin to make her way over to me. She's wearing a light blue, longish dress, which is tight round the chest with a wider skirt, with cream-coloured heels, handbag and hat, plus a laptop bag. The outfit is very nice and with that and her striking dark curls and tanned skin she's attracting a lot of attention as she walks towards me, which she doesn't seem to notice at all.

'Morning.' I double-cheek air-kiss her because that's what I do with anyone I don't feel awkward around, and I'd like to pretend there's no awkwardness between us. 'You're walking very differently from how you were last time I saw you.'

'Ha, yes, all good now.' She sticks a foot out and smiles at it, which makes me laugh. 'I've got a pair of flip-flops stashed in with my laptop too, just in case.'

'Good thinking,' I admire, and she twinkles at me.

'It's platform nine,' I tell her, and we begin to walk over there. As we go, I suddenly wonder why I suggested that we meet on the concourse; my ticket includes an allocated seat and Nadia's probably does too. So we won't be sitting next to each other. And so we didn't have to do this; we could just have met at the other end. My guilty conscience over I'm not even sure what has clearly come into play and made me overcompensate.

Well, never mind. We *are* going to be hanging out today, or the others will notice, and now is as good a time as any to start. I'll be very happy not to sit next to her on the train, though.

'I'm in seat C17,' Nadia says. 'So... see you at the other end?'

My ticket is C19. We must have bought them at the same time. For all I know it's at the same table.

I make a quick decision and say, 'Absolutely. I'm further down.' I'm going to carry on walking and take my chances with an empty seat in a different carriage.

* * *

We reconvene at Basingstoke station.

'How was your journey?' Nadia asks politely.

'Very pleasant.' I found a free double seat several carriages down from her. 'I'm proud to report that I spent less than half of it playing Brawl Stars.'

'Wow. Impressive willpower.'

'I know, thank you.' I smile politely at her and then look around. 'Taxis are over there, it looks like.'

When we get out of the taxi on our opposite sides (the driver told us before we got in that he doesn't like people sitting in the front because he views that passenger seat as his work office, so we both sat in the back, slightly uncomfortably effectively hugging our own doors, not really speaking), Carole's standing a few metres away with her back to us.

Nadia thanks the driver and then says to me, 'Oh look, there's Carole,' and heads straight over to her.

'I'm so pleased to see you again,' Carole tells us.

'You look amazing,' Nadia tells her. 'I love your new hairstyle.'

Oh, *that's* what's different about her.

'I've gone dramatically to town as a spurned woman,' Carole says. 'Kicked him out, changed the locks, new hair, personal trainer, already signed up to a dating app, booked a very nice holiday with the kids without Roger – you name it I'm doing it.'

'Nice,' says Nadia approvingly, and I nod.

Carole steps between us and links her arms though Nadia's left arm and my right, and says, 'Let's go in.'

* * *

The ceremony is perfect, pitched exactly right, not too long, not too short, great hymns that everyone recognises. Bea and Ruth both look dignified and beautiful at the same time, in their different ways.

There are maybe a hundred people in the church – family and friends gathered over long lives – and it feels like an honour to be one of those friends.

* * *

Afterwards, Carole, Nadia and I join the other guests on the lawn outside the church and are given champagne while the photos are done. Everyone's been struck by the good humour that accompanies a wedding that feels *right*, and the vibe is friendly delight.

I strike up a conversation with two men a few years older than me who turn out to be Ruth's nephews and Arsenal supporters. I see out of the corner of my eye that Nadia and Carole are talking to a group of women; there's a lot of laughter coming from their direction.

I'm not listening to the wedding photographer's instructions, because they clearly aren't going to involve me unless we do a whole-wedding-guest group photo at the end, which I'll notice anyway, because everyone will be doing it, so I'm surprised when Nadia pops up at my elbow with Carole behind her.

When there's a lull in our conversation, she smiles at my companions and says, 'Hi, I'm Nadia. Sorry to interrupt, Tom, but we're up. Photo.'

'Us?'

'Yes. A Waterloo Five one.'

'Oh, that's very nice.'

I say, 'Great to meet you,' to my fellow Arsenal fans and off we go.

'Honestly,' Nadia chides. 'The Arsenal obsession.'

'You're just a philistine,' I tell her. 'Football *is* better to watch than tennis.'

I catch Carole looking at us with eyebrows slightly raised. Maybe she isn't a football fan either.

* * *

Bea and Ruth arrange the five of us in a row, the two of them in the middle, with Carole on one side and Nadia and me on the other. For the first couple of photos we all just stand and smile, and then the photographer directs us to loop our arms round each other's shoulders. And, quite ludicrously, I'm very conscious that I'm standing very close to Nadia, and my arm's along her shoulders and hers is around my waist. It shouldn't feel odd. I also have my arm round Ruth, and that doesn't feel odd at all.

I can feel everywhere Nadia and I are touching. She's taller than usual because she's wearing heels, and her hair's brushing my face. It smells lovely, as it did when I carried her down the steps.

The whole thing is weird.

I don't have long to analyse it (a good thing) because the photographer, on hearing that we met at Waterloo station, has the bright idea of asking us to line up holding each other's waists like we're doing the locomotive.

So Ruth has her hands on my waist (fine) and I have my hands on Nadia's waist (less fine, because it feels weirdly intimate. I mean, it is absolutely *not* intimate because we're in the middle of a lot of people at a wedding and lots of people are looking at us and we aren't doing anything intimate whatsoever and I've been *told* to place my hands there. But it stills feels odd).

I'm very pleased when the photos are done.

While we're still grouped there, but slightly separately from the other three because Bea and Ruth are asking Carole about Roger and she's given in after they said no they *really* want to know about him, even though yes it is their wedding day, and she's now filling them in on lots of details (that I think Nadia got while I was talking Arsenal), Nadia lowers her voice and says, 'Could I possibly ask a huge favour? A very low-maintenance fake-plus-one thing?'

'Er, yes, I think so. If I'm free,' I find myself saying,

because even though I really don't want to how can I say no when she went to such great blister and frilly pant lengths to help me.

'Ha, your face is a picture. Don't worry, no mingling with my colleagues required. I'd just love to get a selfie with you if that's okay. And then I can post it on our work group chat and that'll be confirmation that I'm still with the same person three weeks after they met you.'

'Oh, that's genius,' I say. 'You're right; very low maintenance. Definitely.'

'Would you mind if we…'

'What?' I ask, alarmed. *Surely* she isn't going to suggest that we *kiss* or something.

'Put our heads fairly close together? In one of those heads-next-to-each-other beaming kind of poses?'

'Oh, yes, no, absolutely.' I've lost my mind; of *course* she wasn't going to suggest we kiss. There are so many reasons that she wouldn't. Not least because it's the middle of the day and we're at someone else's wedding. And it would be incredibly awkward because fake snogging is a whole other level beyond fake dating. Which we are not even doing right now.

'Sooo,' she says. Oh yes. I think I might have been internally panicking for weirdly long.

'So,' I say.

She takes a step towards me and I take one towards her and then she gets her phone and holds it at arm's length and kind of tilts her head up towards mine and I tilt mine down towards hers, very, very conscious that we're really very close to each other now and that I can smell that lovely shampoo she uses and that if one of us moved just a very little we could easily actually kiss, which is just extremely odd.

'Smile,' she says and takes a few photos.

Then she brings the phone back in and we look at the images.

'Erm.' She looks at me. 'Do you not have a photo smile? Like one that looks like you're actually smiling?'

'Erm. Do you not either?'

We both peer at her screen again. Yep. We both look... pained, I think is the best word.

'Yes, fair enough,' she says. 'We *both* look incredibly fake. Maybe we can have another go?'

'Yep, no problem. Natural-looking smiles it is.' I can do a photo smile. People want photos and selfies all the time and I see the results of the photos I'm in and I *can* look like I'm smiling perfectly photo-naturally. I really can.

I really cannot remember how, though, right now.

I focus on the very beautiful hotel building beyond the gardens and produce a perfect photo smile, and then, holding it, look at Nadia.

Nadia presses her lips together.

'What?' I say, still perfect-photo-smiling.

'It's just...' For some reason she looks as though she's trying not to laugh.

'Just take the photo,' I instruct. I'm not joking, it's genuinely hurting a little holding the smile for so long.

'Erm. Okay.' She moves closer to me and clicks away.

The photos are not good. One of us looks not at all as though he is smiling naturally for a photo – he actually looks as though he's trying to prove that he isn't hungover or maybe desperate for the loo – and the other looks as though she's trying really hard not to laugh.

Now, she *is* laughing.

'How is that so hard?' she splutters through her sniggers.

'It's the on-demand nature of it,' I explain.

'All posed photos are on demand, though?'

I consider for a moment. 'That is a valid point,' I concede. 'It's the *acting* part of it.'

'Try to ignore the acting thing and just remember that you aren't standing next to a fake girlfriend, you're standing next to a regular friend and having a photo taken like people do all the time?'

'Yes.' I nod. 'I can do that.'

The next photos are still dire. I have this crazily wide smile on my face and Nadia's looking up at me with one eyebrow raised, as though she's genuinely alarmed.

She starts laughing and then after a moment I do too and then she says, 'Dammit, it seemed like such a good idea.'

'*I* know,' I say. 'Let's get someone to take one of us from *behind*.'

'Nice.' Nadia pauses and frowns. 'How do we ask for that, though? *Hi, could you take a photo of us from behind and make it look as though we're early-days dating? Thank you!*'

'It'll be easy. Watch.'

I turn to the little group nearest to us and when there's a gap in their conversation say, 'Hi, so sorry to interrupt but could you possibly do us a huge favour and take a photo of us?'

'Sure.' A man in a very conservative grey suit and a bright pink tie with one very large orange fish on it (head down) and matching orange (suede) shoes takes my phone.

'This might sound weird,' I tell him, 'but can we just turn round – we have this thing with our friends where we all post photos of ourselves with our backs to the camera.'

'Each to their own,' the man says. 'Sure.'

I put my arm round Nadia's shoulders and she leans into me, and after a moment, the man says, 'Done,' and we turn back round.

'Sure you don't want any of your *faces*?' he asks. 'Are you on the run or something?'

'Ha, ha,' says Nadia. 'Yes, please that would be great, actually.'

So I put my arm back round her shoulders and she leans against me again (we're getting good at it; it's like a jigsaw piece going into place now), and the photo's taken.

We have quite a long chat with the fish-tie guest (who turns out to be an ex-colleague of Ruth's) and then end up in a wider group (all very nice people), before everyone's called for a big, final entire guestlist photo, so we don't immediately get the opportunity to look at the photos.

'Want to check the results of our photo shoot?' Nadia asks me when we're all told that we're very free to use the hotel facilities for a couple of hours while the brides rest and get changed, before the reception proper starts.

'Sometimes I amaze myself with my own genius,' I say on sight of the photos of us with our backs to the camera. We could totally pass for a happy couple. I have my arm round Nadia and she's leaning into me just like a girlfriend would.

'You know, I did fall for your near-genius for a moment, but couldn't we just be *anyone* in that photo? As in, any two people with their backs to the cameras? As in, I could just have sent *any* photo of *any* two people?'

I shake my head. 'No-one else has hair like yours. And also, I don't think anyone *would* send a photo of two other people and pretend it was them?'

'Would anyone fake-date though?'

'I think you'd more fake-date than you would do a completely fake photo?'

Nadia scrunches her face at me. 'Very true. You know what, fake daters *should* just do fake photos.'

I laugh and we look back at the phone. And the last ones, where there was no pressure on either of us, are perfect for our purposes. They make me feel a little queasy, though. Like... weird again.

We really do look as though we're in a happy, early-days relationship. We must have only just turned round from the behind photo. Nadia's laughing, looking straight ahead into the camera, and I've removed my arm from her shoulder and stuck both my hands in my pockets – I think for somewhere to put them that isn't touching her – and I'm looking at her and wearing what would definitely pass for a very fond, if not besotted, smile if you didn't know better.

We're both silent for a tiny bit longer than is comfortable, and then simultaneously, I say, 'Wow, I am a *good* actor,' as Nadia swipes to the next photo.

'You *are*.' She nudges me. 'Finally.'

'Ha, yes,' I say.

'So are you happy for me to use that one and maybe one of us from behind?'

'What, are you not going to use any of the ones where we look like people who've never smiled before?'

Nadia grins at me and I think to myself how *that*, right there, is a gorgeous smile, and then she says, 'Okay, I'm going to post them now. Thank you very much. That's going to keep people off my back for weeks to come.'

I watch the concentration on her face as she adds them to her work chat, and I wonder again *why* – if she wants to meet someone so much – she hasn't managed yet. When she does find the right person, she'll be an amazing partner for them.

11

NADIA

My fingers are fumbling like nobody's business as I post the two photos to my work chat, accompanying them with heart and smiley emojis, and I know why. It's because I'm just stupidly flustered by that last photo. Well, all the photos actually. In fact, the whole photo-taking experience unnerved me, and, to my shame, while we chatted to those other guests I very much enjoyed their evident assumption that Tom and I are together.

Basically, since we started taking the selfies, I've had this incredibly stupid, foolish, idiotic, ridiculous feeling that it would be very, very nice if we *were* together, because what's not to like about Tom? I mean, not just what's not to like but what's not to *lust* about Tom. And, kind of, if you weren't very careful, *love* about him.

And seeing that photo, with the way he was looking at me, I mean, I *know* that he was only acting, I *know* that he's in love with Lola, I *know* that we don't have that much in common (although really who cares about that; I don't think I do actually) and I *know* that I should not and do not want to allow myself to fall into the trap of putting myself in a position where

I'll get hurt again, *but*... it's really difficult not to feel a little bit... well, flustered.

'Done,' I say. I'm already getting *Aww* comments and hearts in response to my message and I have to say I'm enjoying them. It is a *lot* more fun being the object of 'OMG you have a boyfriend and he is *hot*' envy than 'Shh, yes, she's the one who got dumped in the middle of the work canteen' pity. (My last proper boyfriend was a colleague – thankfully he recently left the company – who dumped me very publicly at work, which was why I embarked on my series of disastrous first dates.)

'Cool. So for the next couple of hours—' Tom looks at something over my left shoulder for a moment before clearing his throat, which I have to say reminds me very strongly of the canteen dumping '—I'm thinking I'll probably just go and chill in the garden somewhere with a book.'

'Great!' I say very, very brightly, like *I do not mind at all that you just basically mini-dumped me because actually wouldn't it have been a lot more natural for us to have hung out, and what a complete and utter muppet I am for having thought for one moment that there might be a tiny little thing developing between us*. 'I'm going to...' Er, what *am* I going to do now, given that I obviously can't go anywhere in the gardens in case I look like I'm stalking Tom? 'Get on with some work. I have work emails to go through. Quite a lot of admin actually. Because I'm actually supposed to be doing half a day of working from home today and I didn't get through everything I needed to on the train.'

Yes, I am overexplaining.

'Great, then,' Tom says.

I nod.

I turn to go... somewhere, anywhere, and I see Carole walking a little unsteadily towards us, champagne slopping over the rim of the glass she's holding in her right hand.

'Tom! Nadia! Let's go and get a drink together on the hotel terrace.'

I try to look at Tom without looking as though I'm looking and catch him doing exactly the same thing to me.

'Great,' we say simultaneously after a little pause.

We all start walking towards the building, Carole between Tom and me.

A few paces along, I remember that I told Tom I had work to do.

'I might have to dip out for a bit, though,' I say. 'I have a couple of emails to catch up on.'

'Nadia,' Carole says in chiding tones. 'This is Bea and Ruth's *wedding*. We all need to participate fully.' She accompanies the *fully* with a big swing of her glass-holding arm, spraying the surrounding area with champagne. I jump very successfully out of the spray zone and am able to enjoy my success for maybe half a second before I land very *un*successfully, due to my heels.

My right ankle turns over and I topple straight onto the ground.

It hurts. It hurts so bloody much.

I'm dimly aware of Tom and Carole (who's drunkenly wailing something about being sorry) crouched down next to me, but don't have a lot of time to think about them because I'm busy trying hard not to faint.

'Nadia.' Tom's very firm and very loud voice, right in my ear, cuts through the cotton-wool feeling that's enveloping me. 'I'm going to put my arm round you and lift you to stand on your good leg and then I'm going to carry you over to a chair.'

I try to say, 'Okay,' but the sound that comes out is a lot more like, 'Owwwwwwww.'

Tom has arms of steel. He literally picks me up from the ground like you would a toddler. I'm not an enormous person but I am also not a tiny person, and I don't think many people could do that.

I'm momentarily relieved before I begin to feel extremely sick.

I close my eyes because the easiest thing to do would definitely be just to give in to the faintness that's washed over me.

'Nadia.' Tom's speaking far too loudly. Stridently, actually. I don't like it, so I ignore him and carry on with my nice sleep. '*Nadia.*'

I feel him bend down and place me onto a lounger-style chair. I could just sleep here for a while, although actually the pain in my ankle's waking me up now.

I open my eyes and blink in shock at the two faces looming large right in front of me.

'Nadia,' cries Carole, 'I'm so sorry. All my fault.'

'Not at all,' I say, inaccurately.

'How are you feeling now?' Tom says. 'Do you think you're going to faint again? Carole, do you think you could go and get Nadia some water?'

'Water.' Carole pushes herself up from where she's been holding on to the lounger and wobbles quite alarmingly until Tom shoots an arm out and pulls her into a vertical position. 'Thanks. On it. Back in five.' And off she lurches across the garden.

'I think Carole could do with some water too,' I observe, in what I have to admit is a somewhat pathetic, I'm-not-feeling-at-my-best voice.

'Yep.' Tom squats next to me and I admire the way his thigh muscles, which are right in my line of vision, strain against his suit trousers. 'Right. How's your ankle feeling? Can you move it?'

I shake my head. I'm pretty certain that moving my ankle would be a very, very unwise thing to do right now.

Tom sits himself down on the grass next to me.

'Is it still hurting?' he asks. 'Do you mind if I have a look at it?'

'Yes, and no.'

It does feel a little odd, though, having Tom peering at my leg and foot.

'Can you take your shoe off?' he asks.

'Not sure I'll ever get it back on if I do.'

'You have your back-up flip-flops?'

'Oh yes.' I can't believe how pleased I feel that he remembers our spare footwear conversation from this morning. The shock's obviously getting to me.

Thank goodness I painted my nails properly rather than putting my shoes on and just painting my nails inside the peep-toe bit (I have been known to do that). I was really tired yesterday evening after a day of soul-destroying conversations about spreadsheets (I really need to look for another job) but luckily remembered in time that by the end of the day I might want to switch to flip-flops, especially if dancing, so I did them properly, in a very nice shade of reddy-orange that I bought a couple of weeks ago.

'Would you like me to help?'

'Definitely not. Thank you.' I reach my hand down and my leg out and up to the side and do an experimental little tug before letting go fast. 'Whoa. That's sore.'

'You know what. I'm sure you're fine, but why don't I just go and see if I can find Ruth's doctor son to give you a very quick once-over.'

'Nooooo. He won't want to do that at his mum's wedding.'

'I'm sure he won't mind sparing one minute. And then we'll

know you're fine and that I'm not going to maim you for life by helping you get the shoe off.'

'Okay. Thank you.'

'I might just wait until Carole gets back with the water.' He looks all round as though she might materialise out of a tree or from the sky.

'I feel like she might have forgotten, or got distracted, or gone to sleep in a bush or something. And I'm fine. Really. Definitely not going to faint again and I have my phone.' I take it out of my clutch and wave it at him.

'Okay. See you in a minute.'

My foot's really throbbing now. I get going on a game of Brawl Stars to distract myself.

There's still no sign of Carole when Tom returns with a big bowl of ice and a towel, a glass of apple juice and a bottle of water and Ruth's son, who introduces himself as James.

'We brought you apple juice for a bit of sugar for shock,' James tells me. 'Just in case it really hurts when we take the shoe off.'

It *does* really hurt taking the shoe off and I'm very grateful for the juice.

It hurts even more when James very gently (which I am extremely grateful for) examines my ankle, which, when I look at it, has already ballooned and is quite an odd colour.

When we've gone through lots of questions on things like whether I can turn it in various directions (no) or push with it without pain (no), James says that he thinks it's likely that I have a small fracture and that I should go to A&E and get it X-rayed.

I sit very still and think about that. I have a lot of important client meetings this week that I really can't miss. Hmm. I wouldn't actually *mind* missing them if I have a really good reason like a broken ankle. In the very short-term, though, I don't want to miss the rest of the wedding. The reception is karaoke and I absolutely adore karaoke. Thinking ahead to the weekend, I have plans, and most of them involve having the use of my ankle. And I have a holiday to Menorca with three girlfriends booked soon. I don't want to have a broken ankle. Also, if I *do* have anything wrong with me, I don't want to go to a hospital here, I want to go to St George's in Tooting, which is quite near my flat, in case I have any follow-up appointments.

'Is it definitely broken do you think?' I ask.

'Not definitely but probably.'

'Not badly, though?'

'Probably not.'

'Okay.' I smile at him, because I always think people seem more convincing when they're smiling nonchalantly. 'I'm guessing that it won't really matter – even if it *is* broken – if I just *treat* it as though it's broken but don't go to A&E for a couple of hours longer.'

'That *is* probably true,' James concedes.

'So I'd like to stay for the reception but not walk and just do the karaoke and I'll get a taxi to the train station here and one home at the other end.'

I look at James and smile nonchalantly again. 'I really don't want Bea and Ruth to know about this because I don't want them to be upset or worried. And I don't want Carole to know if it's broken either because there's no point her feeling bad and I know she would even though she shouldn't.'

James nods. 'In my capacity as a GP I would advise you to go now. But as a fellow wedding guest... I'd say if you actually *are* sensible, it probably can't hurt to wait a few hours. I have bandages. We can ice it now and then I'll strap it for you to support it. And please don't put any weight on it. And don't have any more alcohol.'

I tell him that he's very strict and then promise to do everything he says. Then he goes off to get a bandage and painkillers and I put ice on my ankle while we're waiting for him.

'Nadia,' we hear Carole calling just as James has gone out of sight. 'I forgot where I'd last seen you and couldn't find you. I'm so sorry. How are you feeling? I have your water.' She hurries towards us and, as she approaches, lowers her volume. 'I have to admit I was feeling a little sozzled but I've had several glasses of water myself and am quite sober now.'

When she reaches us, she sits down heavily on the end of the lounger, partially on my leg.

'Carole!' I squeak, in *real* pain, as Tom hauls her off.

'Why don't you sit on this one?' Tom pulls another lounger closer.

'Good idea.' Carole seems unaware that she's just sent red-hot searing pain up my leg and through my entire body. 'How are you feeling now, Nadia?'

I really can't speak because I'm focusing very hard on not allowing the contents of my stomach to emerge. I'm never sick, I remind myself. I can do this.

I lean my head back against the lounger again and wait for my ankle to return to a more manageable level of throbbing pain.

Everything's going far away and misty again, which to be honest I'm quite happy about, but apparently Tom isn't keen for me to faint, because he's speaking very close to my head again, saying, 'Nadia, drink some water.'

I open my eyes and look straight into his. And blimey they're *beautiful*. Big and dark and fringed with lovely thick lashes, with gorgeous little I've-lived-some-life-and-am-no-longer-young-and-inexperienced crinkles at the sides, and right now they're looking right into mine and are topped by a slightly furrowed, concerned-looking brow, and the whole effect is so heart-stoppingly gorgeous that for a moment the pain from my ankle recedes far into the distance.

'You'd make a very good anaesthetic,' I tell Tom foggily.

'Oh.' His eye-crinkles crinkle more and he laughs. 'I'm going to take it as a good thing that you're speaking and assume that you meant what you said and are not hallucinating. I'll ignore the fact that it does *not* sound complimentary.'

'No, no, it's a big compliment,' I tell him, still foggily. If I leant even a little bit forward now, and tilted my head just a little, our lips could meet and...

'Okay, I will accept that weird compliment. Are you okay?'

I love the way the corners of his mouth lift when he's semi-laughing as he speaks. He has very nice teeth too.

I open my mouth to say so and then realise that, no, that is not a normal thing to say to a friend.

'I'm completely fine,' I say, blatantly untruthfully.

'I'm so glad to hear that.' Carole pulls her lounger closer. She definitely seems soberer than she was before. 'I was really worried that I'd caused you to injure yourself when you fell.'

'No, no,' I say. 'And even if I had done something bad to myself it wouldn't have been your fault; it was all me being clumsy and over-reacting to a tiny drop—' it was a *deluge* '—of champagne.'

'Exactly,' Tom agrees. I side-eye him. He didn't need to sound *so* certain that I was basically a complete muppet. He smiles at me and I melt a tiny bit more inside, which, now that I'm no longer feeling faint, I realise is not a good thing. Tom is in love with Lola. And I am not in the market for getting hurt by anyone again, especially not someone who is fast becoming a good friend. Unrequited love is not something I want to do.

'Finally back.' James has popped up wielding a black

doctor's bag, of the type that you would never expect a twenty-first-century doctor to actually own.

'Inherited the bag from my father,' he says, as he opens it and begins to rummage inside it. 'He was a community GP, always out on visits. Right. Here we go.'

I've never seen anyone put a bandage on so *briskly*. It's genuinely not even that painful to have my ankle handled by him, and the more it's strapped the more secure it feels.

'You're *good*,' I tell him.

'Why are you bandaging it?' asks Carole. 'I thought you said it was fine?'

Tom rushes into loud speech, interrupting James. 'Just a precaution, is what James told us. She's fine, just a bit bruised, and James thought a bandage would be a good idea.'

'Exactly,' I agree.

James nods and says nothing as he carries on with his very neat bandaging.

When he's finished, he says, 'I'm proud of that. I don't do a lot of bandages now but apparently it's like riding a bike.'

When I've swallowed the paracetamol and ibuprofen tablets he hands me, and thanked him profusely, he picks up his black bag to return it to his car, and Carole says, 'Are you absolutely certain that it's nothing serious?'

'Yes,' Tom and I answer as one.

'Don't think I'll be drinking anything else today,' she says. 'I think I downed too much champagne from the shock of being at a wedding without Roger.'

'You're going to get through this, Carole,' I say. 'Okay, that sounded extremely trite, but you *are*. You're an amazing woman.'

She sniffs. 'Thank you. Do you know what Roger is?'

I want to say *tosser* but am not sure that I should, just in case she's re-warmed to him, so I just shake my head. Tom's doing the same.

'A complete fucker,' she says, suddenly cheerful. 'Come on, let's go and have some non-drunken fun. The main reception will be starting soon.'

'Good idea.' I move my legs round to the side and reach for my bag to get my flip-flops out. Oh. I did not think this through. The flip-flops fit very snugly into my bag. My heels do not.

Carole sees my dilemma. 'I'm staying overnight,' she says. 'Let me look after your shoes for you. I'll take them to my room now. I'll dash. Meet you back here?'

Tom sits himself down on Carole's lounger and we stare at each other for a moment before both looking away.

'It's a really nice spot here.' I hadn't totally registered it before; we've been busy since we got here and I haven't had a chance to just sit and take things in. The hotel itself is an ancient abbey, built of honey-coloured stone and very beautiful. It's surrounded by stunning rose-covered-walled gardens and lawns that are so vibrant green it's clear they've been breaking the hosepipe and water sprinkler ban that's been in place across the whole of the south of England for the past fortnight despite the deluge the night we met at Waterloo.

'Gorgeous,' Tom agrees. 'I really like the way all the gardens lead into each other, like a kids' fantasy.'

I'm about to suggest that he go and explore the gardens properly – I feel very guilty that he's stuck here with me – when Carole turns up, at a bit of a run.

'Sorted,' she says. 'Ready to go inside? People seem to be congregating.'

I swing my legs left, so that my good foot hits the ground first, and then sit there, wondering how I'm going to stand up because I'm very nervous about putting any weight on my right foot.

'Help?' Tom's appeared at my elbow and is holding his arm out.

'Yes please.'

'Honestly,' he says as he hoists me up onto my left foot. 'Every time I see you you have a foot issue.'

'Oh, what other foot issues have you had?' Carole asks, looking between us like a cartoon detective.

'I trod on Nadia's foot the first time we met, at Waterloo,' Tom says.

'And then we met up a couple of weeks ago for a drink and I got a blister,' I add, ignoring Carole's raised eyebrows.

'Not just any old blister,' Tom clarifies, 'but blisters plural, mega ones.'

'And on that occasion I didn't have any flip-flops.'

'Thank goodness you have them now.' Tom adjusts his grip on my arm. 'I wonder whether I should just carry you over there to avoid you putting any weight on it.'

'Very kind but no thank you,' I say firmly. I don't want to make Carole think I'm properly injured and also I'm alarmed by the lovely little fantasy of being held close in Tom's arms that just passed through my mind. 'I'm an excellent hopper.'

'Okay. Would you like some hopping help? Even though I'm sure you can indeed hop excellently by yourself?'

'Yes please.' I'm pretty sure that I'm not a good hopper at all.

* * *

Hopping as your actual mode of transport rather than just a few hops while drunk or on the beach is extremely hard work. Personal trainers should recommend it for exercise. I'm *exhausted* within only about ten hops. And ten hops don't take you very far.

'I might just have a break when we get to that tree,' I pant. It's like my left foot has cement on the end and my thigh is *burning*.

'The big oak tree?'

'No, the little thin red one.'

'Oh, right in front of us. Got it.'

Thirteen excruciating hops later, we're next to the little red tree. Honestly, I'm almost seeing stars from the hopping effort. When my vision clears, I look down at where I'm still holding on to Tom's arm for balance and notice that, even through his shirt sleeves, you can tell that his forearm is very nicely muscled.

I think I really might be falling in lust with him, which can't be good.

12

TOM

I'm spending a lot more time with Nadia than I bargained for today.

Obviously I knew that I was seeing her. And obviously I knew that I only knew two guests at the wedding. But I wasn't really expecting *this*.

To be spending *so* much time being *close*.

You can't help sticking with someone when they're injured, though. Clearly, she needs someone to help her, and clearly, I am the only person who can be that someone, because she doesn't know any other guest other than Carole who a) still isn't entirely sober and b) will not benefit from being made to feel guilty, so we do need to continue to pretend that Nadia is basically fine.

So here I am, physically helping her.

I don't like it. I don't like how much I notice things about her when I hold her in my arms, or indeed when I'm *not* holding her, just looking, or even not looking, just listening to her. Or breathing in her scent.

Right now she's holding a tree with one hand and leaning on my arm with her other, and I am necessarily standing very close to her so that she won't fall over.

Carole's hovering nearby and you'd think that her presence would stop me being incredibly aware of the softness of Nadia's skin, the rueful smile that she just shot at me, the line of her slim neck, but no.

I think we should just get this torture over and done with. I want to deposit her on a chair inside next to Carole and then go off to the bar and have a drink (or several) with some of the other very nice wedding guests that I met earlier.

'Hopping seems pretty tricky,' I say.

'Trickier than I expected,' Nadia agrees.

'So I'm wondering whether maybe I should just carry you or give you a piggyback? Quickly. From here. Given that very few people – you would think – could hop up the steps, so you'll need to be carried then anyway?' I'm not sure why I'm making such a big deal of it; I'm making it sound a way more significant thing than it is. I should stop talking.

'I'll help.' Carole's words are a statement, rather than a suggestion. 'We'll link hands under Nadia's bottom and she'll put an arm round each of our necks.'

It's very difficult not to laugh at Nadia's open-eyed over-my-dead-body expression.

'I get the feeling Nadia wants to get this over and done with as quickly as possible,' I say. 'Probably fastest if I just carry her myself.'

'I insist that I help. Let's go. Chair lift.' Carole moves so that she's next to Nadia's right side and holds her arm out towards me.

'Erm.' I look between Carole and Nadia.

After several seconds, Nadia says, 'Thank you,' very miserably.

'Okay, then.' I transfer Nadia's weight to my left arm while Carole and I are getting our arms locked into the chair position, and then we're off.

For two steps. And then Nadia says, 'Sorry, no, please put me down on my left foot *now*. Now. *Now!*' We scramble to lower her as she continues, 'Carole, I'm sorry, I don't want to upset you and you must know that it was in no way whatsoever your fault that I fell over – *anyone* can splash a drink and it is not normal to dodge out of the way in quite such an overenthusiastic manner – it really was entirely my own fault – but James thinks I've broken my ankle and I agree that it feels as though I've done myself an actual injury and I don't want to be dropped. And again I don't want to upset you but being chair lifted is *really* unpleasant and I felt as though I was going to be dropped on your side, which is my bad foot side, and I just want to go inside and sit in a chair and enjoy the karaoke but not drink and not breathe a word to Bea and Ruth and then go home tonight and sort it. I'm sorry – I didn't want to offend you.' She turns away from an open-mouthed Carole and says to me, 'Could you possibly just carry me to the room as fast as possible and get me onto a chair and then I'll be fine? Thank you.'

Carole's recovered. 'So sorry, my love. Tom, what are you waiting for?'

'Yep, sorry, on it.'

I hoick Nadia up into my arms and stride off, and, actually, with Carole trotting along next to us giving directions it's all fine. Her presence stops me from feeling as though it's any kind of intimate experience; it's just like I'm carrying a regular friend who's hurt her foot.

Shortly afterwards, Nadia's on her chair in the dining room

of the hotel, Carole's finally stopped apologising for apologising, and I've discovered that I will not be leaving Nadia and Carole to it and going and propping up the bar with some nice new friends, because there's a seating plan and, yay, I'm seated between the two of them.

* * *

It's fine, though, I realise, once we're all at the table and chatting. The others on our table are great, Carole and Nadia are both good company, and I can totally ignore the entirely inappropriate feelings of attraction for Nadia that I'm experiencing.

We eat fantastic food, we talk, we laugh; it's a very nice way to spend a Tuesday.

The speeches are brilliant too. Warm, entertaining, and a little risqué but staying on the right line of appropriate, and after the toasting we all clap and cheer for a long time.

Eventually we've quietened down from House of Commons rabble levels to mere loud chatter and wolf whistling and Bea takes the mic and hollers, 'Okay, everyone, karaoke time. Every table has to do at least one song, or you're out on your ear before the cake cutting, which is happening later.' She looks pretty serious and I can't imagine anyone daring to not comply.

We're the third table up.

'I'm coming,' Nadia tells Carole and me.

'Let's go for an arm round the waist each and basically drag her across the floor,' Carole says.

'Er, thank you?' Nadia says, laughing.

She holds her injured foot up bent at the knee, flamingo-like, and off we go.

A flip-flop slide across a polished wood floor works a lot

better than a flip-flop hop on grass, it turns out, and the hauling is very successful; I don't even think we look particularly odd as we go.

Our song – appropriately – is Abba's 'Waterloo'.

None of our table are that drunk but we do not hold back. Nadia, in particular, goes for some truly spectacular soprano harmonising, ably backed up by Carole, at a more contralto pitch, with me belting the words out in my best bass.

While I am always happy to join in, I am not a natural singer. It's only because my voice is low that I don't make people cry with my singing. I love music but the notes just don't come out the way I was expecting. Nadia, though, her voice *soars* in a truly wonderful way.

'You could have been in Abba yourself,' I tell her when the song ends.

'Yeah, kind of gutted not to have been Swedish in the nineteen-seventies. I *love* the flares and the platforms.'

'You have to do a song by yourself,' Carole commands. 'We'll be your backing group.'

We all bow to her natural CEO demeanour and form a line behind Nadia, who gets going on 'Super Trouper'.

It's amazing. Nadia's voice is *stunning*. We all stop singing quite quickly so that we can just listen to her.

'You could have a career in singing,' Carole says when we're finally off the stage and have slid Nadia on her flip-flop back to her chair. 'Can I pull some strings for you?'

'Ha.' Nadia buries her face in her drink for a moment and then says, 'Oh, I love this song,' as the group on the stage start singing Miley Cyrus's 'Flowers'.

I haven't seen such a blatant subject avoidance since my mum asked my nephew Rafe where the rest of the chocolate log had gone last Christmas.

'*Are* you a singer?' I whisper while Carole's looking the other way.

'Shhh.' Nadia looks all round like she's imitating a Cold War spy and says, 'For very obvious reasons I don't like to mention this in certain situations, but on the side I am—' she leans very close and lowers her voice even further '—a wedding singer.'

As she pulls back, I stare at her. 'I did not know that.'

'No,' she agrees.

'How come you've never mentioned it? How many weddings do you do?'

'Shhhhh.'

Oh, yes. I see her point. If you aren't involved in your friends' wedding it's clearly awkward to mention that you have a wedding-related side hustle.

'Sorry,' I whisper. 'But wow. Cool job?'

'Very cool. A lot better than accountancy, which I'm not saying is bad, because it isn't and loads of people love it, but isn't really for me. And to answer your questions: I do maybe twenty weddings a year; and I've never mentioned it because—' she looks at me a little oddly, her head slightly tilted and her eyebrows up a bit '—we really hardly know each other.'

For some reason, which I cannot immediately put my finger on, her words make me sit back, like I've been almost physically struck.

She's right, of course. We do barely know each other.

I nod. 'True.'

And that seems to be the end of that conversation. I have nothing else to say now, even though a minute ago I had a lot of questions about the wedding singer thing, and Nadia evidently doesn't think we're still chatting because she's moved her chair slightly and is clapping and swaying to the music.

Karaoke makes for a great wedding reception. It's fun. It's noisy. It's interactive. It really is good.

Except I don't like sitting next to Nadia like this any more because somehow it feels as though a barrier has sprung up between us. I keep noticing it, but I don't want to, because I don't want to analyse it.

A lot of singing later, some people are dancing in a space they've made at the end of the table, while others are still sitting, which, as Carole points out, is handy for Nadia.

'How are you feeling?' I ask. The painkillers have probably worn off by now.

'Fine, thank you.' Her face looks a little pale. 'I think I'll make a move, though, soonish. Maybe in about half an hour so it doesn't seem too early. I have my eye on the door; I don't want to be the first to leave but I think I might definitely be the second.'

'I'm thinking there's no shame in being the first. Someone's got to be.' I pull my phone out of my pocket. 'And I'd like to go now too. So why don't I get us an Uber?'

'I don't want to be the first to break the party up, though. The domino-effect thing. I don't want other people to copy us and leave too and ruin the wedding-party vibe.'

'It'll be fine if we go quietly. People will just think we've gone to the loo. Let's have a chat with Bea and Ruth when they get to our table—' I can see them two tables away, clearly trying to get round all their guests '—and we'll tell them we're leaving quite soon, and then we'll just sidle out.'

'That's actually very tempting.'

'Why don't I go and let Carole know as well—' Carole's displaying some fairly outrageous moves on the dance floor '—so that we can get going as soon as we've said goodbye to Bea and Ruth?'

***

Our Uber driver is very chatty and very keen to hear details about the wedding, so Nadia and I aren't alone together until we get to the station.

'So. Many. Fecking. Steps,' she says, glaring at the big flight down in front of us.

'I know you don't want to be carried, but the next train's in three minutes.'

'Yes. Fine.' She looks sideways at me. 'That might have sounded a teensy bit grumpy.'

'Not at all,' I lie.

She laughs. 'What I mean is, thank you and I'm very, very grateful for all your help today.'

And just like that, it seems the most natural thing in the world to lift her and carry her down the steps and onto the train that's just pulling in.

'I'm going to go straight to A&E from Clapham Junction,' Nadia says as soon as we're seated.

'Good. That has to be the best idea. Can I come with you?'

'That's very kind but I've already accepted *way* too much help from you today and I've already texted Marisa and she's going to meet me at the station and come in an Uber with me.' She does a little gasp. 'Oh my goodness.'

'You're going to struggle to get out of the station without me, so Marisa will see me?'

'Yep.'

'Perfect, though, for boyfriend fakery? On top of the photos today.'

'Oh, very true actually. Thank you.'

'We have to stop thanking each other. We're just friends helping each other.'

She opens her mouth and then clamps it shut, and I laugh.

'Can't say anything without a thank you?'

'Pretty much.' She starts typing into her phone. 'Just occurred to me that I need to explain why I asked Marisa to go with me and not you. You've got a flight to catch at 6 a.m. to somewhere glamorous, I think. Good job *I* wasn't supposed to be catching a flight tomorrow.'

'Hopefully if you do have a broken ankle it'll heal quickly and won't impact on any plans.'

'Well. Given that we have an hour on the train and it's throbbing and I'm not enjoying it, I might list my ruined plans for you in a cathartic-wallowing-in-self-pity way.'

'Go for it.'

Nadia's in the middle of a description of the padel class she's joined that she *really* doesn't want to miss because she (in her words) is not as fit as she should be and is loving it and doesn't usually stick at exercise, when she suddenly interrupts herself and says, 'Oh for fuck's sake. I *like* those shoes and I've left them in Carole's room.'

'You'll be able to meet her to get them and, at the risk of not cheering you up at all, it doesn't seem that likely that you'll be able to wear them in the very near future.'

Nadia heaves a very big sigh. 'True. Very, very true. Honestly, it's *so* annoying.' She rolls her eyes *hugely* and then says, 'Well. It is what it is. Tell me something funny.'

So I read her highlights from the one hundred and thirty-nine messages I just found on my family chat relating to a mouse that ran across the kitchen earlier this evening while my incredibly mouse-phobic mother was making a soufflé. (Panic over; my father tempted it out from under the oven with cheese and caught it under a bowl – to everyone's admiration – and my mother won't tell us what happened next because, even though she hates mice, she doesn't like animals being killed unless they're going to be eaten.) I hadn't told Nadia before because she seemed quite focused on being pissed off about her ankle.

'I *love* your family,' she says when we reach the end of the messages. 'And I *love* your mother's sweariness. She knows some serious *words*.'

'She's an English lecturer.'

'Oh well that explains it.'

'Yeah.' I grin at her and then say, 'So tell me about the wedding singer thing. Twenty a year's a fair number? An actual business?'

'Yep, I started with the wedding of some friends who were very brave and trusting, but mainly skint and out of any other options, and went from there with word of mouth, and it just kind of escalated. I only do weekends because I work full-time, which is kind of limiting, because I have to turn down offers, and also it takes up a lot of my Saturdays *but* I do love it. I love the singing and you meet a lot of fun people and it's so nice to be involved with their happy day. I honestly haven't had a single bad experience.'

'What, *none*?'

'I mean, stuff *happens* occasionally, but it's always okay. Your average person is nice. There are always enough of those people around to help on the odd occasion that something *nearly* happens.'

I decide not to dwell on the somewhat terrifying thought of Nadia's trust possibly being misplaced. It's nice, *lovely*, that she's so glass-half-full.

We chat about inconsequential stuff for the rest of the journey until we get to Clapham Junction.

We do a hop-carry combo to get out of the station. Marisa's waiting with a taxi and they hop straight in. (I mention that pun out loud – it sounded better in my head – and Marisa looks at me pityingly while Nadia gives me a bless-you-it's-cute-how-bad-your-humour-is smile.)

It feels weird waving them off.

I feel as though it should have been me going to the hospital with Nadia.

13

NADIA

'I've said it before and I feel like I'm going to say it again.' Marisa's craning her neck further than you'd think possible to get one last look at Tom out of the back window 'Tom is *hot*.'

I nod, a little miserably. Objectively, she is of course right. Subjectively, too, now, I can't help being very aware of his gorgeousness pretty much the whole time I'm with him.

Marisa turns to face me. 'Where's he going in the morning?'

I panic for a moment and then say, 'Las Vegas.' (I've just been reading a book set there.) 'With friends. He's away for ten days.' I am so bad at lying. It makes me feel very hot and clammy-handed and unable to look people in the eye without making a very big effort and doing it weirdly consciously. So I should really stop embellishing my story and change the subject. 'Thank you so much for coming to the hospital with me. I'm very, very grateful. Once I'm in there and being seen you should go home.'

'Nope. I'm staying. I'm working from home tomorrow morning; I'll be fine.'

I am such an idiot. I really didn't think this through. The

reason I asked Marisa to meet me was that she also lives in Wimbledon, only a few roads away from me. I can't expect her to stay up half the night with me, though.

Maybe, with hindsight, I should have asked Tom to help me to the hospital and then he could have left and I could have managed by myself.

We could be there for *hours*. I mean, we almost certainly *will* be there for hours. I cannot do this to Marisa. I'm a grown-up. I can totally wait there by myself.

I'm almost tempted to tell her the truth but I really don't want to hurt her feelings and she would definitely be hurt, because I've been lying to her. I could have told her that Tom was a fake date before taking him to the work drinks. She wouldn't have told anyone else.

We have to stop. All this lying is an absolute nightmare.

I think I'll finish this when Tom fictitiously gets back from Vegas. I'll have fictitiously realised while he was away that our relationship was in fact just a fling. And I will never, ever again do any fake-plus-one-ing.

So now I'm detoxing from blind dating, app dating *and* fake dating.

'Nadia? You look as though you're in a lot of pain?' Marisa's concern makes me feel even guiltier; she's obviously misinterpreted my uncomfortable thoughts for physical pain. Although, to be fair, my ankle *does* hurt a lot again after the train journey, despite the second round of painkillers I stocked up on just before we set off. Basically, if I'm not moving it at all, it kind of throbs, and if I do move it or put a bit of weight on it it's borderline screaming agony and it makes me feel really faint.

'Just a bit. I'd be very grateful if you'd get me to A&E but then I *really* want you to go home or you'll be so tired tomorrow.'

'Nadia.' Marisa's using her sternest voice – the one she uses to get her clients to pay her on time; she has way better payment stats than the rest of us – and it's genuinely scary. 'Remember the time when you spent the entire night with me in A&E when Benny put the pea up his nose?' She had her seven-year-old nephew to stay for the weekend and it wasn't great. 'And when you stayed up all night with me after the Christmas party?' She had four glasses of punch after someone had played an oh-so-hilarious-and-not-at-all-stupidly-dangerous prank and added large amounts of neat vodka to it, and that wasn't great either. 'I could go on,' she continues, still super stern.

'Yes,' I say meekly.

'Right. So you are sober right now and way better company than I was when off my face and vomiting post-Christmas party. And you are thirty-three and not seven and, no offence to Benny, it's a lot easier to chat all night to an adult woman than a seven-year-old boy because I'm not that into Star Wars or Lego or poo. And therefore, even if I stay there all night with you I will still owe you and I'm *glad* you asked me to help.'

'Okay, thank you,' I say, still meek. Obviously it'll be much nicer having her with me than sitting by myself all night. Even Brawl Stars wouldn't carry me happily through more than an hour or two of solo waiting. 'I'm very grateful.'

'No more thanking.'

Hmm, that's very reminiscent of what Tom said earlier. Maybe I do thank people too much. *Or* maybe with this fake-dating thing I'm just making too many unreasonable demands of people and it's causing me to over-thank.

'Okay,' I say. 'Can I interest you in an addiction to a phone game that Tom introduced me to?'

* * *

It is not at all fun at the hospital and the wait is long and Brawl Stars would indeed not have seen me happily through, but Marisa does; she's brilliant. The doctor I'm seen by – once I do actually get to see her – is also brilliant. And *obviously* – as Marisa and I point out to each other quite regularly during the hours that we're there – the long waiting times are no-one's fault but due to successive governments underfunding the NHS; every professional we meet is amazing. (Not every patient we encounter is amazing but that's kind of par for the course in the middle of the night in A&E.)

My ankle is indeed broken. It's a very straightforward fracture and should heal very well; I just have to wear a foot boot for the time being and follow a few simple instructions about caring for it.

Tom's texted me periodically during the night to check that everything's going okay and to see whether I've changed my mind about him coming to the hospital, and when I message him to tell him the final diagnosis, he replies immediately.

'Cute,' Marisa says every time she sees me messaging and asks if it's Tom I'm talking to and I confirm that yes it is. (I'm pretty sure that no-one else I know will be awake at this time.)

'It *is* cute,' I say, wishing that my heart didn't beat a little faster every time I see his name come up on my phone.

We finally make it back to my flat at quarter to five in the morning.

Marisa insists on coming upstairs to make sure I'm in safely, even though now I have the boot I'm all good to walk.

Once we're in there we decide that we're very hungry. We have pancakes and berries from my fridge, and then Marisa falls asleep on my sofa while I'm in the loo. I try unsuccessfully to wake her and then put a blanket over her and tuck her in and take myself off to bed.

Tom messages me in the morning while Marisa and I are spoiling ourselves with croissants for breakfast after our bad night.

'Is his flight delayed?' she asks.

Shit.

'Yes,' I say. 'Very annoying for him but never mind. More coffee?'

I'm definitely ending the fake relationship when Tom fake gets back from Vegas. The lying is a killer.

* * *

Tom of course does not go to Vegas but he does go for a long weekend to Lisbon with some teacher friends. He has a good time there, managing to fit in a lot of sightseeing, a lot of good food and a fair amount of drinking and partying. I know that because, even though we are no longer fake dating (on my side anyway, which I'll tell him soon), we're messaging several times a day.

It began the day after the wedding with him checking up on my ankle and asking how I was coping with life as an injured person, and me asking what he was up to in his school holidays while I battled spreadsheets. I told him about the wedding I was singing at and he was very interested in my song list, and when there was a huge mouse incident (one in the honeymoon suite no less) naturally I told him, given his mum's incident while we were at Bea and Ruth's wedding. And then we just carried on messaging.

And now Tom has just texted to say he's home from Lisbon and that he has a little present for me and do I fancy meeting at Waterloo on my way home from work in the next couple of days so he can hand it over.

I say yes of course and decide that that will be the ideal time to fake break up with him.

* * *

Tom's waiting when I hobble over to the clock at Waterloo three evenings later. I knew he was already there because he messaged me when he arrived to say I was a loser because he'd beaten me to it. I sent him a middle-finger emoji back.

He's looking *handsome*, lightly tanned from his weekend away, big, solid, square-jawed. My fanciful mind thinks that he looks like a dependable oak tree in a storm as people (pretty much all smaller than him) swirl around him as he just stands and grins at me.

I can't believe that I didn't really notice the first time I saw him how very attractive he is. I mean, I did notice that he was attractive, but in a very objective way; it didn't almost floor me like it does now every time I see him anew.

'Hey.' He leans down for a quick hug (I'm proud to say that I release him slightly before he releases me, rather than *clinging* in lust). 'Looking good with your attractive grey boot.'

'I know. Rarely do you get an item of footwear that allows you both super speed and high fashion. Nike should take note.'

'Fancy taking your high fashion boot to the pub?'

'The football one?'

'No, and also there's no football on this evening.'

'Dammit, what a shame. Yes. Cool.' Eek. I'm already kind of dreading our fake break-up. Maybe we'll both feel as though there's no point messaging any more. I hope not.

* * *

Tom puts my glass of white and his pint on the little round table we've found and sits down opposite me.

'First things first.' He takes a little bag out of his pocket. 'I'm not saying this is a big present, because it isn't, but I'm pretty confident you'll be happy with it.'

I pull it out of the bag. 'Oh, wow,' I breathe.

'I know. Incredibly proud of myself.'

It's a Portuguese cockerel made entirely out of jelly beans. And it's particularly apt because Carole let slip that, after we left the wedding, they'd handed out lots of puddings involving jelly beans, and I was *gutted* to have missed out (yes okay maybe that's a little childish but in my defence I did have a broken ankle) because jelly beans are one of my biggest guilty pleasures in life.

'It's *perfect*. Thank you.'

He's going to make someone – Lola or whoever – an amazing real boyfriend one day. So thoughtful on top of all his other attributes. I really can't understand why he wasn't snaffled by some lucky person long ago.

'It's so pretty as well,' I say. 'Really it shouldn't be eaten.'

Tom mock gasps. 'So are you not going to eat them?'

'No, no, they'll all be gone by the time I go to bed,' I say happily. 'It's an amazing present.' I'm already imagining myself chomping away. 'You're an excellent present buyer.'

'I will accept that compliment. And I would like to make it very clear that the present was entirely separate from the big favour that I'm about to ask.'

'Tom.' I purposely widen my eyes and drop my jaw. 'Were you trying to *buy* my help?'

'I was not. But I would say that if that's what it takes I'm more than happy to buy as many jelly beans as you can eat.'

I shake my head. 'I really don't think any normal person could afford that.'

'Okay,' he amends, 'I'm happy to buy a lot more jelly beans than you *should* eat but not as many as you *could* eat.' He pauses. 'Because I'm a little bit desperate. But also, obviously, please feel very free to say no. And I will *still* feel beholden to you just for having asked it, which I will bear in mind next time I pass a jelly bean shop.'

'Okay, you have to tell me your request now. Your desperation's making me a little nervous. And I'm obviously very happy if it results in more jelly beans.' I'm presuming the favour is fake-girlfriend-related, and I'm not totally sure how I feel about that. On the one hand, there's the whole lying to people thing. It's horrible. And his family are *lovely*. But on the other hand it's an excuse to spend more time with him and I'm really not averse to that I realise. Basically, I'm very conflicted.

'It's my grandmother's ninetieth soon. She very specifically wants you there.'

'Ohhhh.' That's *bad*.

'Yeah. I had a panic and thought of a lot of different scenarios. One, tell her the truth now. The thing is, I can't really do that. My family have been a bit worried about me on the romance front – for various reasons, well, one particular reason, a nasty break-up – and she specifically told me that she's very relieved that I've finally met someone nice and she has high hopes for our future together and she's so pleased that she doesn't have to worry about me any more.'

'Oh dear, that's bad.'

'Yep. So. Not keen on telling her the truth at this point. So the second option is you coming.' He looks at me and I look back at him, keeping my expression as neutral as possible.

'The thing about that...' He pauses and looks almost as

though he's regrouping. 'Well, the thing is that my family loved you. And they want the best for me. So... as it turns out... we weren't just keeping them off my back, we were properly lying to them. And that's awful.'

'Yes, it is,' I agree.

'Oh.' He says it as though he hadn't realised that I would feel the same way. Which I *would* find insulting if it weren't for the fact that I also hadn't realised that he would be feeling the same way.

'I feel the same about Marisa,' I clarify, feeling a sudden need to make it very clear that I am also not someone who *likes* lying to people they care about. 'I don't, if I'm honest, feel the same way about Sammy in particular.'

'Fair enough. Total arse.'

'Yes, he is,' I say, pleased. 'But anyway, everyone else – my actual friends at work – I hate lying to them. Marisa likes you. She's pleased for me. And it's awful. So I know exactly what you mean.'

'Had you also in fact resolved to stop with the faking?'

'Yes. I was thinking that we could grow apart while you were in Vegas.'

'Am I still there?'

'Yep. You aren't supposed to be getting back until the end of the week but I'm thinking you might extend your stay because you like it so much and that might be my first inkling that we aren't really meant to be.'

'Nice,' he says, in a congratulatory tone. 'Hopefully we'll be able to think of a way of us splitting up in due course that won't upset my family too much.'

'I think we'll just have to fizzle out? That's got to be the least upsetting way for everyone to hear about it. Just growing apart through circumstance.'

He nods. 'You're very wise.'

'I've had a *lot* of experience of failed relationships.' I really don't want to go to his grandmother's ninetieth. It would feel awful. 'So... what did we decide about your grandmother?'

'Oh, yes, sorry. I think there might be a third and better option, which is you working abroad for a while like me going to Vegas, and sending birthday wishes from there so that it doesn't just sound like an excuse.'

'I like it. I like it a lot. Maybe I could make a birthday video.'

'That's a relief.' Tom's beaming at me. 'And that's a great idea. Maybe – and please do feel very free to say no – you could sing "Happy Birthday" in it. *Very* cheesy, I know, but my grandmother does love a singalong.'

'"Happy Birthday" it is. Do you want to record it this evening? Maybe we're having a meal out together the last evening before I leave. Where am I going to, do you think?'

'Somewhere far, far away. So that it would be very difficult for me to visit you.'

'I'd like to visit New Zealand,' I say. 'I've always wanted to go there. Very far and also very expensive to get to.'

'New Zealand it is.'

'Another good thing about New Zealand is the time difference. It would probably be very difficult to call me from the party. I'd probably be asleep. That's why I'm recording the video.'

'Even more perfect,' Tom approves.

'And then,' I say, because utterly, utterly insanely, the thought of our fake break-up makes me feel a little melancholy, and I'd rather say it myself than have to listen to Tom saying it, 'I'm guessing that while I'm away the distance will push us apart. We won't have any big bust-up, no-one will cheat on anyone, we'll just realise we've drifted apart.'

Tom nods and we kind of stare at each other for a few seconds, and then he nods again and says, 'Yeah, that's definitely the least bad way to finish a relationship. Sad, but just the way it is.'

We stare at each other a bit more, and then Tom suddenly does a weirdly big intake of breath and then says, 'It *is* sad when relationships finish just because of circumstance. So it's a good job that this is all fake.'

'Yes, ha, ha,' I say, very over-jollily, 'a very good job.' Hmm. I think I might have sounded a bit peculiar there.

'Yep.' Tom takes a really long glug of his beer and then looks at me. 'So when would you like to do the video? Maybe outside somewhere? Maybe next to the river?'

'The river's a good idea. Romantic.'

'Yeah.'

Our conversation is gentle and fun and absolutely *lovely* while we finish our drinks, and then we get up to leave.

I really like walking (limping) across the pub with Tom just behind me. It makes me feel as though – at this moment – he's *mine*. As in, as though we're together. Just for this moment.

The door's heavy and he reaches over my head and helps me to pull it open, and I like that too.

It's still very – well, almost – romantic, as we wander at my hobbling speed along the road under the railway arches and then over to the South Bank. As we walk, we discuss very earnestly and in great detail (turns out Tom knows this area as well as I do) exactly where I should stand when we do the video. Tom's grandmother loves Central London but isn't as mobile as she was and isn't really able to travel into town, so we need to get the background right.

'Surely it's obvious,' I say. 'We need to include the best night view in the world.'

'The best *city* night view,' Tom clarifies.

I nod.

'Waterloo Bridge at night looking up towards St Paul's,' he says.

I nod again. 'Of course. Maybe we should record each line of the song in a different place. Maybe some of the bustle around the London Eye and then panning across to Big Ben as well, because who doesn't love a Big Ben shot.'

'*Or* maybe we do an intro together, maybe in front of the London Eye. Then you sing the whole song in front of Big Ben. And then we close it with a together thing on the bridge. She'll like that. She used to bring me into town for dinner when I was little and we'd stop on the bridge and she'd tell me how my grandfather proposed to her from there.'

I stop walking and look at him. 'We *can't* do a video of us from there, then. Knowing that we're *definitely* going to break up, which she will *definitely* find out. It could tarnish her Waterloo Bridge memory.'

'Oh my God, you're right. I'm an idiot. What if...' He frowns for a moment and then his brow clears, in a *ping*-I-have-it way. 'Maybe we never break up. Just for her. Or maybe for everyone else. We just have a long-distance relationship forever.'

'Erm.' It's quite hard to know how to refer to someone's relatives' mortality but it's *very* relevant. No. I can't do it. I can't say out loud: *well, maybe it'll work until your grandmother...* no, I don't even want to think it. I'll just point out that while it might be feasible with an older relative (although who knows; a ninety-year-old could easily live another ten-plus years), with his younger relatives this really won't work. 'You can't lie to your sister forever, can you? Like if you have a *real* relationship – with Lola, or you meet someone else – how do you split up with New Zealand me? Without looking like a total arse? You'd have to tell your family that I was staying in New Zealand, and you'd have to keep your new partner hidden for a bit so you wouldn't look like you'd been cheating on me. It would be very, very complicated.'

'I mean, I don't think Lola's going to be beating down my door any time soon. And I don't think I'm going to be meeting anyone else either,' Tom says. I try very hard not to care that he clearly has no thoughts whatsoever in his head about *me* as a person he might meet. I shouldn't have any about *him* either.

'But you're right,' he continues gloomily. 'We should never have started this. But since we *did*, I feel like we should cross the splitting-up bridge when we come to it.'

'I feel like there's a pun in there to do with Waterloo Bridge just waiting to jump out.'

'Yeah.'

We both stand and think for a few moments.

'Yeah, no, I can't do puns,' I say after a bit.

'Me neither. Although I do *admire* a pun.'

'Same. Okay, so we're going to find somewhere without the bridge in the view and say a few words and then sing?'

'Perfect.'

We start walking again, and are soon weaving our way through the crowds at the bottom of the Eye.

'Hmm,' I say.

'Is your video director instinct telling you that it's too busy here?'

'Yep.'

We begin to walk east from the Eye, along the South Bank.

'I do love it here.' I do a big sweep with my arm. 'I travel in and out of Waterloo all the time, but I don't come down here very often and just enjoy the atmosphere; I'm always in a rush to go somewhere. When I *am* here, I always wonder why I don't come more often.'

'Yeah, same.'

I love the buzz, the variety of people, the way anything goes. There are elderly people, people on their own, people in groups, people dashing straight through, people sitting and enjoying the moment, other couples just strolling together like we are.

Except. We are very much not a couple.

I need to remember that.

14

TOM

'Why don't we grab some dinner?' I say on impulse. 'Take advantage of being here. I still owe you big for the blisters and frilly pants. Let me treat you. After we've done the video.'

'Oh, I...' Nadia hesitates and then says, 'Dinner would be fab. But only if we go halves. I choose; we both pay. That was the deal.'

'We did the deal before either of us realised the terrible sartorial and blister lengths you'd have to go to at my mother's hands.'

She laughs but shakes her head. 'I insist on going halves.'

'Fine,' I concede. 'But you are absolutely choosing where we eat.'

'Done.'

'Okay, so shall we get the video done? It's actually fairly quiet here? And we can get Big Ben in, in the distance.'

Nadia nods, before checking, 'So we're going to do it as a selfie video and I'm going to say something and then we're going to sing?'

'Exactly.'

'Okay. Let's do it.'

We stand together with our backs to the river at an angle, with Big Ben in the distance.

'Maybe before we start recording we should take a couple of photos so we can see how we look?' Nadia suggests.

We kind of both just stand there and then I take a couple of photos and we check the screen.

'If you don't mind,' I say, 'I think we should put our heads closer together.'

'Definitely. The way we look as though we're trying very hard not to touch each other really doesn't scream *in love*.'

Yeah, I think the reason that we look like that is that I really dislike the way I can't help... just... *noticing* her a lot. Like, being really aware of her. It makes me feel like a disgusting lech, because no-one should feel like that about people they aren't *with*, or *might* be with, and that is not us. So, yep, I don't like it. However, needs must.

I adjust closer to her and take another couple of photos, and we pore over the screen again.

'I think it'll be fine once we're talking and singing,' Nadia says. 'No-one would expect us to be *actually* touching. No-one likes seeing too much PDA.'

'Yep, okay, so are we doing it?' I switch to video and press the red start button.

'Hello!' Nadia beams into the phone. 'I'm so sorry that I'm not going to be with you for your party, because I have to leave for my overseas work placement, but I just wanted to wish you a *huge* happy birthday. And Tom and I have a song for you.'

She looks at me and I look at her, and we smile – I smile because she's smiling and it's a smile that you can't not smile back at – and then she says, 'Aaaaaand,' and launches into 'Happy Birthday' and I join in.

When I say join in, I mean that I do my best to match the notes she's singing, but I'm pretty sure I fail. Her voice is *amazing*.

'You should go on *X Factor*,' I say. 'Or whatever they replaced it with.'

'Been on it,' she says, 'but I didn't get beyond judges' houses.'

I stare at her. She isn't even looking at me. She has her head slightly tilted and is gazing up the river, like she's in full sights-of-London appreciation mode.

'Actually been on it or joking?'

'Actually.'

'Wow!'

'I know. It was very cool. And if I'm honest I didn't even mind not making it into the live rounds, because it's kind of obvious that a lot of the people who make it through do get a little messed up by it. And I love my wedding singing.'

'My word.' I have a lot of questions for her and I just ask all of them. Which judge. Which songs. How much of it was staged. Outfits.

'This is so funny.' She's nearly choking with laughter. 'It isn't *that* cool.'

'It *is*. If I'd been on it, I would've been the comedy terrible act. I could *never* do what you did. Nor could most people.'

'*Loads* of people have good voices.'

I shake my head. 'Not like yours. Do all your recent friends and colleagues know about the *X Factor* thing?'

'Actually, no. You can't just say oh by the way I was partially on *X Factor*.'

'Very true.'

'Come on. Dinner.'

'I still have more questions,' I tell her, which makes her laugh again.

We try a few restaurants along the river, and they're all fully booked for at least the next couple of hours, apart from one that's really empty, which Nadia points out is not a great recommendation.

'I think all the signs are pointing us in the same direction,' she says.

'What is that direction?' I ask, not wanting her to say that the signs are saying that we shouldn't get food and should just go home instead.

'We should phone the very nice-looking Italian restaurant we walked past on the way to that sports pub and see if they have a table.'

'A very good idea.' I'm *ridiculously* pleased that the evening's going to continue.

'Hang on. Have we even looked at our video? To check it's okay? Did we get distracted by your *X Factor* questioning?'

'Okay, let's phone the restaurant first and then check.'

'One table, a cancellation,' I mouth a minute later as I'm on the phone to them. 'Serendipity.'

'Perfect. It looked *so* nice.'

I smile again because she's doing the smile that I can't not return, and then say, 'Let's look at the video just in case we need a reprise.'

Well. Objectively (I think), we are *cute* together. We make a very convincing couple in the video. That makes me feel a little... odd, but then I think most people if they stuck their heads close to each other and self-videoed would probably look schmaltzy-happy in each other's company. They just would.

Unfortunately, however, unnoticed by us (not sure how), there's a man doing really remarkably rude gestures just to the right of my head. And then he manages somehow to get his hand between our heads.

'Erm. I'm not sure I can edit those out,' I say.

'I'd be impressed if you could. And even if you could it would probably be quicker to just record it again.'

'Sure you don't mind?'

'Totally sure. And if I'm honest, out of vanity, even though I will never see any of your family again, I'd be *more* than happy to get my hair a little more under control.'

'What? Your hair looked lovely, as always.' I mean it. I like her hair a lot. It's big hair, and it's *great* big hair. 'But we do kind of need to do it again if you're up for it.'

'Definitely. But shall we do it after we've eaten so we don't lose the table?'

'Oh, yes, very good point. Let's go.'

We almost speed-walk to the restaurant; Nadia really wants to eat very specifically at that restaurant and I really want to eat at *any* acceptable restaurant because I'm starving, and now she has the boot on she can get around at a pretty good pace.

'It's a warm evening for hobbling that fast.' Nadia fans herself as we wait for our table having almost catapulted ourselves through the door.

* * *

They seat us at a round table for two in a corner at the back of the restaurant, one on each side of the corner so that we're both somewhat facing out into the rest of the room and we're immediately given tap water and glasses, together with the menu.

'This looks as good as I expected,' Nadia says. 'If I'm honest I couldn't believe that you would walk past here on your way into the pub that time. And choose pie and mushy peas over lovely Italian.'

'Okay. I'm very grateful to you for the video work you've already done and are going to do, not to mention the pants and the blisters, obviously, but I cannot let that pass. I'm sure this restaurant is amazing, but it is *not* going to beat pie and peas.'

Nadia just stares at me. 'Nonsense,' she says eventually. 'You know what I'm going to do? I'm going to point out how much you owe me for those frilly pants in particular and ask if you'll let me order for you.'

'Well...' I just want steak and salad.

She gives me the evil eye.

'Okay,' I say hastily.

A few minutes later, she's ordering for me... in fluent Italian. With a very genuine-sounding Italian accent.

'My mum's Italian,' she explains when I state the obvious and say wow she speaks amazingly fluently. 'And I used to spend a lot of my summer holidays staying with relatives in Rome.'

'Well I did not know that,' I say.

Nadia smiles and I wonder what *else* there is to find out about her that you wouldn't expect. Although actually I'm not surprised that she's half Italian and speaks the language or that she's been on *X Factor*. More... *interested*.

'Funny how you can find out all these things about someone *after* you start fake-dating them,' I say.

'I like it,' Nadia says. 'Finding things out about people as you go along. It always happens with new friends.'

'True.' I'm not really sure actually why I'm so struck by getting to know Nadia better. It isn't *her* I'm getting to know better, it's *facts* about her. *She* is the person I met on the

Waterloo clock evening and the more I know her, the more she just seems *her*.

A waiter interrupts my thoughts with a bowl of steaming arancini and a big platter of antipasti plus some bread.

I'm actually starving, I realise.

'This looks amazing,' I say.

'Better than pie and peas?'

'Nearly as good as. And that's a huge compliment.'

Nadia frowns. 'Eat and then you'll realise that what you just said was total sacrilege.'

Three mouthfuls in of some stuffed peppers wrapped in Parma ham, I'm already wavering. If I'm honest, there are very few pies as good as this. And once I've had one of the rice balls, I'm a convert.

I contemplate for a moment pretending that pie still wins, but she's looking very fierce.

'I will say that a good pub pie is better than a lot of the stuff that I would usually order from an Italian,' I settle on. 'But I didn't know what the best things to order were.'

'What would you have chosen?'

'I'm not really sure, but probably none of this.'

Nadia tsks. 'Honestly.'

'So do you cook Italian food too?'

'Yep, but only for friends and my dad's side of the family, never for my mum's. They'd disown me. What about you? Do you cook?'

'Kind of. As in, not as much as I should. Very basic. But I did learn a couple of things from my ex-w...' I nearly said ex-wife there. Out loud, which I rarely do. 'From my ex. And am not too proud to use them still.'

Nadia looks at me for a moment, like she's wondering

whether to say anything or not, and then says, 'So talk me through your top cooking tips.'

We talk about food for quite a while (possibly a little over seriously on my part until I feel that we've definitely moved far away from any ex mentions) until the conversation shifts somehow to the first cars we ever drove. (Nadia drove straight into a wall on her first time out – no-one was injured – and didn't drive again for five years and then passed her test first time; at seventeen I thought I was an incredibly skilled driver and was astonished by every one of my five failed tests.)

The stunningly delicious food keeps coming (I love listening to Nadia's Italian whenever a server comes to the table) and the conversation's as good as the food.

We've just finished sharing a truly spectacular tiramisu, when Nadia says, 'Whoops, look we're almost the last in here.'

'Oh yes.' I hadn't noticed; for however long we've been here it's like I've had everything I need in the world at this one table. 'We should probably let the staff clean up and go home and get back down to the river and do our reshoot. If you still have time?'

'Definitely.'

* * *

As we walk, Nadia says very naturally into a lull, 'It sounded difficult with your ex?' And suddenly I find myself telling her all about the nightmare ex-wife thing. Which I never, ever do if I can help it because usually I just don't like talking about it.

'Yeah,' she says simply at the end. 'That was her, not you. Which I hope you know. She didn't deserve you. You're wonderful.'

And I feel very, very, well, just *warm* when she says it.

'Thank you.' I smile at her and give her a quick gratitude hug that I have to fight with myself not to prolong.

And then Nadia – just in the nick of time so the moment doesn't get too maudlin or full of regrets or embarrassment about what an idiot I was to marry someone so entirely wrong for me – says, 'Wow, that's a *seriously* garlicky smell coming out of that restaurant,' and then we talk about garlic (and, yes, with the right person, you really can have a garlic chat).

* * *

We go back to the same spot where we shot our first video and get ourselves into position again, standing close together.

It's *really* hard not to just *inhale* the scent of whatever shampoo Nadia uses, but I have to make sure I don't do it, because she'd be able to *see* me because we're basically watching ourselves.

I shift a little closer to her to get both our heads fully into the frame.

It's ridiculous how well we seem to fit together, like we were made to shoot selfie videos as a pair.

I press the red button just before she looks up at me, smiling, and asks, 'Ready?'

'Already recording,' I reply, smiling back, because her smile is infectious again.

She rolls her eyes slightly. 'Then... start again.'

I laugh, and then realise that I'm still recording. I pull my eyes from hers – when you look at them properly you realise just what a stunning and unusual shade of green they are, and there's something about the shape of them, and the way her eyelashes and brows frame them that it's hard not to just stare at – and press the button again.

'Aaaaand go?' Nadia suggests.

I swallow. 'Yep.'

And we're off again. She repeats her little voice message and then we sing. This time, I can hear that I'm not keeping the tune anywhere remotely near the actual one. I try not to laugh but fail, and then Nadia begins to laugh too but carries on singing. (I've given up.) I wrap my arm round her shoulders and stand there grinning as she continues to the end, making 'Happy Birthday' sound like the most amazing musical composition ever (she sticks in some gorgeous twirly operatic bits at the end).

'Honestly,' she says, still laughing, when she's finished, and then I stop recording. 'Do you think there's any chance that worked?'

'Worth checking?' I hold the screen so that we can both see it and press play.

It looks like an amateur video of a woman who could be a professional singer saying a few lovely words and then making 'Happy Birthday' sound incredible while her boyfriend attempts to join in and fails and just stands there looking at her adoringly.

That's what it looks like.

There's quite a long pause, and then I say, 'It's perfect. She'll love it as is. No need for any more recordings I think. Thank you.'

'Absolutely no problem at all,' Nadia replies extremely politely. 'I'm only sorry I have to be in New Zealand and can't make the party.'

'Ha,' I say, also very politely.

'Sooo, I should probably get going.' Nadia glances up at me as she speaks.

I'm looking down at her as she moves her head and now we're kind of hovering, just staring at each other. I sense her chest move as she takes a deep breath and find myself swallowing in response.

I could so easily just lean a little closer, brush my lips against her forehead, her cheeks, her lips, gather her into my arms, where I already know she fits very well.

It would be so easy.

I'm so very tempted.

I can't move from where I am now. It's taking so much energy to stop myself doing any of the things I want to do, like taking my finger and gently moving the few strands of her hair that have blown against her face, or, obviously, just kissing her to high heaven, that I don't have any left for working my legs or feet.

She has her lips slightly parted and is gazing as hard as I am.

When her eyes move from mine to my mouth and then to my throat, I find myself swallowing so hard I feel it through my whole body.

And I realise how very much I would like to feel *her* body against mine. Starting with a kiss, and then...

That would be an extreme instance of short-term gratification destroying a great friendship, though.

How often do you have such an instant fantastic friendship with someone?

She isn't Lola. She isn't the kind of woman I usually go for. She's my *friend*.

And I would do very well to remember that.

I try very, very hard to gather myself. It feels like I'm making more physical – or mental, I'm not really sure which now – effort than two years ago when I had to pull out of the London Marathon in the last mile. (I *know* without asking that Nadia would say that she could never do a marathon, but she absolutely could, even with blisters.)

She's gorgeous. She's fun. She's my friend.

She is my friend.

'It's late.' My voice is hoarse like I've drunk a couple of bottles of vodka and smoked a couple of packets of cigarettes since I last used it. 'We should go. Don't want to miss the last train.'

'Very true.' She's croaky too.

She takes a little step backwards, away from me, and I move sideways away from her. I'm surprised that my legs do in fact work.

'So.' She looks all round like she isn't entirely sure where she is, and then shakes her head slightly. 'That way.'

'Yes, exactly. That way.'

Our conversation's less easy than it has been. I say it's less easy. It's actually non-existent. As in *what a beautiful evening, yes isn't it* levels of emotionless banality. Well, not emotionless. Certainly from my side there's emotion; I'm just not sure what the emotion *is* and I feel like that near-kiss moment, because that's what it was, is now a big barrier between us.

'Do you have an early start tomorrow morning?' I want to make this better; I want things to be straight back to the way they were before the video. It isn't like anything actually happened. I glance over at Nadia, to see that her brow's furrowed like she's thinking hard.

'Erm.' She looks at me. Eventually, she says, as though she's having to make as big an effort to be normal as I am, 'Ha. Losing my mind there for a moment. I was just trying to remember what day of the week it is. It's Tuesday today and it will be Wednesday tomorrow.'

'Nice day-of-the-week knowledge,' I say, pleased to be able to get in a non-emotional weak joke.

'Thank you.' She gives me a small smile. 'Yes, so tomorrow

morning I have a particularly exciting meeting first thing to sign off on some accounts and then I'll be segueing straight into a few more light-the-world-up accounting meetings before sneaking out for a client lunch with someone who's actually an old uni friend. Genuinely a client, but also a very good friend.'

'Nice.'

'I know. A we've-got-to-the-middle-of-the-week genuinely legit treat for ourselves. What about you? Early start tomorrow?'

'Year 8 basketball club at 8 a.m.'

And we go from there, feeling our way back to our usual chat, and by the time we're at Waterloo, things kind of feel – almost – as though *that* didn't happen.

Only almost, though.

We semi-run together for a train, at Nadia's best speed-hobble, and if I'm honest, I'm relieved when, after Nadia has said extremely vehemently that she absolutely does not need to be escorted home, I leave the train at Clapham Junction.

Walking along the road home, I check what messages I've had through the evening. And I realise that, as usual, I'm a little disappointed that there's nothing from Lola, even though *obviously* there was never going to be.

And then I feel very guilty. Because it feels disloyal to *both* of them that I'm thinking in that kind of way about two women at once.

15

NADIA

Well.

I'm still wondering what *happened* there – or rather did *not* happen – as I let myself in through my front door and plonk myself down onto my sofa.

Tom was *totally* thinking about kissing me. As much as I wanted him to. I could see it in his eyes. And feel it in the way things were definitely awkward afterwards.

I almost reached up and started the kiss, but – thank goodness – was massively inhibited by the memory of a hideous first date where I tried to initiate a kiss but *completely* misjudged the situation and he turned away just as I was going in, lips puckered, and I ended up planting one right in the middle of his ear, a place that no-one kisses anyone ever.

And clearly Tom did not want to kiss me because I'm pretty sure I was looking embarrassingly keen, so he would have known that I'd have been very happy for him to.

I undo my boot and rub my leg before going over to put the kettle on. When tormented, drink mint tea. I'm not having coffee now because I do want to sleep tonight.

I turn the tap on viciously hard and water sprays everywhere.

As I'm mopping it up, I tell myself that it does not matter that Tom didn't kiss me.

We're friends. He's a nice person.

I just need to act very normally, nothing-to-see-here around him the next few times I see him, and then he will hopefully think that he was mistaken and I was just gazing at the moon or something. I mean, who doesn't love a full moon? Or a crescent. Or whatever it was.

I don't know what it was because for me at that moment the whole world was about Tom.

Pathetic.

I finish clearing up the water and run the tap very gently to fill the kettle before deciding that actually I just want to crawl into bed and pretend the eager-for-a-kiss madness never happened.

* * *

Sometimes it's a blessing to be really busy with work, and today is one of those times. I still keep getting flashes of embarrassment, but they're really quite spaced out (I mean no more frequently than one every five to ten minutes rather than one long gaaaaah moment) and by the time I'm having lunch with my university friend-client I've felt a tiny moment of positivity, which is that, actually, these things *do* occasionally happen between people and in fact how would Tom know about my paranoia about initiating kisses on first dates? (It wasn't even an actual date.) For all he knows, I didn't really want to kiss him but was too polite to break the moment. Or was indeed staring at the moon.

What I need to do is act entirely normally so he'll think I was definitely cool about everything.

Maybe I'd already decided that.

'Nadia?' Holly, my friend, is staring at me. 'Are you okay? Do you have Covid again? Is it your foot?'

'Sorry, no, nothing.' Eek. I do *not* want to be rude to a good friend. Or anyone. I'm behaving like a teenager. 'Tell me about your holiday.'

* * *

My phone's stalking me, as they do, and articles about pies have been popping up all day in my feed. One of them – 'How many pies is too many?' – which I see as I'm lugging myself and my boot onto a train after a long day at work, makes me think of Tom, because, according to the writer, *any* number of pies is too many. I begin to forward it to him, before stopping and worrying that I'm stalking him. And then I worry that uncharacteristic silence would be weird. And then I decide that I've gone mad because I'm overthinking everything to do with Tom.

And then I play a quick game of Brawl Stars to calm myself down and decide that I just need to act normally and the normal thing to do in this situation (if the non-kiss had never happened) would be to forward the article.

Tom comes straight back with his response:

> Rude. And wrong.

Which makes me smile. And just like that I feel a little bit better. I've been normal and now I can simply – very normally and totally relaxedly – not send any more messages for a bit, and all good. Even if he knows that in that moment I would have been up for a kiss (gigantic understatement) he'll probably think – from my extreme normality and relaxedness – that it was very much just in that moment and not at *all* what I usually think when I'm with him.

It's all fine. Definitely.

* * *

By Saturday, I almost believe that I'm over any stupid infatuation I had with Tom.

I could even see him again without feeling embarrassed.

I'm on the bus on my way to meet friends at the cinema when I get a message from him:

> My grandmother LOVED the video. Thank you again!

And then a second one a few seconds later:

> Sorry, sorry, I should have asked – how's New Zealand?

> Clearly your grandmother has excellent taste because there could not have BEEN a better video. New Zealand is beautiful. A big change after London but I'm really enjoying it.

> Ha.

I wait for a minute (okay, fine, probably – to my shame – quite a few minutes) but that's it.

* * *

And, it gradually turns out, that really is it. When I sent the pie article, Tom's reply was a conversation-closer. And our polite conversation about the video ended with another conversation-closer from him. So for my own self-respect I'm not initiating any more text conversation.

And he doesn't either.

So… eventually I realise that my gorgeous, wonderful, kind, sexy, actual-man-of-my-dreams-despite-our-on-paper-differences fake-plus-one Tom is no longer really in my life.

We do both participate in the ongoing Waterloo Five chat but that's it. Nothing that's only between the two of us.

When I go through Waterloo, I often wonder if I'll bump into him. I never do.

When I'm wondering whether I'll bump into him, I occasionally wonder whether he'll give us a Lola update on the chat. He never does.

I stop mentioning him to my colleagues and eventually I tell Marisa and a couple of others that I felt that his extended stay in Vegas demonstrated that we weren't right for each other but it was good while it lasted (kind of almost true).

* * *

And eventually it's a good six weeks since I last saw him, which is longer than the time I *knew* him for, and I've stopped looking out for him at Waterloo and I'm busy enjoying my life and continuing with my date detox.

The date detox is a lot easier than it was before, actually, because currently – and truly pathetically – no-one else really appeals to me romantically. Because they aren't Tom.

Who I am probably never going to see again.

Which I think is a good thing.

***

Except one day Carole puts a message in our chat saying that she's having a divorce celebration party (she got a quickie divorce, which she said was only fair given the number of *quickie*-quickies it's emerged that Roger's had over the course of their marriage). And she wants the four of us there as guests of honour.

I don't know whether Tom's going but I very much like and admire Carole and if she wants a divorce party I'm going.

Bea and Ruth are straight in there too with their acceptance.

Tom doesn't reply until the next day:

> Sorry, sorry, sorry for the late reply – away for the weekend in the Brecon Beacons – not much signal. Love to come – congratulations again, Carole!

And there we go. I'm going to – very normally and relaxedly – see Tom again, at Carole's party. Which is going to be very fancy and fun, and that's what I will focus on.

She's hired out a whole country pub near her house for a Saturday evening in a month's time. It's black tie, and the rooms have different themes, including a casino, and she's putting all her non-local guests up either at her house or in rooms at the pub.

So I have one month to decide on the perfect dress for in no way (obviously) trying or looking like I want to seduce Tom but at the same time making sure that were he to be seduceable my dress might help. And hair, make-up and shoes (I haven't had to use my boot for a couple of weeks now).

***

One month later, I'm in wide-leg jeans, Adidas shoes and a jumper on the train to Carole's. This time, unlike before Bea and Ruth's wedding, Tom and I did not discuss in advance which train we'd be on (because we haven't had any one-on-one contact since the my-grandmother-loved-the-video message). I have therefore been jumpy since I got to Waterloo, and have reapplied lip gloss at least ten times, so my lips are now extremely sticky and my hair keeps getting stuck to them. I'd like to say that I didn't think about him at all when I was choosing which jeans to wear today but that would be a lie. So I'm wearing my most flattering ones and my favourite jumper (pale pink, loose turtleneck, orange cuffs and hem).

* * *

'Hey,' says Tom's voice the second I get off the train. Unbelievably, given how exceptionally on possible-Tom-sighting edge I've been for the past two full hours, I get a huge shock and drop my cross-body bag, which I unfortunately didn't put across my body when I stood up to get off. The bag was open, so stuff falls out all over the platform. Fortunately no-one else got out of my door so it isn't getting walked on.

'Let me help.' Tom's already joined me on the ground gathering up items. It's amazing, really, how much you can fit in a small bag, and how little of it you actually need on any given day.

He hands me some tampons (which I clearly do not want back now they've been on the ground but do have to accept), a scrunchie (maybe I can put it in the washing machine), some plasters (I also do not want those back) and my purse.

'Thank you.' I stuff everything back in for the time being, close the bag and stand up. Tom stands up too. 'I should really remember to zip my bag up. In my defence I got a big shock when the train drew in.'

'Because you... didn't know that we were getting off here?'

'Because I might have been having a teensy snooze,' I say with dignity. I had a wedding singer job yesterday evening and it was a *big* night.

'Well, all good now,' Tom says very jollily.

'Exactly,' I say, equally jollily.

'You look like you're moving well on that ankle now.'

'Yep, fully better, thanks.'

'Great news. Hopefully this will be a foot-injury-free day for you.' He slightly winces as he finishes speaking, as though he'd thought he was going to make a joke but it didn't come out funny.

'Hopefully,' I agree.

Then we look at each other. It'll be weird if we don't get a cab together. It will also be twice as expensive for both of us. But... is either of us going to suggest sharing? I know already that I'm not going to because Tom is the one who effectively stopped our text conversation and I'm not going to risk further humiliation by setting myself up to be turned down now.

'Share a cab?' He says it a few seconds too late, like he doesn't want to but knows he has to.

I spend too many seconds trying to think of an answer, and eventually come up with the only possible one. 'Good idea.'

'Great, then.' He's still jolly.

'Yes!' So am I. 'Looking forward to the party!'

I'm just wondering whether to pull a sickie or tell him I can't actually talk to him when I hear Bea hollering down the platform.

'Nadia. Tom. Taxi?'

Thank fuck for that. I want to be alone with Tom even less than I thought I did.

'Perfect,' Tom and I call as one, and then, still as one, and without looking at each other (well, more accurately, I'm trying not to look at him but I do sneak a glance out of the corner of my eye and see him not looking at me while also slightly looking at me) we begin to walk along the platform to meet Bea and Ruth.

'You're both looking very well,' Ruth tells us.

'So are you.' Tom and I are still speaking as one.

We all share hugs (well, Tom and I each hug both Bea and Ruth; we do not hug each other) and then we set off towards where it says exit.

Soon, we're in a taxi together, with Tom in the front next to the driver, and me in the middle of the back squished between Bea and Ruth.

'This is lovely, isn't it,' Ruth says. 'It's so nice to see each other again.'

'And it's wonderful that Carole's throwing this party,' Bea says. 'You have to be positive about the future rather than having bitterness or regrets about the past.'

'Exactly,' Ruth agrees. 'Your past is just a journey to where you are now, and the future is yours to mould and we all have to let go of previous disappointments and view them as development.'

I *love* the way they're such a *couple* in the way they speak, like they're taking it in turns to express the same thought. Even if that thought is a little irritating in the very specific circumstance of me and Tom right now. Because I *do* regret that evening and that moment where, if I'm honest, I was sending out the biggest kiss-me-now signals in the entire history of signalling. And I *am* disappointed that it's clear that Tom has no interest in me and I am also embarrassed and I am also quite sad that after we had so much fun together being fake partners we've got to the point where we politely go fake jolly about even a small thing like sharing a taxi.

'Yes. And *also*,' Bea says, 'I'm *really* looking forward to the party.'

We all chuckle a little bit and then somehow, with Bea and Ruth there, helped by the fact that we can't see each other's faces, I think, Tom and I join in the gentle chat.

The taxi gets slightly lost (Bea instructs the driver very strictly on where he should have gone and then Ruth asks very gently whether he was trying to stitch us up and overcharge us – he blatantly was – and he apologises and says that his dad always taught him to do that with rich-looking out-of-towners, and Ruth, still very gently, tells him that that's appalling and he should stop, and he practically bursts into tears) and the journey takes a good half hour.

By the time we pull up at the pub, it's feeling (from my side anyway) surprisingly normal with Tom.

Once we're out of the car, we all exclaim how beautiful the building is. It's very ancient-looking, stone-built, with a huge timber door, and is surrounded by trees and shrubs.

Inside, it's a warren of little rooms (already decorated for this evening), beautiful oak floors and stone steps, cosy seating round huge fireplaces, lots of nooks and crannies, your basic dream country pub.

The four of us are all staying upstairs overnight.

Two people escort us up the stairs, which rise from the middle of the ground floor. At the top, a man directs Bea and Ruth left, telling them that their room is at the far end, and a woman indicates that Tom and I should follow her to the right.

Our rooms are the last two along the corridor and are opposite each other.

'They're both en-suite,' the woman tells us, which I am extremely happy about; I don't want to be bumping into Tom on the way to the bathroom in my pyjamas.

I purposely avoid looking inside Tom's room when she opens the door for him and he goes in, because it is *definitely* nothing to do with me what his room's like.

My room has a white ceiling with timbered joists, a polished oak floor covered in a big Persian-style rug, huge antique mahogany wardrobe and chests, and a very impressive four-poster, complete with curtains. It's all decorated in pale blues and jade greens, which go beautifully together. The shower room is lovely in a different way – very modern and angular, with jade-green floor tiles and white walls and pale blue towels.

It's utterly gorgeous.

I just wish Tom wasn't opposite.

I'm glad I brought my favourite (and most flattering) pyjamas.

Although I will certainly not be seeing him during the night, obviously.

* * *

I've just finished washing my hands and face and sorting my stuff out when there's a little tap on the door.

It must be Tom.

I check my reflection in the mirror above the fireplace and adjust my hair slightly, before arranging my features into a nonchalant smile and opening the door to... Ruth.

Over her shoulder I see Bea at Tom's door.

'We thought it might be nice to have a little walk around the village before we're due downstairs. I think we have an hour before we're meeting for drinks?' Ruth says.

'Perfect,' I say. Infinitely better than sitting in my room annoyed with myself for feeling awkward about Tom.

Tom also agrees to their suggestion and the four of us troop downstairs and begin to walk up the road.

Bea and Ruth set an extremely fast pace.

'I hope I'm *half* as fit as them at their age,' I say to Tom as we match their strides.

'I know. We're literally going to be out of breath and need serious showers at this rate.'

We continue our speedy march until Bea tells us that it's time to go back to the pub and get changed.

'We'll see you downstairs in the main bar at six,' Ruth says as we part at the top of the stairs.

Which means, I think, as I nod, that I will maybe have to walk downstairs with Tom.

I really don't know why I'm making such a big deal of *seeing Tom* in my head. It's actually all very easy and simple and there is no need to be like this; I'm being very silly.

Except... he's basically drop-dead gorgeous. In every way – right now I'm remembering the way his forearms flexed under his rolled-up shirt sleeves when he pushed open the very heavy pub door and how he carried *all* our bags upstairs without appearing to even notice – and I don't want to allow my thoughts to even get started on the way his thighs are filling out his jeans. And the gorgeousness of his face.

And also he's very funny and very kind and very nice and very good company.

It's really almost impossible not to love him.

And that is a problem for me because it is not fun loving people who don't love you back. I mean, I'm sure he quite *likes* me, as a person. But he definitely doesn't love me, and he never will. And I think he might suspect that I like him more than I should. And therefore I do feel awkward around him.

I shouldn't, though. He's nice and he wouldn't think less of me, and also, he *must* be used to it. A *lot* of people must find him very attractive.

Tom interrupts my thoughts to say, 'See you later, then.'

I nod.

'Want to go down together?' he asks.

'Yes, sure,' I say, like you would when a fully platonic friend makes a sensible suggestion. Not at all like you would when the hottest boy you've ever met asks you out. *Because he is not asking me out and never will.*

* * *

I take a lot of care over preparing for the evening and I'm also careful to be done in good time (I'm pretty sure that Carole doesn't suffer fools, or late people, gladly), so when Tom knocks on my door I've been ready for several minutes, and am playing a game on my phone to distract myself from thoughts of the evening ahead.

'Sorry,' I say, a few seconds later when I make it to the door. 'I was deep in a Brawl Stars game and didn't want to die.'

'No sorries necessary; I'm there with you. I'd practically miss a plane rather than go back a level.' He takes a step back and says, 'You look... lovely.'

'Thank you.' I *am* pleased with my dress (dark green, satiny, halter neck, tight on the top half and flared out from the waist into a long skirt) and my hair is – currently – under control following a lot of effort with heated tongs. I take the legitimate opportunity to study him hard, and have to make a big effort not to allow my eyes to widen. 'So do you.'

His black dinner suit, white shirt and matching turquoise cummerbund and bow tie *really* suit him. Like really, *really* suit him.

'Ha. Thank you. Shall we?' He sticks his arm out as though we're in *Bridgerton*, and I take it (hoping that I'm not doing too *Bridgerton*-esque a bosom-heave), and off we go.

I'm grateful for Tom's arm on the stairs, because I actually do stumble slightly a few steps down, although chicken and egg – it happens a second after I look down at where our arms are locked together and think about how we're kind of pressed up against each other and momentarily forget how to work my legs – and he effortlessly clamps me to his side until I've regained my balance.

'Okay?' he asks, sounding a little odd. Probably due to internal laughter about how I just cannot stay upright.

'Yes, thank you,' I say breathlessly.

'I can't decide whether I think it's incredibly likely or statistically incredibly unlikely that you're going to be unable to walk properly by the end of the evening.'

'Well.' My inner maths nerd emerges. 'Statistically you might say that it's incredibly likely, because the only statistics you have are that every time you see me I get a foot-area injury. On a micro level. But then on a macro level statistically it's incredibly unlikely because most people don't most of the time. But then again on a micro level my feet and ankle might be weakened by past mishaps.'

Tom's staring at me as though I'm slightly mad. 'So if you were going to make odds on yourself what odds would you give me?'

'Literally a billion to one. I will not be injuring myself in any way this evening,' I say, very haughtily.

'Not tempted to touch some of this inn's fine wood now to prevent tempting fate?'

'No need,' I say airily, while with the hand that isn't holding his arm I reach surreptitiously for the edge of the wooden banister.

'Ha. Come on, let's go and find the others.'

* * *

Bea and Ruth – dressed respectively in a very sophisticated fitted navy velvet trouser suit and killer navy patent heels and a long wine-red dress with a matching bolero jacket – greet us in the tap room, which has been turned into a cocktail bar for the evening.

'You have to try this,' Ruth splutters, pointing at her glass. 'Catches you in the back of the throat, but it's delicious.'

'She's already squiffy,' Bea says, 'but that's ideal because I'll be able to have my way with her later.'

'Bea. Shhh.' Ruth beams at her wife and Tom and I exchange an *aww* look.

'Waterloo Five!' Carole's hurtling towards us across the room, her arms outstretched. 'Hello, hello. I'm so pleased to have you here.' She hugs us all in turn and then says, 'Tom and Nadia, you both need drinks. You'll be pleased to hear that I'm on the mocktails, because I'm determined to enjoy and remember every moment of this party, so I'm not going to allow myself to drink anything alcoholic before midnight, but let me encourage you to try any cocktail you like. I have it on the authority of everyone else – half of whom are, frankly, already fairly sloshed – that they're *all* good.' She pauses for breath and waves at one of the servers behind the bar, who scoots straight over. 'Lily here will sort you out with drinks. Thank you so much, Lily. I'm going to go and say hello to everyone else now, but just to warn you, you'll be heavily mentioned in my little speech in a minute.'

I look at Ruth's drink and then at some of the other already-unsteady-on-their-feet guests and decide that a mocktail would be a very good idea to start off with.

Tom asks for one too.

We chat to Bea and Ruth, and then we all find ourselves talking to different people and it's all very nice, because everyone here is a friend or relative of Carole's, and they're all great in different ways, and everyone wants the best for Carole, which is lovely.

I've just got myself a second mocktail (despite some serious encouragement from the little group I've just been chatting to to try a fierce Blackberry Mule), when we all hear the clinking of cutlery against glass and turn to see Carole standing on a chair in the corner.

'Don't worry,' she tells us all. 'I'm still sober. And I've taken my shoes off so I'm not going to break an ankle.' She directs a pantomime wink in my direction. 'So. Time for a little speech from me.

'You're all here as my guests because you're very important to me and I've been through what can only be described as a very shitty experience followed by the realisation that I have wonderful people in my life who I'm very grateful for and who make me very happy. I'd like to thank all of you for being *you*, and I'd also like to make some specific thank yous.

'Firstly, our wonderful Waterloo Five group. Guests of honour. Four strangers who were there when I found out what a dick Roger was, and who could have turned their backs on the screeching, blubbering wreck that I immediately became, but who instead helped me when I needed help the most, and basically adopted me and we became a kind of family. Bea and Ruth—' she points at them and we all clap (and yes I do try out the wolf whistle that I have finally just learnt to do courtesy of my nephew and yes it is satisfying) '—had just got engaged and might have been expected to want some privacy. But not only did they look after me in that moment, they also insisted on the five of us going out for dinner. *And* they hosted me overnight – the night they got engaged.'

Everyone claps again, and then Carole moves on.

'And then there's Nadia.' She points at me and, even though this is her party and I *absolutely* want her to have a good time and say anything she likes, I don't really, if I'm honest, want everyone here to know about my unfortunate dating history. And Carole is great, she really is, but you never entirely know what she's going to say at any given moment. 'She'd been stood up by the most stupid blind date ever because he hooked up with someone else the night before and forgot to tell her.' Oh, okay, well there you go, yes, everyone knows now, but it could be worse, at least she didn't say it was my seventh dating disaster in six months. Oh, God, I hope she isn't going to.

Tom's looking at me quite wide-eyed, and mouths *Sorry* in my direction. I nod a thank you.

'Look at Nadia,' Carole continues. Everyone was already looking at me. 'She's wonderful, beautiful, kind, funny. She pretended all the way through Bea and Ruth's wedding *not* to have a broken ankle and sang angelic karaoke while in terrible pain.' She seems entirely unaware that Bea and Ruth are now looking quite shocked. 'That blind date was an *idiot*. But I'm very grateful to him because his failure to turn up was our gain.'

I *think* she's done. Thank *goodness* for that.

Everyone claps and I decide to laugh because it's my best option.

'And finally Tom,' Carole says when the claps have died down. Eek. I feel very selfish that I was concentrating on my own discomfort, because I'm guessing Tom isn't going to enjoy this. I see him shift his weight between his feet and try to send him sympathy vibes. 'Like Nadia, Tom was supposed to be meeting someone, a woman he made a ten-year pact with.' As Carole smiles around the room, I glance at Tom, who's standing motionless. Mentioning his pact with Lola is *so* embarrassing for him.

'And again,' Carole plunges on, 'his date's failure to turn up was our gain. Tom's just as wonderful as Nadia, and we're all the richer for knowing him. And I'd just like to say, for the record, that Tom and Nadia seem to get on *very* well, so watch this space. Perhaps their dating disappointments will lead to future joy. Personally, I'm hoping for an invitation to their future wedding.' She holds her glass up high, apparently oblivious to how Tom and I might feel right now. 'A big toast to my four wonderful new friends, our Waterloo Five, and I hope we'll remain friends forever.'

Tom's smiling and toasting but his back is very rigid.

I'm not sure that he and I will in fact be remaining friends forever.

16
TOM

Carole is a force of nature. And she's a very kind and generous woman. I'm pleased to know her.

I didn't enjoy that Lola reference, though. And I *really* didn't enjoy that Nadia-and-me reference.

Anyway.

It was worse for Nadia really.

And it doesn't matter.

With regard to Nadia, I doubt we'll see each other again after this weekend.

And with regard to Lola, I should really have moved entirely on by now. It's hard, though, when you aren't sure exactly what happened and why. I haven't made any attempt to find her, because she clearly just didn't want to see me, and I have to accept that, but I still find it difficult not to think about her at times, and wonder.

Carole's still talking, thanking people. There's more toasting.

I tune back in.

Yep, it isn't just Nadia and me she's overshared about. To

name but one fellow victim, a red-faced man named Barry has just recovered from a septic vasectomy that we now know all about.

Carole's very open. It's endearing. Lovely. Genuinely.

* * *

Eventually, Carole finishes her speech. 'And now I want everyone to party like there's no tomorrow. Starting by downing a *lot* of cocktails.'

Everyone cheers, we all toast again, and then, basically, we're off.

And when I say we're off, we really are.

It's like the mood in the room immediately changes. There's a near charge on the bar as everyone clearly decides that they need to take Carole's last words extremely literally.

As I join in the surge (I'm weak-minded enough, and also pissed off enough at Carole's speech, that a real cocktail suddenly very much appeals), I catch sight of Nadia, her bare shoulders looking extremely stiff, a man I was talking to earlier speaking in her ear.

Nadia moves a little and I see her profile. She looks as though she has her lips clamped together, and I get the strong impression that whatever the man is saying to her is not going down well.

I think he told me he's a colleague of Carole's (i.e. he works in her company). He's definitely on the pull; he told me earlier that he'd love the irony of meeting someone at a divorce celebration party.

I can imagine that Carole's well-intentioned words about Nadia might have given someone who was already inclined to be looking for a snog – or a lot more – the impression that Nadia would be fair game.

The man places his hand – like a paw – against Nadia's lower back. She steps away and his paw follows her.

I can't in good conscience not go to her rescue.

A few seconds later, I'm by her side, saying, 'Nadia, hi, I lost you over there.'

She looks up at me and rolls her eyes in the man's direction.

I nod at him. 'Excuse me.' I put my arm round Nadia's shoulders and draw her away, towards the edge of the room.

'Thank you,' she says. 'What an arse.'

'I think his name's Richard.'

'And Dick would be a very appropriate nickname.' She rolls her eyes again. 'Honestly. I *would* just like to say that under normal circumstances I could and absolutely would have got rid of him by myself. I do not *need* to be rescued by anyone. It's just that it's particularly awkward this evening; I didn't want to make any kind of scene and ruin Carole's party.'

'I know that,' I say. 'And it wasn't because I'm a man that I was able to rescue you. Could equally have been a girlfriend.'

'Thank you. And that is very true.'

'And also usually no-one would have announced that you were recently blind dating.'

'Also true.'

I smile at her. 'Come and try the real cocktails?'

There's still a big crush at the bar, so we're stuck there together for the next fifteen or twenty minutes with nothing to do except chat. And that's a good thing, because we do chat, and soon we're laughing, the way we did before I lost my mind on the South Bank, and it's nice. And also handy, because it would be nice to enjoy each other's company, because I feel as though it would be a little mean not to stick around Nadia for the duration of the evening, after Carole's inadvertent signalling that she's single and up for meeting someone.

I mean, she *might* be up for meeting someone, actually, because obviously she might have binned her dating detox, but at least with me around she won't be harassed.

'Want to go and begin to explore the other rooms?' I suggest.

'I think it would be rude not to.'

* * *

The first room we enter has been set up as a casino. As we go in, a black-clad man hands us each a velvet bag containing a pile of chips and then leans in, as though confiding a secret that he won't tell absolutely everyone who walks through the door, that, while there will be no gambling for money, there *will* be prizes for the people who end up in first, second and third place when their chips are counted at the end of the evening.

'*Really.*' Nadia has a very competitive gleam in her eye. 'Let's get gambling. What do we have?'

We begin with roulette.

'How does it work?' Nadia asks the very professional-looking croupier.

Surprisingly, it turns out that most of the people round the table haven't played before. Once we're all up and running with the rules, we all begin to place our bets. I go red to start off with. I like a fifty per cent chance of winning. Nadia goes number seventeen. I place three of my chips. Nadia places one.

It lands on seventeen. Which is black. And Nadia gains a *lot* of chips due to the unlikeliness of anyone choosing the right single number.

'Well, that was cool,' she says.

Then she places one chip on number thirty-one. I put another three on red.

Black thirty-one it is.

Nadia gets lots more chips.

She's already got a crowd around her, because – as is obvious whether or not you're a roulette aficionado – this does not usually happen.

'Wondering whether I should quit while I'm ahead,' she says.

'I don't feel like you're going to make much of a dent in your massive pile if you carry on only gambling one at a time,' I point out.

She goes for a row of numbers this time.

And wins.

'Unbelievable,' I say (very unoriginally; everyone round the table is saying it). 'If only you were playing for real money.'

'We are,' Nadia says very seriously. 'There are prizes at stake.'

When she places her fourth single chip on a red sixteen, no-one is more surprised than everyone except Nadia when she loses.

'I'm going to take my winnings now,' she announces to the table. Everyone cheers and Nadia laughs and bows.

Once she has all her chips stashed in the two extra velvet bags the croupier gives her, I say, 'So what are we doing now?'

'We?'

'I would very much like to see how the rest of your gambling pans out. Should you choose to continue your winning streak.'

'Is it a streak, though?' She says it like it's a very serious question. 'Given that I lost on that last bet?'

'Er it was a big win overall, though?'

'Hmm, we'll see. I'd like to play something involving more skill and less chance next time.'

We look around the room. There's also poker and there's blackjack.

'Poker's definitely very skilled,' I say, 'going by what everyone says. I never know how, though. You have so few cards. How can you work out what anyone else has? I've played a few times and I'm terrible.'

'*Really*?' Nadia studies me. 'Is that true, or are you being cunningly poker-faced so that you can fleece me of all my hard-earned winnings?'

I smile at her. 'Who knows?'

'Hmm.' She continues to look at me through narrowed eyes and then says, 'Okay. I'm going to go for it. How bad can it be?'

Yesssss. I'm going to fleece her.

It becomes immediately apparent that she's never played before. She has to ask for a chart of all the poker hands, plus she keeps forgetting how to play. So it *would* be easy to fleece her of her roulette chips except her aversion to betting big continues and she folds really easily (once she gathers what folding is).

Soon I give up on the idea of fleecing Nadia and just concentrate on winning money from the others in the game. It goes very well. I'm going to need another velvet bag or two myself.

'Okay,' says Nadia as I pull another pile of chips towards myself. 'This is ridiculous. I want another go. Your luck's going to run out soon like mine did with the roulette. There's no way you can carry on like this for long.'

'It isn't entirely luck, though?' I point out for the sake of honesty. 'I mean, for example, you have the world poker championships and you don't get complete beginners winning them, do you?'

'Really?' Nadia has her elbows on the table (that is really not good poker-playing etiquette but obviously she doesn't know that and I'm not going to be petty enough to point it out because this is a party, not a serious poker evening) and her hands propping up her chin, and is looking searchingly at my face. Her eyes move to the table and the cards. 'How is that possible, though? There aren't enough cards used in the game. How can someone work out what everyone has, given how many there are left in the pack?'

Okay, I've done enough honesty. I want her chips.

'Fair point,' I say, trying hard not to glare at her elbows. 'I still think I'm going to stay lucky though.'

'Well...' Nadia folds her hands under her chin, elbows still rudely in place. 'I didn't stay lucky at roulette. No-one stays lucky forever. That's the classic gambler's issue isn't it. Not knowing when to take your gains and run.'

'Yeah, no. That's not going to happen to me.'

'Oh-kay.'

It's actually lucky for Nadia that she's so *nice* (and so pretty) because the other players are a lot more proficient than she is and – now that she's decided she isn't folding immediately – would definitely be getting irritated with how she's slowing the game down with all her questions if she weren't just so lovely.

In fact, an older man called Howard (not un-Roger like) seems to be positively enjoying explaining, in *the* most patronising manner possible, how to raise someone. He's mansplaining in a way that will give all men a bad name; he's literally telling her how to do very basic mental arithmetic. As in literally how to add two and two.

It's halfway through Howard's explanation that I suddenly realise.

Nadia is lovely, and kind. But she isn't a *saint*. I've seen her get irritated before. She's *too* tolerant of Howard. I think she knows how to play poker.

I begin to watch her very carefully, and realise that the careful watching is reciprocal.

With the exception of me, everyone at the table is very surprised when Nadia says, all eyes wide open, guileless smiles, 'Am I right in thinking I got lucky?' as she places four aces on the table, straight after I've shown my full house.

I laugh. She's clearly played before but she also clearly did get lucky, because it's obviously fairly rare to get a full house.

Several increasingly intense rounds later, I have discovered that Nadia now seems to get lucky every single round, be it with a good hand or a bad hand. She knows when to fold, she knows when to gamble big, she just *knows*. And the weird thing is, I'm pretty sure that I've begun to be able to read her, except... it doesn't *work*. It's like she can read me *better*. Or alternatively she is in fact having the luckiest evening of her life and it's unfortunate that she wasn't playing for real money.

When I've demonstrated the gambler's crucial failing of not quitting while I was ahead and she has a lot more chips stowed in two more velvet bags, and we stand up from the table, she says, 'Well that was fun. Who knew someone could get so lucky at both a game of chance *and* a game of skill in one evening? Assuming it *is* skill.'

'Ha,' I say. 'Do you play a lot?' Clearly, she does.

'In your words, who knows?' She laughs. 'I did warn you. I'm having a lucky evening.'

'So what next?'

'I'm not good at blackjack. I'm quitting while I'm ahead. Also, I want to see what's happening in the other rooms.'

After we've given our chip bags to a man on the door and he's recorded our names, I follow her out of the room. I don't *have* to stay with her (although it's obviously better if I do, so that she won't get harassed by anyone else) but, if I'm honest, I'm loving her company.

'You know what I *really* loved in there?' Nadia murmurs to me as we move towards the next room, from which we hear music.

I lean in to hear her answer.

'The way you couldn't stop looking at my elbows,' she says, just for me, fixing my eyes with hers. 'Like they were offending you *so* much, but you very tolerantly weren't going to say anything because how was ignorant me to know. *Loved* it.'

I laugh – she's completely right – and try not to *adore* the way she's standing so close to me right now. And not to wonder what else she's completely right about. And why I'm wondering that.

I'm still looking at her, and she's still looking at me.

I have no idea what we were just talking about. She has some shimmery make-up on round her eyes, which makes them look mysterious and as though you could drown in their depths. Her lips curve in a smile that makes me question whether she knows what I'm thinking about her eyes, not just her elbows.

'Would you like...?' she asks.

I lean even closer. Our faces are barely an inch apart now.

'Yes?'

'To go to the silent disco?'

'Oh. Yes. Sure.' What was I *expecting* her to ask then? I don't know.

'*Sure* sure?'

'Yep.'

And in we go.

Meet Me Under the Clock

* * *

I've been to silent discos before. I've laughed in them, pulled ridiculous moves in them, had the odd snog in them. I have never before just adored watching the way someone else moved, be it fully throwing herself into the music, or just swaying, depending on the song.

To be fair, I've only been to them in groups with friends, not with just one woman, and I doubt I've been to one sober. And I haven't been to one recently. But even given all of that, this is different.

We're definitely listening to the same channel and dancing to the same things at the same time. Taylor Swift's 'Shake it Off' has just finished and now we're listening to Dua Lipa. And I can't take my eyes off Nadia.

It's weird. We're several feet apart. We came in together and we're dancing near each other but we're certainly not dancing together. But...

I'm watching every move Nadia makes and she's looking at me too. As she leans one way, I lean the same way. Until she leans one way and I lean the other and then we're asymmetrically mirroring each other and everything that she does I copy. Her body is... I mean, yes, it's... well, I don't even want to allow myself to think the thoughts I'm thinking. She's basically bloody gorgeous and frankly, wearing that dress, which is not in itself anywhere near as risqué as some of the dresses that are being worn tonight, it's no wonder she's getting lecherous glances from far too many people.

On that thought, I move a little closer, still watching her the whole time.

There's something very... *physical*... about dancing with someone, mirroring their movements, but looking into their eyes the entire time. Like you have this connection with them because you're only seeing their body in your peripheral vision, *sensing* it but very in tune with it.

And then suddenly the music switches several decades back to a Bryan Adams ballad, and without thinking, I stretch my right hand out to take Nadia's and give her a twirl under my arm, and then I don't release her hand, but give it a little tug, and she comes right in against me, and I slide my left around her waist, and we begin to sway together.

It is, hands down, the most erotic dance of my life. We're still looking into each other's eyes, and just *feeling* everything else that we do. And when I say feeling... I can feel her everywhere we touch, the slight warmth of her hand inside mine, the curve of her waist, the softness of her body against mine.

When it finishes and an Avicii song starts, I don't want to move apart, but also, yep, we should, because what *was* that?

I need a drink, I decide.

When I motion towards the door, Nadia nods, and walks out ahead of me.

We bump straight into Carole.

'You have no drinks,' she accuses us. 'Hang on.'

Before we can say no thank you to more cocktails, she's pressing bright red drinks on us.

We take sips at the same time.

'Blimey,' Nadia says when her eyes have stopped watering.

'Exactly,' I say, still blinking.

'I knew you'd like them,' Carole says fondly. 'What have you been doing? I heard that a beautiful woman with amazing hair and a lovely green dress did very well at both roulette and poker. That can only have been you, Nadia? Drink up.'

We both sip and Nadia says, 'That's a very over-flattering

description so maybe someone else did well, *but* I would say that I was on fire in there.'

Carole and I both laugh, and then Carole says, 'Maybe you'll be in with a shot at the prize. In the meantime, have you seen the fortune teller?'

'Oh, no, I don't think...' Nadia says, while I shake my head (I've just taken another gulp of the red drink under Carole's forceful gaze and have temporarily lost the use of my vocal cords).

'You have to go. She's very good and always right but also, the beauty of it is, you *can* tell yourselves it's all utter nonsense and then ignore her. I insist. But finish your drinks first.'

The drinks are big, but Carole is fierce, and I find myself meekly downing mine, and Nadia does the same with hers.

When we've both finished coughing, Carole pulls us along the corridor and round the corner behind the stairs to a small room, which has very low lighting. Sitting at a table is a woman dressed very stereotypically in a black dress with a fringed shawl round her shoulders and a kind of head-dress thing.

'Enjoy.' Carole basically shoves us towards the table and closes the door behind us.

'You do not look very happy,' the woman observes.

'Ha,' I say.

'We're very happy to be here,' Nadia says.

'Have you been to a clairvoyant before?'

We both shake our heads. Which clearly in itself tells a story because we're obviously both old enough to have chosen to see one if we wanted to.

'I have a queue.' The woman isn't looking too happy herself; she must prefer a more obviously receptive audience. 'Let's begin immediately. Show me your hands.'

We glance at each other and then put our hands out for her.

She bends her head over them and then says, very rapidly, 'It's clear that you have only been together for a short time but that you are very much in love with each other. You will remain together for the rest of your lives and will have two children, a boy and a girl. You will live long and happy lives. Thank you.' She pushes our hands back towards our bodies and looks at the door.

'Um, thank you.' Nadia stands up and moves towards the door.

'Yep, thanks.' I follow.

Nadia's giggling almost before we've closed the door. Which I'm delighted about, because otherwise things could have felt very awkward right now.

'I can't remember the last time I've been so thoroughly dismissed by someone,' she hiccups. 'And how long were we in there? Thirty seconds?'

'Complete charlatan.' I sound like my own father. Nadia just laughs more.

'Let's get some food,' I say. 'We've had a lot of drink on empty stomachs.' And now I'm sounding like my own mother.

A few minutes later, sitting at a table with plates piled high with food, and glasses of wine, in the corner of a room with a long buffet down one side, Nadia says, 'If *I* were going to say that I could read fortunes, I wouldn't make a statement straight out that might be right or wrong. So silly. We might have believed her if she hadn't told us first that we're *already* a couple.'

She looks up and me and freezes, her hand halfway to her mouth with a mini sausage roll. I freeze too.

'I don't mean *we* would have believed her,' she clarifies, and I relax. 'I mean *other people* in our position, i.e. very much not, certainly not, a couple, but in there talking to her together by chance, might have believed her. But they wouldn't have done because she made the incorrect statement before she said anything else.'

'Yeah,' I say, and take a really long slurp of wine, because for a minute there I had a vision of being old with Nadia, and our son and daughter coming to visit us with their kids, and I liked it.

17

NADIA

I chomp my sausage roll hard and hope that I just made a good recovery. My words came out very wrong and I definitely sounded as though I wanted the fortune teller's words to be true.

I keep on chomping. Very attractively, I'm sure. I kind of do want her words to be true about us. Me and Tom. If I allowed myself to think about it, I imagine I would *really* want her words to be true.

But her prediction is not correct, and Tom and I have not spoken for a few weeks and he is clearly still hung up on Lola – which if I'm honest is kind of stupid because she's clearly as interested in him as he is in me, i.e. not at all, and it's just not going to happen – but whatever, the point is he's not interested in me.

I swallow the last bit of my sausage roll and wash it down with quite a lot of wine.

Tom hasn't said anything for a while. Nor have I.

'So, poker,' I say. 'How much do you play?'

Tom returns from wherever he seems to have drifted off to

in his mind – possibly wondering how he'll get away from the deranged woman he's with who wants the fortune teller's words to come true, possibly thinking about Lola, possibly just grappling with a bit of indigestion – who knows – and says, 'I'm not sure whether I should tell you that.'

'And why would that be?' I ask, pleased that he's brought the conversation back to normality with his answer.

'Because you are—' he looks me right in the eye and empties his glass '—clearly a poker hustler.'

'Me?' I place my hand on my chest and feign hurt. And then laugh.

'No, no. No laughing. This is a serious matter.'

I'm still laughing but I'm also staring at Tom. Because that seemed, almost... flirty.

And we don't flirt with each other. Not for real.

I take a *big* gulp of my wine.

And then I say, 'Oh really? How serious?' And take another gulp.

'So serious—' Tom leans in so far that I can feel his breath whispering across my cheek when he speaks '—that I think we should have a rematch.'

My stomach dips and I reach for my glass. Oh. It's empty.

'When?' I croak.

'Now?'

'Um.' I don't like to play poker when I've been drinking, and I definitely don't feel sober right now.

'Are you... *scared*?'

'Certainly not.' What I actually need, I realise, is another drink. 'But can we finish our food first? Because this is delicious.'

'Of course,' he says. 'Never look a gift burger in the mouth.'

There are tiny cheeseburgers and also spicy chickpea and mushroom ones, both in brioches.

'Yummmm,' I say after my first mouthful.

'Stunning,' Tom agrees, and we munch happily on.

We don't really talk about much at all, just a bit of commentary on the food and how Carole is an amazing hostess and how much fun it all is.

We're just finishing our burgers and saying how tempted we both are by the mini pavlovas and treacle tarts that are calling to us from the table, when Bea and Ruth join us.

I realise, to my shame, that I'd completely forgotten about them this evening. My mind's been too full of someone else.

'Have you had a go on the rodeo yet?' Bea asks.

'Rodeo?' I query.

'VR,' Ruth explains. 'There's a gaming room.'

'Hey.' Tom nudges my foot with his. 'I wonder whether they have Brawl Stars.'

'Porn stars?' Ruth queries. 'I'd be surprised.'

'Brawl,' I say loudly. 'It's a phone game that Tom got me into. I've been addicted for ages now. Really annoying, actually.'

'Hello.' Carole appears holding bottles of red and white. 'The Waterloo Five together. So lovely to see. How was the fortune teller? White or red?' She sloshes wine into all our glasses without waiting for an answer.

'She was wonderful,' gush Bea and Ruth.

'Mmm, yes,' Tom and I both say.

'When you've finished eating, come to the big room at the back,' Carole commands. 'The main part of the evening is barn dancing. Ideally everyone will have a partner, and you are very handily already paired up.'

I look sideways at Tom and see that he's looking sideways at me.

The only thing I can do is bury my face in my glass. And keep on drinking while Bea and Ruth eat.

* * *

'Twirl me now,' I pant some time later. Tom obliges immediately but we're still half a beat behind the rest of our set (who are much older and on paper you would think less fit but are actually *amazing* at barn dancing).

'Back to back. Two steps right.' I keep on instructing out loud because Tom's even worse than I am. He had some *great* moves in the silent disco (if I'm honest I couldn't have looked away if you'd paid me) but right now he's basically laughing too much to concentrate.

I, however, have decided that I want to get it right, so I tut and just keep on going.

Tom carries on too, but I can see that his heart isn't in it.

And now people are tutting at both of us and if I'm honest I'm feeling a bit sick from all the backwards and forwards and turns.

'Maybe we should take a break,' I whisper to Tom next time our heads are close.

'Good idea. Right now?'

'No. At the end of this dance. We can't let our set down.' Although we *are* letting them down right now by constantly going *so* wrong. 'Now focus, just for the next few minutes.'

'You're very strict,' Tom grumbles.

* * *

Eventually the dance is over and we march ourselves straight over to the door.

On our way out we encounter a bartender carrying a tray of cocktails, which he offers to us.

'Rude not to.' I take one for each hand.

Tom raises his eyes at me.

'The tray looks really heavy,' I point out. 'We're doing him a favour.'

'Oh yes, you're right.' Tom takes two too, and then we go and sit on a little window seat near where the fortune teller was, and drink in companionable silence.

'I feel like we should go for a walk,' I say, when I've finished the first cocktail. I feel like I'm getting hiccups so I decide not to drink the second one for now, and stash it carefully by the side of our bench. 'Blimey,' I say admiringly. 'You're very good at drinking.'

'I am actually, yes. Also, this stuff has grown on me. What did you just say we should do?'

'Walk.' I stand up and sway a little, so I hold on to the wall for a moment. 'Outside in the garden.'

'Good idea.' Tom stands up. He isn't swaying at all, I notice.

'You're very clever,' I say.

'Thank you.'

We wander off down the corridor and then Tom halts.

'We missed a room.'

We poke our heads inside. It's a kids' party game room but for adults.

'I *really* want to play,' I say.

'Me too.'

'This one first.' I advance to the other side of the room. 'Pin the tail on the donkery.'

'Donkey,' Tom corrects.

I shake my head at his pedantry and also because he's wrong. 'Donkery.'

'Donkey,' he persists.

'It's donkery.'

'It isn't, though.' He's like a dog with a bone.

I stare at Tom and think, hard. 'Maybe you're right. Or wrong.'

'I'm right. It's donkey.'

'I've known that word for a really long time, like thirty years.' I'm really confused now. 'Donkey or donkery?'

'Donkey,' confirms the black-clad man who's helping with all the games.

'Well! I'm very surprised by that. Why did I get that wrong?'

'You've had too much to drink,' Tom says. 'That's why.'

'No, no, no. You've had more than me. Anyway, shut up. I need to get blindfolded and pin that donkery.'

I don't like the blindfold because it makes me feel sick but when I take it off it's worth having worn it: my tail is in *exactly* the right place.

'Look at that,' I crow. 'I win again.'

'You've pinned it to its face,' Tom says.

Oh. I look more closely. I think he might be right.

'Stupid game anyway,' I say. 'Let's go for our walk.'

Tom decides that we should drink a lot of water before we go. He thinks we should have two pints each, which takes quite a long time to drink. Eventually, though, we've finished our second pints and we're on our way to the garden.

'It's really nice out here,' I say. 'I like it.' I wave my arm around and nearly fall over. 'My arm's really heavy,' I explain.

'Hold mine,' Tom suggests.

'Good idea.' I *love* his arm. All of it. From sexy shoulder to handsome hands. If hands can be handsome. I feel like doing alliteration though. Eek. I freeze and look up at his profile. 'Did I say that out loud?' I ask.

'Say what?'

Thank goodness for that.

'Nothing,' I say airily.

We stroll along and comment on the moon and stars. (The sky is very clear. It's the countryside.)

'I don't really think hands can be handsome,' Tom muses a minute or two later as we pass some big trees.

Oh dear.

Okay. I'm going to style it out. Just engage in reasonable conversation about it.

'I think they can, actually,' I say. Very reasonably and conversationally.

'Oh, right. What about... elbows?'

'Um. Extremely elegant?'

'Nice. Legs?'

'Loose? Long? Lithe.' I'm pretty pleased with *lithe*. 'Anyway, enough alliteration. Isn't the moon nice?'

'Still lovely,' Tom agrees.

'Ooops,' I scream, as my heel catches in something.

Oh no, it's okay. I haven't fallen over. Tom has his arm round my waist and all is well.

'For a moment there I thought you were going to have *another* foot incident,' he says.

'No. There's no chance of that. It would be ridiculous. As previously discussed.'

'Yeah. Should we maybe sit on this bench, though, for a bit?'

'Good idea.' I'm very happy with Tom's idea, actually, because his arm that was round me kind of stays round me as we sit down, although now it's round my shoulders, and it feels very right there, like it belongs.

'I know we've said this before,' I say after a bit, 'but the stars *are* very, very nice. Twinkly.'

'Yeah.'

We sit there some more, just looking at the stars, and then – I'm not really sure why, well, just because I want to, I suppose – I kind of snuggle into Tom a bit more.

'Cold?' he asks.

Am I cold? No. Do I want to un-snuggle? No.

'Not now,' I settle on saying.

He hugs me in tighter.

I do fit very well inside his arm, actually.

I sense him shift to look at me, and turn my face up to his.

And then, like it's the most natural thing in the world, he bends his head and kisses me. At first, his lips just brush mine, but then he kisses me harder, and I kiss him back, and it's exactly like you always imagine the best kiss in the world would be like. It's delicate, and tender, and urgent, and almost desperate, all at once. Tom's lips are firm and soft and gentle and hard, and I never want this to stop.

It *doesn't* stop, for a long time. We just sit there, nestled together on the bench, kissing and kissing.

Until one of us moves, and then, frankly, we have hands *everywhere*, and it's amazing and I could *totally*, basically, have al fresco sex, except, also, I couldn't, and, suddenly, I slide out of Tom's arms and take his hands and pull him to his feet and hurry him back down the garden.

We have our arms wrapped round each other as we go. We're kissing, I think we definitely have arms under clothes, and now we're almost running, and then I trip and Tom picks me up and carries me upstairs to our rooms.

'Mine,' I say between kisses.

Tom slams the door closed with his back, and then we're on my bed and... it's amazing. *Nothing*, other than Tom himself getting up and walking away – which seems pretty unlikely right now – could stop me now. It's *so* good.

* * *

I wake up very confused for a moment. The sunlight is bright on my face, painfully bright. My head is fuzzy, my eyes feel scratchy like I didn't take my make-up off, and there's a solid man-sized weight against me, and legs across mine.

And ohhhhhh, all of that is because last night Tom and I had glorious, amazing, wonderful, divine sex for a very long time, in this lovely four-poster bed, and I didn't close the curtains or take my make-up off, and I might have had a teensy bit too much to drink, which would account for the headache (and possibly the sex, although I would *very* happily have done that entirely sober, and in fact I *was* sober by the time we were really doing stuff, thank goodness, because I remember it all very clearly and that is a memory I would be *very* sad not to have), and the solid weight against me is of course Tom. Who I know that I love very much. And with whom, from my side, I know that I was making love last night, as opposed to just shagging.

Not to say that the sex wasn't superb and worth it just for itself. In fact, I'm remembering my conversation with Tom right at the beginning, the night we met, and I'm wondering *why* I had this belief that no-strings sex was a bad thing. Because even if we never do that again (I really hope we do, many, many times) it will have been worth it.

Although... maybe it was only that good *because* I'm in love with him. Which I very clearly am.

I move my arm a little, because it's going a bit pins and needly, and Tom stirs.

I look at his lovely, kind, stubbly, square-jawed, ridiculously handsome face, and smile, and wait for him to wake up.

'What the bleurgh, what, where, what,' he says.

'Morning,' I say.

And, 'Oh my God,' he yells.

Not in a flattering way, if I'm honest. His tone is *what the actual*, not *oh wow lucky me*.

His eyes are swivelling a little, and I can feel his whole body drawing back.

While I summon up my best acting skills, I turn my face into the pillow on my side and tip my head so that my hair falls over my face.

And then I say, really hoping that my voice won't sound as though I'm crying (which, okay, I am a bit – my eyes are suddenly moist and internally I'm absolutely *wailing* with misery because it's *so* obvious that he's just full of regret and nothing else), 'I know.'

Which is the perfect phrase. I'm just agreeing with whatever he's saying. Because I do not wish to be humiliated on top of everything else.

'Um.' He's pulling further away from me, so I scoot right over to my side of the bed and drag a sheet around myself (the bed linen is in complete disarray) so that my nakedness is fully covered.

Then I wait for him to continue.

'I don't know what to say,' he says. And waits.

I say, 'I know,' again.

And then he says, 'I'll get my clothes and go and have a shower.'

Out of the corner of my eye I see him pluck a sheet from the bed and wrap it round his waist, so that his lovely, solid chest and abs are still on full display, and then I close my eyes because he clearly isn't mine in any way, and I shouldn't be ogling his (gorgeous) body. I hear him move round the room, and then he says, 'Okay, well I'll go then.'

And I say, 'Great,' and then I hear the door open and close. I wait for a moment, before getting up and locking the door, and then I crawl back into bed and hug one pillow into my body, putting the other one over my head and allowing myself to really just *sob* for a few minutes.

Because there is nothing good about realising that you are hugely, probably irrevocably head over heels in love with someone who… just regretted your night of mad, passionate sex.

I think it might take me some time to recover from this, and the first thing I need to do is not see Tom again.

18

TOM

It's rare to feel like a total dickhead first thing in the morning, but I do.

Carole has organised for everyone from last night's party to meet for breakfast.

I'm sitting with Bea, Ruth and Nadia. Fortunately, we're in a row, me and Nadia on the ends, Bea and Ruth in the middle. I'm chatting to Bea and the two people opposite us and I'm trying extremely hard not to catch the sound of Nadia's voice or her laugh, because every time I do I feel incredibly guilty. In my head I have unfinished business with Lola, and I also have unfinished business with Nadia in that we are *friends* and we had *sex* last night. A lot of sex. A lot of mind-blowingly good sex. And we are *friends*. And sex is not a good thing to do with a friend who you would like to stay friends with but not have a relationship with.

Why do I not want to have a relationship with Nadia?

Because she's my friend and because of Lola.

'Have *you* been, Tom?' Bea's enquiry means nothing to me. I have no idea what we're talking about. Or rather what the others have been talking about while I nod and smile as my thoughts go in circles.

I need to message Lola, I decide. Tell her something once and for all. I mean, she's obviously ended whatever non-relationship we had by airing me, but I want – need – to round it off from my side. Or, equally, make one final attempt.

'Tom?' Bea repeats.

I look at her kind (but always quite stern) face and try to think of a good catch-all response. I fail.

'Sorry. Really tired. Miles away for a second,' I confess. Bea's forehead furrows just a little and she tilts her head slightly, like she's disappointed in me, so I continue, 'I had a very, very late night, and I might have drunk a bit too much. So I might just have nodded off for a second. But I would very much like to know where it is that we're talking about visiting and I will undertake to not nod off again.'

'Gibraltar,' the woman opposite me says.

'Gibraltar?' I query, confused again.

'Have. You. Been. To. Gibraltar?' Bea says.

'Oh. Nope.'

The conversation pretty much carries on like that. I am uninspired and uninspiring. I just want some peace and quiet to decide what I'm going to say in my message to Lola (because I definitely am going to message her) and what I'm going to say to Nadia (I have to say something) and then I want to send the message and say the thing and then I want to go back to my flat and watch TV by myself to take my mind off everything else. And then get a full night's sleep in my own bed.

Finally, everyone's draining the last dregs of tea from their cups and looking ready to go. I don't want to be the first to leave (I feel as though Nadia would think that it was because of her, which would of course be true, but I don't want her to feel bad), but I'll be very happy to be the second to leave. I just want *someone* to make a move.

There's definitely a bit of shuffling and gathering of handbags now; this is it, hooray.

And then Carole, at the end of our table, stands up and says, 'Thank you for coming, everyone. You've made a newly divorced woman very happy.' After she's said some more nice things, she continues with: 'We have some prizes to announce.' It takes a bit of time to get through them all. She concludes with the casino winners. 'And in first place, to no-one's surprise, I'm sure, is Nadia.'

I make sure that my cheering and clapping are at least as loud and generous as everyone else's.

'Come and collect your prize, Nadia.'

Nadia looks a little dark under the eyes this morning, and to me it seems as though the big smile she's produced is a little forced. Her lack of sleep could be the reason but I can't help worrying that it's because she's miserable.

We all clap again as Carole hands Nadia an envelope.

As Nadia opens it, Carole explains to us all that it's vouchers for a massage in the spa of a nearby country hotel and a champagne lunch in the hotel's restaurant. For today. *For two*.

'Thank you so much,' Nadia says. Her smile isn't reaching her eyes and her demeanour is that of a rabbit in headlights. She clearly has absolutely no choice but to stay and use the tickets. And, oh God. Oh no.

'I thought, Tom, you might like to share the treat with Nadia.' Carole's smile is a lot realer-looking than Nadia's.

Fuck.

I sit, also entirely a rabbit blinded by headlights, staring at Carole's beaming face and Nadia's pained expression.

I cannot think of a single thing that I can do other than say what a great treat. I can't let Carole down or indicate that there's any awkwardness between Nadia and me. I can't consign Nadia to having to spend the day with a stranger. I really can only say thank you and then grit my teeth and bear it.

'Wow,' I say. 'Great. Thank you.'

As everyone claps again and Bea and Ruth both tell me that I'm going to have a *wonderful* day, I go for some positive thinking. How bad can it really be? We can agree to read the news, catch up on emails while we're having the lunch, and it can be a quick one. And who doesn't love a massage? During which we obviously won't have to talk.

It will be absolutely fine.

Definitely.

* * *

Forty-five minutes later, I enter the massage room in a white towelling dressing gown, very aware that Nadia will be in the same room and very aware that under the dressing gown I'm wearing only trunks and that Nadia is likely to be similarly under-clad.

Fortunately, the room contains two massage therapists and no Nadia yet.

Under instruction, I hop onto one of the beds and lie face down before my therapist switches my dressing gown for a towel.

I have my head turned away from the door, so that I won't lock eyes with Nadia when she comes in, so I'm disappointed when it turns out that there are two doors and she's come in through the other one, so I'm staring right at her dressing-gowned body for a moment. I give her a quick smile and turn my head the other way (trying my hardest to look as though

I'm just adjusting into a better massage-receiving position rather than whipping my eyes from her as fast as humanly possible).

I'm going to enjoy this massage. I like them but I rarely get one. I am determined to take advantage of this.

'You're very tense,' my therapist tells me.

Well of course I bloody am.

Actually, with the soothing music and the expert hands of the therapist, I do relax and begin to enjoy it, and I'm almost asleep and really not pleased when he quietly tells me that he's finished.

Nadia's has finished too, and I know that because her therapist tells us both that we can leave the room in our own time.

And there we are. Together. Semi-naked under undone dressing gowns, with a very big sexual elephant in the room.

Nadia is saying absolutely nothing.

I'm really keen to be on my feet and dressed, so I bite the bullet. I swing round with my back towards Nadia to do my gown up and hustle myself back to the changing room.

It's easier said than done because some of my muscles have gone to jelly due to the firmness of the massage, but I manage not to groan out loud (I don't want to remind either of us of last night, during which I think there might have been a fair amount of groaning) and say, 'Good massage. I'm going to get changed. I'll meet you in the hotel restaurant shortly. I think Carole said the table was at one. I'll see you then.'

'Great,' says Nadia, her voice sounding distant, I'm guessing because her head's still turned away from mine.

I take my time getting changed and then I slide out of the changing room – there's no sign of Nadia I'm pleased to say – and then take myself off for a brisk, brain-clearing country walk.

*　*　*

I'm back for lunch and in the restaurant by five to one, because I don't want to seem rude.

I slightly wonder whether Nadia will turn up at all, given that I'm the one who left her room this morning and how she didn't sound super happy at that moment, but I think she probably will, because she won't want to let Carole down.

Clearly we just need to eat the lunch and drink a bit of champagne, while making polite conversation, take a cab to the station together, and then sit separately on the train (I hope).

Nadia turns up at one minute after one.

Once the waiter has her seated, he immediately pours us both a glass of champagne before telling us he'll be back in a few minutes to take our orders.

Nadia looks me right in the eye and says, 'What a lovely restaurant; what a lovely treat. The massage was great too. Carole's very kind.'

'Yes, she is,' I agree, very carefully. I *think* Nadia's signalling that she will not under any circumstances be initiating a discussion about last night, but I don't want to *assume* that.

Nadia opens her menu and begins to read it very intently.

'This looks lovely,' she says after a few seconds.

I open my own menu. 'It does.'

We make desultory conversation about the menu. Nadia is careful to bolster the incredibly mundane food chat whenever it starts to wane, and I do my best from my end too. We continue our dull conversation after the waiter has taken our orders (unbelievably annoyingly Carole has very kindly prepaid for us to have starters, mains and puddings; I'd been planning on going for just a main).

'Yes, the décor *is* lovely,' I agree, dutifully looking around the room. This is such hard work.

'Our starters!' Nadia says, with the most genuine enthusiasm I've seen her display all day.

We both direct our full attention to our plates.

'Your scallops look lovely,' I say.

'So does your terrine.'

And then we both start eating, both of us going really slowly – a full mouth is an excellent excuse for not talking much – and not saying anything other than how good the food is (actually it *is* good).

We time the end of our slow starter-eating very well, because our mains arrive within only two or three minutes of our plates being cleared.

We eat the mains slowly too.

We eat our puddings quite fast, both of us as though we're pulling a sprint finish out of the bag after an arduous long-distance run.

'Can I get you a cup of coffee to finish?' the waiter asks as he clears our plates.

'No thank you,' we say simultaneously.

'I have to go very soon,' Nadia says the second he's gone. 'I have things to do in London. I'm going to call an Uber.'

'Great.' I spy an early reprieve. 'I'll probably just relax here for a little longer. I'm not in a rush.'

'Good idea,' says Nadia extremely politely. 'I'd love to relax here too. But I can't. Have a lovely afternoon.' And she stands up, kind of nods at me, and walks off across the room.

I can't help watching her go and I can't help thinking that she's very beautiful and kind and cool, and marvelling at the fact that last night we... yep. We did all of that. Together.

I get my phone out and check train times.

I think she might just miss one and they aren't that frequent because it's Sunday. So I need to give the station a wide berth for several hours.

I decide to take myself to a pub for a few hours and go back to London this evening.

* * *

In the pub (a different one from the one we were in last night; I do not want to run into Carole or any of the other guests), I read the news on my phone. I watch some tennis and some golf on the pub TV. I try very hard not to think about Nadia. I fail. She likes watching tennis. I wonder whether she likes golf. I order a birthday present for my mum from John Lewis. I wonder whether Nadia would think my mum would like the top I've chosen. I play Brawl Stars (which makes me think about Nadia).

It's ridiculous how much I'm thinking about her but in fairness to myself we did have a lot of sex last night so it's probably natural.

Eventually I decide that it will be safe to go to the station and catch the next train back to London.

I'm a little bit on edge walking onto the platform, but all good, there's no sign of her.

Once I'm on the train that arrives within five minutes, I'm still thinking about Nadia.

It's really annoying me. I just can't stop.

I'm also thinking sporadically about Lola. Who I don't even have a photo of other than a grainy one from ten years ago.

I search through the pictures on my phone and look at the grainy old one. Lola is beautiful. Blonde, sleek, but with a naughty side-eye to her. And ten years younger of course.

Suddenly, I don't know why – maybe it's just the kind of

thing you do when you're feeling sad and guilty (which is how I am feeling because I don't think I should have slept with Nadia and it's very sad that our friendship is effectively over) – I decide to rewatch our 'Happy Birthday' video.

Yeah. It's a nice video. My grandmother loved it. Anyone would have.

We made a very convincing couple. It's actually horrifying. I don't know how I'd describe how I'm looking at Nadia in it. Fondness I think. Definitely strong friendship. Very strong friendship. Very fond. Very, very fond.

The way she's looking at me... well, yeah. Also very, very fond. There's no poker face there. She's wearing her feelings right there on her face.

I am an arse.

And suddenly I know what I have to do. I have to round off things with Lola one way or another. I have to message her. And I either have to say just to let you know that from my side it's over, or I have to ask one final time if she'd like to meet. Or something.

I don't know what I'm going to write until I begin.

And then I say:

> Lola. Hey. It's Tom. Would you like to meet one final time?

And, to my utter astonishment, she immediately reads the message and then she begins to type. And she sends a reply.

> Yes please. Can you do Wednesday?

19

NADIA

I look hard at my hob and give it just one more wipe. With the under-cabinet spotlights beaming onto it, its gleam is almost headache-inducing. It literally could not be any cleaner.

Likewise the floor, the sink, the worktops, the cupboard doors, the fridge, the oven, you name it. Also every single part of the bathroom.

I *would* declutter the cupboards but they've all already been decluttered, following all my terrible dates over the past year.

Obviously you could say it's a good thing that when I'm stressed I clean to avoid thinking, but it doesn't really work in a flat where you definitely couldn't swing even a kitten, because there just isn't enough cleaning to *do*.

I'm almost tempted to offer to clean my neighbours' flats.

Or my friends'.

I put my cloth back in the (currently stunningly clean and tidy) cupboard under the sink.

I'm going to have to allow myself to think about Tom at some point. It should probably just be now.

Okay.

I go over to my sofa and sit down. Then I stand up and plump the cushions. Maybe I should give them all another vacuum.

No. Maybe I should just actually woman up and address in my mind what happened.

I sit back down.

So.

The sex. The amazing, out-of-this-world, fantastic sex. Well, it was at the time. Now it should probably be re-categorised as huge-mistake sex.

It just cemented the realisation that had been dawning on me but which I hadn't really been allowing to filter through properly that I am – obviously – deeply, probably irrevocably, in love with Tom.

And this morning, the way he slid out of my room as soon as he could, just cemented the knowledge that I already had that he is not, and never will be, in love with me.

It's ironic, because it's like him and Lola. He's interested in her but she is blatantly not interested in him now and might never really have been. (The woman is clearly mad.)

The whole time I've known Tom I've thought that he should actually just move on from Lola. Obviously that's easier said than done. Hope is the killer of recovery from unrequited love. So I think you have to kill the hope. I think Tom should have killed his hope that Lola would come back to him. He should have told her that he was moving on and didn't want to be in contact again. And then he would have found it easier to stop thinking about her.

I stand up to go and put the (lovely, shiny, vinegar-and-bicarb-of-soda-descaled) kettle on.

And while I'm filling it I realise that I should take my own advice.

It's not like I can be any more humiliated by this situation. I just need to help myself recover from this.

I'm going to do with Tom what he should have done with Lola.

I'm going to send him a message.

I know this is the right thing to do, so before I can change my mind (because let's face it I probably *can* be even more humiliated by this), I pick up my phone and type.

> Hi Tom. I'm going to get straight to the point. I love you. I am in love with you. Clearly you do not feel the same way and there's no reason that you should. So I need to get over you, basically. And so I can't see you again. I'll explain to Carole, Bea and Ruth if they want the five of us to meet again. Perhaps you and I can meet them separately if you'd like to stay in touch with them. (I would.) Anyway. I wish you all the very best. Nadia

And then, without rereading it or questioning whether or not I *should* send it, I *do* send it.

Tom is not Lola. He reads the message almost immediately, and he replies almost immediately.

> I don't know what to say. I'm so sorry for having hurt you. I would never want to do that. You're a wonderful person. I wish you the very best too. Tom

I read it through dry eyes, and then through tears, and then I can't read at all because I'm crying so hard.

It was the right thing to do.

I'm not going to see Tom again. He's out of my life. End of.

20

TOM

I really want to message Nadia.

Obviously I can't do that, because she doesn't want to speak again and I have to respect that.

She's the main – only – person I want to speak to right now, though.

It would be the most selfish thing in the world to message her.

I want to tell her how nervous and full of anticipation I am to finally be seeing Lola. It's like Nadia's been on a lot of my Lola journey with me. And I'd like to tell her about this part of it. And I'll want to fill her in on the end of it. Which will hopefully be the beginning of something else.

I miss Nadia.

Not seeing her is of course entirely my fault.

I look up at the station clock above and then over towards the other side of the concourse. And oh my God, I think it actually is her. Lola. After all this time.

As she draws closer, I kind of want to take a photo and send it to Nadia so that she gets to see the end of this story – like *look, it's actually her*.

It really is her. Ten years on.

She's beautiful. She's graceful. She's aged – well, not aged, she's matured – in the most perfect way. Exactly as I would have expected her to.

My heart's beating like the clappers (an expression I think Nadia would use).

Lola's here now, right in front of me.

'Tom.' Her voice is exactly as I remembered it. Confident, poised, the hint of a laugh in there.

'Lola.' And mine is, I have to admit, a little shaky. In my defence, this is a big moment.

I hold my arms out and she walks straight into them.

We hug for a long moment. It feels odd, if I'm honest. I don't usually hug a woman, knowing that I'm hoping to start a relationship with her, only a few days after having sex with another. All I can think is that she doesn't fit into my arms the way Nadia does, which is really not what I want to be thinking right now.

'I've missed you,' she says.

'Me too.' I push away the thought that I've particularly missed her since *she* got in touch with me five months ago and then *she* didn't turn up. I don't want to ruin this reunion by negativity. I'm sure she had a very good reason for not coming. I mean, she's here now, isn't she?

She tilts her face back and smiles. God, that smile's bewitching. Slightly mocking. Enticing. *Very* flirty. It's the one I've dreamed of for years on and off. Her lips are slightly parted and I get the strong impression that she wants me to kiss her.

I…

Yeah, it's weird.

It feels too soon after... Nadia.

This actually all feels as though it's happening to someone else. Lola is a very attractive woman who I... am not quite ready to kiss properly.

I kiss her cheek.

'Very... gentlemanly,' she says, one eyebrow raised.

'Yep.' I smile at her.

I can't actually believe that she's here.

'It's really you,' I say.

She laughs. 'It really is.'

Given everything that's happened – or rather *not* happened – it's odd how very mundane this seems. Two people meeting again.

Maybe it's because we were meant to be. Maybe it's like we're just slotting into place together. Maybe that's why it seems so peculiarly unremarkable given the facts.

But I'm just not as excited or as full of anticipation as you would expect at this point. I think I felt more excited and anticipatory *before* I saw her.

'I booked dinner,' I say. I chose a restaurant on the other side of Waterloo from the places I've been with Nadia. Since I can't tell her about this evening, I don't really want to be reminded of her. And, also, it kind of feels slightly disloyal to go to the same place with both Nadia and Lola. As though I'm betraying both of them. Similarly, I'm really not loving being under the clock with Lola. Even though it was – originally – our place. It belongs to our group, the Waterloo Five, now.

'Can't wait.' She slips her hand into mine as we begin to walk. Our paces adjust easily to each other, and, yes, it's easy. Weirdly easy. But also weirdly... asexual, I suppose.

'You have gorgeous hands,' she purrs as we walk.

'Ha. Thank you. You too.' I nearly point out two pigeons scrapping over some bread and then remember that she is not Nadia and that she probably wouldn't find it that funny.

We don't chat that much on the way to the restaurant; it's like we're just enjoying being in each other's company again. We don't really *need* to talk that much.

Although, no, we *do* need to talk, I think, as we're seated. In fact, there's a lot to say. A lot to *ask*. And I really don't want to spend time ordering drinks. I just want to be able to ask all my questions immediately.

I admire Nadia for having dived straight in after... that night... and having immediately texted what she wanted to say. I should do the same with Lola. Really, the only question is *which* question I should ask first.

Why did she contact me again back in June?

Why did she not turn up?

Why didn't she reply to my message?

Why did she then reply immediately to this one?

How is she?

What's she been doing?

Does she love me?

I open my mouth to begin, just as Lola says, 'I was waiting for you to contact me again.'

I close my mouth and stare at her, before asking, 'When?'

'Now, silly.'

The *silly* is strangely... grating. No, it isn't. It's just that this is a weird situation. It's like Christmas Day when you're a kid. It takes such a long time to come that you can't really believe on the day that you're actually *in* it and it doesn't always live up to expectations. And there are *loads* of Christmas Days compared to this. One a year. And birthdays. So together that's two a year.

This is a once-in-a-lifetime experience. And it's been ten years and five very anxious months coming. So it isn't surprising if things feel a little odd, and if we're both behaving a little differently from usual.

I've been sitting just *looking* at Lola for ages. And she's looking at me, apparently waiting for me to speak.

'So you were waiting for me to contact you again?' I clarify. 'Now? After the last time we were in touch in June?'

'Yes.'

I look at Lola's perfectly symmetrical features. I can't help wondering whether she's had lip fillers. I don't think her mouth looked exactly like that ten years ago.

Then I think about Nadia's lips and kissing them, and feel terrible, before pushing that thought away.

I look down at the menu and consider beginning to read it.

And then I look up again. We aren't going to get anywhere if we can't mention things. Really obvious, big things.

I can't put it off by thinking about Lola's face or reading the menu.

'Why didn't you reply to me in June?' I ask. 'Or contact me yourself?'

'I needed to test you,' she says, like it's obvious.

'Because?' I ask; it is not obvious to me.

'Because I've been let down by men in the past and I needed to know that you wouldn't let me down?' She says it like it's a question, like it's a completely *duh how-do-you-not-know-that* answer.

She must have been let down very badly, I decide, feeling guilty for the flash of irritation I felt before she explained.

Instead of feeling irritated, I should be trying to understand exactly what she means, so that I can reassure her.

'Are you ready to order?' a waiter asks.

'I'd like a Caesar salad, please.' Lola flashes her smile at the waiter.

He blinks and smiles back, before saying, 'We don't serve Caesar salads.'

I realise that Lola hasn't opened her menu at all. Fair enough; we've had weightier things on our minds.

'Really?' She frowns a tiny bit. 'Would it be possible to make me one, though?'

'Oh. Well, I think so. Maybe. I'll check with the chef.'

'Thank you.' She throws another smile at him before saying to me, 'Where were we?'

'Well I...' I was going to order but the waiter's gone. But no problem; he will obviously come back and I'll order then.

The weirdness of the situation really is getting to me.

'So,' I say firmly. 'You got in touch in June to see if I wanted to meet but then you didn't make it. Which I completely understand; things do just happen sometimes.' I'd love to know *what* happened. 'I was a little worried about you, though, because from your messages it sounded as though something bad might have happened to you. And then when I—' yep, I'm just going to say it, or where will we ever be able to go from here '—told you I loved you, you didn't reply. And so I suppose I thought that my feelings weren't reciprocated.'

Lola takes my hands across the table and smiles at me. 'Silly. Of course they're reciprocated.'

I let my hands stay holding hers, but out of nowhere I think, *I miss Nadia*. It feels odd being here with Lola; it's like I'm almost homesick for Nadia's presence. *She's* the one I go to restaurants at Waterloo with. Weird. I really don't know why I'm thinking that right now.

I focus and take a deep breath. 'What was it that stopped you from coming in June?'

She shakes her head, and says, 'Details. What matters is *now*. I love you, Tom.'

She's smiling in her mocking, intimate way again, and looking into my eyes. And I'm... confused. This is all I've wanted for a very long time. But...

'Excuse me; we can do a Caesar salad for you,' the waiter interrupts.

'Thank you so much.' Lola doesn't move her gaze from mine. 'Make that two. And a bottle of champagne, I think.' She points at the wine menu. 'To celebrate.'

I don't particularly want a Caesar salad and I... Yep, fine whatever. Not the most important thing right now. I mean, I'm reminded of when Nadia ordered Italian food for me and she *asked* if it was okay for her to do that; she didn't just assume. But, really, whatever. What we eat this evening is not important.

I smile at the waiter and thank him, before looking back at Lola.

Her smile grows and then she very deliberately moistens her lips, and then bites her down on her lower lip with her perfectly even teeth.

It should be a very sexy move – it's definitely, I think, intended to promise exciting things for later – but I'm too confused still to appreciate it. All I can think about is *Nadia's* mouth.

I withdraw my hands from Lola's on the pretext of looking at the wine menu.

Lola pouts at me. 'Champagne, surely, all evening?'

She's right. I should make an effort. I don't know what's wrong with me. This is a huge evening for us. Of course we should be drinking champagne. Although not too much; I don't want to ruin the evening by being remotely drunk.

Maybe things between us will feel more normal, for want of a better word, if we just *chat* rather than plunging straight into the deep stuff.

My mind is actually quite blank, though. Nadia would be astonished if she could see me now; when I'm with her – well, with most people actually, including Lola the first time we met – I'm not usually at a loss for words or conversation topics. Well, apart from with Nadia when we'd just had sex, but that was different. And even then we *could* have talked, it was more just that we *didn't*, because we couldn't talk about what we *should* have been talking about.

'So you like a Caesar salad,' I say after much searching for words.

'I do.' She elongates the *do* so that it's almost two syllables, which makes me laugh, and that feels better.

'Do you cook a lot?'

'Tom,' she admonishes. 'We aren't here to talk about cooking.'

'Right. What *are* we here to talk about?'

'Us. Obviously.'

I nod because that's fair enough. Although we can't talk about us forever. But, no, obviously she just means *now*.

I wait, because I feel like I've said some stuff about *us* and Lola hasn't, so I'd like to hear now what *she* has to say.

'We should have got together ten years ago,' she says. 'Then and there.'

'We couldn't, though?'

'Because you were moving to New York.'

'And also,' I point out, 'because you were in a relationship and pregnant.'

'Relationships end,' she says.

I kind of ignore her words because I've realised that I haven't yet asked about her child (children perhaps), which feels terrible. I've been too overwhelmed by seeing her again.

'The baby you were expecting,' I say. 'I'm so sorry. I didn't ask. What did you have?'

'A boy. He's ten now.'

'What's his name?'

'Tom.' She smiles at me as though she's conferring the most enormous compliment on me. 'He's looking forward to meeting the person he was named after.'

I know it's a bad reaction but all I can do is stare at her. I want to be flattered but... I'm a man she met and had an amazing evening with ten years ago *while* she was with the baby's father... and she named him after me? I am *not* flattered. I'm disturbed.

I wonder what Nadia would be thinking if she were a fly on the wall right now. I think she'd be aghast but would also struggle not to laugh a bit at the utter ridiculousness of my situation.

And why *is* my situation so ridiculous?

Well. I suddenly realise everything.

My situation is ridiculous because I don't want to be here at all. I want to be with Nadia. I want to tell her all about this. I want to tell her everything. Always. I don't care about any of the stupid things I had in my head about us not having that much in common, or her man detox. I just want to be with her.

Oh fuck.

I've been such an idiot.

'Tom?' Lola's eyes are narrowed. 'What were you thinking about?'

I ignore her question and ask, 'Why did you contact me

again this year? And was it because of your son that you couldn't make it to Waterloo on the twenty-first of June?' I realise that whatever her answers are I won't even care; I will just want to tell Nadia so that she knows the end of this pathetic little story, because I owe her that given how involved she's been all the way through.

'Because we always said we'd meet after ten years and you just popped into my head. And, no, I had Tom sorted; he was staying with my parents for the night. No; my bloody husband came home. He was supposed to be on a golf weekend but because of rain he came home early. And when I said I was going into town to meet a friend, he said he'd catch the train in with me and go and see his brother. So I told him my friend had cancelled. It was *soooo* annoying.'

Wow. I cannot believe I was so worried about her. I thought she'd had an accident or something terrible.

'Are you still married?' I ask.

'Yes, but we have a very open relationship.'

'Although not so open that you were willing to tell him that you were meeting me that Saturday?'

'Are you a lawyer?' The edge to her voice is not that attractive.

'Nope.' I signal to the waiter, who comes over. 'Could we get the bill now?'

'I hope you're not expecting me to go halves?' Lola tells me.

* * *

Once I've paid the entire bill, wishing that Lola could at least have bloody ordered the house champagne, not one of the most expensive ones on the menu, I say, 'Well, goodbye then,' and stand up.

'Fuck off,' Lola says.

I'm pretty sure I'm lucky not to have had her glass of champagne upended over me.

I feel... free, I think is the word... as I weave through the tables in the restaurant and out onto the street.

I also feel very, very stupid.

I've been chasing after a youthful dream. In my defence, we *did* have an amazing evening, when we met, and a bruising divorce does (in my experience) make you hanker after better times.

I turn into the station and look over towards the clock. There's no time I'm passing through Waterloo that seeing it doesn't make me think of Nadia.

And that's where I've been *really* stupid. I love her. I want to tell her everything. We can talk about anything and it becomes fun or interesting or deep and meaningful. She's a very kind and thoughtful person. And I fancy the pants off her. I am in love with her and I have been for many weeks. And I was too infatuated with an idea from the past to realise it.

I need to tell her.

The departures boards tell me that there's a train right there for me. (When I'm not, for example, waiting for one that stops at Wimbledon for Nadia, they're very regular – most trains leaving from Waterloo stop at Clapham Junction – and there I go again, actually, thinking about Nadia.) I speed up and manage to get on it just before the whistle goes.

As it pulls out, I reflect for a moment that it feels good to have physical distance between me and Lola. I'm glad I don't know where she lives. Or anything else about her. Other than, of course, that her son is called Tom and she's married to a man I feel very sorry for. Thank God she didn't come in June; I would hate to be involved unsuspectingly in a married person's affair. More importantly, though, I wouldn't have met Nadia.

I have so much I want to say to her, starting with a huge, gigantic, enormous *Sorry*.

The thing is, though, I think, as I stare at my phone screen with my finger hovering over the keys, I'm not sure how to say it.

It feels really wrong to say it the evening I've seen Lola, even though Nadia doesn't know that.

That could make it seem as though I was choosing between them. I wasn't. But it did – to my great shame – take seeing Lola and just wanting to tell Nadia all about it to make me realise how very much Nadia means to me.

I don't think I can message her now.

* * *

I wait two days, during which I think a lot about Nadia and how much I would never want to hurt her and how much I would like to be with her, before, sitting on a bench on Clapham Common in the late afternoon sun, I find the words.

> Hi Nadia. I've really missed you. I wondered if you'd like to meet up this weekend. Or any other time. Tom x

A little reflection told me that you don't leave the room without saying anything after you've slept with someone for the first time and then tell them by text that you're sorry and you love them; you tell them in person. So if Nadia agrees to meet me I'll tell her then that I love her.

Nadia's reading the message.

She's typing.

And the message is here.

> Hi Tom. I'm really sorry but I can't see you. Hope you're well. Nadia

I stare at two squirrels playing in front of me. I wouldn't mind having a life as simple as that. I can't just tell Nadia I love her in a message. But also, apparently, I'm not going to be able to see her in person, because she understandably doesn't want to see me.

Not a good situation, and I've brought it entirely on myself.

21

NADIA

Spreadsheets really don't take your mind off heartbreak. And not to be too dramatic, I do think that is what I have about Tom. I genuinely feel actual physical stomach-clenching misery when I think about him.

So I've been keeping myself very busy and I've been doing okay really. I mean, at least ten people a day this week have asked me if I'm feeling ill, and I'm really not finding many jokes at all funny, which is quite scary, because life is kind of rubbish without finding the humour in things, and I'm even not loving my food any more. But I've been going out with friends a lot, I'm thinking seriously about joining a gym, I've been to the hairdresser's, I've bought myself some new clothes; I've basically lived the trying-to-put-a-brave-face-on-it-after-a-tricky-break-up thing, even though I have not in fact just had a break-up, I just had a one-night-stand with someone who I am in love with who is not in love with me, which I knew *before* I slept with him, so I shouldn't have let it get to me so much.

It doesn't feel good to have told him that I can't see him.

When I got his message I *wanted* to say yes, yes, yes, tell me when and where and I'll jump through hoops to be there (having first touched up my make-up and my hair and maybe changed into a nice new top). But I summoned up some self-respect and said a very polite not-on-your-nellie.

And now I'm feeling *really* miserable.

Not so much because I said I can't meet him, but because when I saw that I had a message from him my hopes rose – soared – and for one second I fantasised that he'd be telling me that he loved me and he just hadn't had the words before and could we be together.

I am so ridiculous.

And so I must focus as hard as I can on this extremely dry spreadsheet (there's a problem somewhere with the numbers adding up – they don't, but *why*?) and then write a quick email to one of my clients (also about a spreadsheet, yay, exciting) and then I must focus very hard on enjoying myself hugely at the cinema with Gina this evening.

* * *

Just over a week later, it's Saturday evening and I'm at Waterloo station, heading towards the clock, to meet Carole, Bea and Ruth. I told them a potted version of the truth (I spent ages trying to word it less embarrassingly and then just gave up – I didn't want to make Tom sound bad in any way – and just said that I'd fallen in love with him and he didn't feel the same way so for my own sanity I can't see him for the time being), so they're going to see him and me separately for now.

Carole wanted to meet Bea, Ruth and me last Saturday but I had a wedding singer job on (I nearly burst into tears during a couple of the songs thinking about Tom because I'm a complete idiot, but did just about hold it together, thank goodness), so we switched it to this Saturday.

I really, really get that Carole needs to keep extremely busy socially to distract herself from her divorce. I feel exactly the same way about Tom and I didn't even know him for that long. It's just that being around the three of them does, obviously, make me think of him, and that's uncomfortable.

I need to get over it, though, because Bea, Ruth and Carole are amazing women, who I care about a lot, and who I'm lucky to have met, and I would like to know them forever.

'Nadia.' Carole walks towards me with arms outstretched and we share a hug.

I'm a little bit surprised by the way she's dressed; she said she'd booked a fancy restaurant with a fancy dress code for us, so I'm in a nice dress, but she's in jeans, brogues and a jumper, looking great but not fancy-dress-code great.

'I have a really big favour to ask,' she says, which reminds me of how Tom and I broached our plus-one requests (what a stupid idea; I can't believe we actually did it).

'Of course,' I tell her.

'Okay. Please don't hate me for this.'

'Carole, I could never hate you.' Although I won't be thrilled if she's organised something I really don't want to do like going to naked-only steam rooms, for example. No. You don't wear a nice dress for that.

'Okay. Well.' Carole is looking very unlike herself. She's practically wringing her hands and standing on one foot and then the other and kind of looking over her shoulder. If I didn't know her better and know that it's basically impossible for her to be nervous, I'd say that she *was* nervous. 'I would only ever want the best for you.'

I nod.

'And you're lovely and I hope that we stay friends forever.' She's still hand-wringing. Very odd and extremely suspicious. *What* am I suspicious *of*, though?

'I love *all* our Waterloo Five,' she continues.

I narrow my eyes. What does she mean by that?

'And so for that reason I have, not to put too fine a point on it, lured you here and I'm going to go now.' And then she envelops me in a gigantic hug, before releasing me and speed-walking away from me without looking back.

Leaving me to deal with the fact that Tom is standing in front of me.

I really, really wasn't expecting to see him.

I can't really move and I can't really think.

My eyes are still working (unlike the rest of me). I can see that clothes-wise he's almost painfully smartly dressed (also painfully handsome); he's wearing a very well-fitting navy suit, white shirt and sky-blue tie, plus shiny black shoes. Facial expression-wise, he's looking very intently at me and his lips are slightly pressed together and his eyebrows a tiny bit raised, which makes him look a little nervous, which makes sense given that I definitely explicitly said I didn't want to see him but he appears to have colluded with Carole to engineer a meeting anyway.

So I should really turn round and walk away, immediately.

'Hi.' His voice sounds a little hoarse, as though he hasn't used it for a while. 'I appreciate that you said you didn't want to meet, and I have to apologise for forcing your hand, but I wondered if we could talk.'

He's right. He *has* forced my hand, and it's *rude*. I feel as though I *should* walk away. And the fact that right now I feel extremely desperate not to leave but to stay and gather any crumbs of his time that I can just tells me that I *really* shouldn't let myself stay.

Especially since, for all I know, the reason he wanted to meet might be something that would devastate me (even though it shouldn't), like, for example, that he wants to tell me that he's reconnected with Lola and is marrying her.

'I don't think I can,' I tell him.

I take one last look at his face, and then turn round quickly, before I can do something extremely embarrassing like bursting into tears, and begin to walk off as fast as my new and very nice wedges will carry me (not as fast as I would like).

'I love you,' someone hollers from behind me.

I freeze, because I'm pretty sure that that was Tom's voice. And I almost think that he must have directed those words at me. Unless someone he *actually* loves has just come into view and he can't help yelling how he feels.

And then he shouts again. 'I love you, Nadia.'

I stop walking and then turn round very slowly.

I stand still and Tom begins to walk towards me.

'I love you,' he says, stopping a few feet away.

I don't say anything because, well, I don't know what I think and I don't know what I should say. What does he mean by *I love you*? Does he mean he loves me like a friend? Does he mean he loves me in an *in-love* kind of way? Does he *really* mean it? If he *does* really mean it, what does he want or expect to happen next?

He takes a couple of steps closer.

I fold my arms across my chest.

He stops walking.

'I...' He moistens his lips and then presses them together and then kind of purses them, and on anyone else what he's doing would just look weird, but now he's doing it I feel like it looks so cool it could catch on. Unfair. 'I've been an idiot and I'm very sorry and I wondered if you'd like to have dinner with me.'

I shake my head because I'm not sure what to say.

'Oh. Okay,' he says.

'No,' I say, 'I didn't really mean no. Or maybe I did. I don't know whether I did or not.' Very lucid.

'Fair enough. Um.' He looks at me for a moment and I just look back at him. Eventually, he says, 'I would very much love the opportunity to talk to you. To tell you some things and, obviously, to listen to anything you might like to say to me. And to apologise for being an idiot. That's why I asked Carole to help me um...'

'Lure me here?' I supply. 'And also Bea and Ruth; they were in that chat.'

'Also Bea and Ruth,' he confirms. 'And for the sake of openness, I should disclose that Carole told me that she spent a lot of her divorce party trying to set us up. The fortune teller was there only for us. And the massage and lunch prize was a spur-of-the-moment thing she dreamt up when she realised that you'd won the casino competition.'

I'm open-mouthed. 'So sly.' I don't know whether I'm in awe or annoyed.

'But entirely done from a position of caring about both of us,' Tom says.

I nod. That *is* true. Carole is the walking epitome of heart-of-gold.

'Well,' I say.

'Well?' Tom asks when I don't continue.

'I don't know.'

We're still standing about a metre apart from each other.

He takes a cautious-looking step forward so there's now only about an arm's length between us.

'Would you perhaps consider going for a walk instead of dinner if dinner seems too much?'

I shake my head. 'These shoes were not made for walking.'

'No flip-flops in your bag?'

'Not really flip-flop weather.'

'Yeah.'

And then we stand there again.

'So not a walk,' Tom says after a bit.

'I could do dinner,' I suddenly decide. Seeing Tom for however long we've been standing here will have set me back quite a long way in recovering from him. So I might as well have dinner and hear what he has to say. If I'm honest, I am extremely curious about what he meant when he said he loved me.

'Are you sure?'

'Yep. If *you* still want to?'

'Yes, I really do.' He takes another step closer. 'You know what? We could just order starters to begin with. And then if you don't want to stay you don't have to.'

I smile at him for the first time. 'Maybe.'

His lips edge up at the sides too, and I realise how very anxious he's seemed the whole time we've been here together until now.

'So shall we go?' he asks. 'If you're sure?'

'Yep.'

As we walk, I'm very careful not to get within arm-brushing distance and I think he's doing the same thing, so there's a slightly unnatural gap between us, but we do at least begin to talk semi-normally.

'No further foot or ankle injuries?' Tom asks as we go down the main steps out of the station.

'None.'

'Congratulations.'

'Thank you. I'm very much enjoying my pain-free walking.'

He directs me across the road in the direction of the embankment. 'I booked an Italian place. It has very good reviews.'

'Great.'

By the time we're shown to our table, I'm completely over the small talk. It's *fine*, but Tom used the phrase *I love you*, and – obviously – I don't really have much interest in anything right now other than establishing what he meant by that.

We're asked for our drink options.

I say, 'Tap water and a glass of house rosé,' without looking at the drinks menu.

'Tap water and a beer,' Tom says, equally quickly.

When the server's gone, Tom says, 'So.'

And I wait.

And then he says, 'I'm so, so sorry for leaving the room like that after we... after that night. For not saying anything.'

'What *would* you have said?' I ask, because now we're here I have to know.

He looks down at the table for a moment before meeting my eyes.

'I'd have said that I was really confused because I thought I was still waiting to hear back from Lola but I'd had the most amazing night of my life with you and I felt as though I was cheating on both of you.'

'Oh.' I'm pretty sure that is not what I was wanting to hear.

'Being honest.' He reaches out and touches my hand very

lightly just for a second. 'That is what I would have said if I was being honest. I was very confused. Because the whole time I've known you I've known that you're gorgeous and funny and had fast become my best friend even though I already had best friends, and also every time I had you in my arms I didn't want to let go, but the moment we met was when I was still thinking about Lola. I mean, at that point I was expecting to meet her and hoping very much to start a relationship with her. I had no expectation of meeting *you*, and at first I didn't think that way about you because I am not someone who would ever cheat on someone, and in my head I was hoping to get together with Lola. And I had – incorrectly – told her that I loved her and I felt as though that was a conversation that hadn't concluded, albeit a one-sided conversation.'

He pauses as our drinks arrive.

When we've thanked the server, Tom continues. 'So falling in love with you crept up on me. I didn't totally realise that I had. And when I realised that I had feelings for you I felt terrible about Lola. So I texted her to ask if she wanted to meet. And she said yes. And we met.'

Oh. I had not expected that. Oh no. Is he trying to tell me that he loves me as a friend and he's together with Lola? But... would he do it like this? I don't know. I'm very confused. I drink half my glass of water to try to clear my head.

'When I was waiting to meet her, I just wanted to tell you about it. And while I was with her, the thing was, I didn't want to tell her about my divorce. Or about wanting to backpack across Europe on a budget after watching *Race Across the World*. Or about my new shoes. All the things that I wanted to tell you about. And I just kept thinking about you. And then I realised that the person I wanted to talk to, be with, *love*, all the time, was you. Is you. And that I'd been the biggest idiot in the world. And I hope it isn't too late.'

'So...' I'm still not totally sure what he means. 'You met Lola and...'

'Quite quickly I told her that unfortunately I needed to leave and goodbye.'

'So...' I don't know how much I should allow myself to hope.

'I realised what you probably already knew, which is that the Lola thing was an insane fantasy, maybe related to my divorce. I love you. I don't think I ever loved her. I never really knew her; she was just an idea.'

'Yep, that's what I thought.'

'Were you tempted to tell me?' He takes a sip of his beer, holding my eyes with his the whole time his lips are on the glass, which I find myself loving.

'Kind of but also not,' I say. 'I think sometimes people have to find things out for themselves.'

'Yeah.' He takes another sip, still looking into my eyes. 'And I did find that out for myself. And I also realised how very much I love you.'

My heart gives an annoying leap.

I don't want my heart to be leaping. Five minutes ago he thought he was in love with Lola. I don't want to get hurt. I don't like getting hurt. I *really* love him, so if we *were* to start any kind of relationship, which is what I think he *might* be suggesting, there's every chance I *would* get hurt, because who's to know whether or not he really loves me.

'Obviously,' he says, 'if I were to tell you that I would like nothing more than to begin dating you, it would sound as though I was to some extent jumping straight from one relationship to another. I mean, my relationship with Lola *was* in fact imaginary. But at the time I suppose it wasn't imaginary to me.'

I think he might want me to say that no it doesn't sound like that. But it kind of does.

So I say, 'Yes.'

He nods. 'Yeah.'

I'm going to have to sniff in a minute to stop myself from crying. I don't want to do that. So I look at the view of the river to my left and try to catalogue the contents of my fridge to take my mind off *this*.

'Could I?' Tom clears his throat and I look back at him. 'Could I possibly... That is to say, could we be friends? For a while? And then if you thought you might like to, we could maybe start dating in due course?'

I stare at his very lovely face, my eyes suddenly feeling a lot dryer. I think that could be a very good idea.

'I have missed you,' I admit.

'Me too.'

'I don't want to do friends with benefits, though,' I say. It would hurt too much.

'Wasn't suggesting it,' Tom clarifies.

I hide a smile. 'Good then.'

'Happy to stay for starters?'

'They do have scallops.'

'And you can never say no to a scallop,' Tom says. He's right.

He looks at the menu, and then looks up again. 'Would you be happy to stay for a main too?'

'The truffle linguine does look very nice.'

'Would you stay if it were pie and mash?'

I pretend to consider. 'Debatable.'

Just after we've placed our orders, something occurs to me.

'Why didn't Lola meet you at Waterloo that evening?' It's always nice to have loose ends tied up. Like if you start reading a compelling mystery, you do want to get to the end.

'Her husband came home early and she couldn't go out,' Tom says. 'Not even joking. And you know, when she said it, I did not care at *all*. It was exactly the same for me as for you; it was an interesting detail to tie up a loose end, like reading to the end of a murder story you weren't even enjoying other than for the secret. She says they have an open relationship. Maybe her husband agrees, maybe he doesn't. Also, full disclosure, her son is called Tom. After me.'

'Wow.' I'm open-mouthed. I have to check my understanding of the situation. 'She named her son after another man she met while she was with the boy's father?'

'Yep.'

'Wow,' I repeat.

'Yep. And as she said it all, all I wanted to do was tell you about it. Because it's so ridiculous. And *I* was so ridiculous, believing that she and I had some kind of relationship.' His features are completely serious. 'I don't really know how, but, as I think I might already have told you, you've become my best friend. You're the person I want to talk to. Every time.'

'Same,' I say simply.

'Can I just say,' he says. 'I really, really hope that you don't think that the fact that Lola's married had any bearing on my feelings. It didn't. I'd already decided to leave when she told me. It was an after-thought question, like it was for you just then.'

I nod. I realise that I really do believe that Lola being married (or not) was irrelevant to the way he feels about her. And me.

And me. I still can't quite believe it.

'So... Starters *and* mains?' Tom says. 'And also... maybe dessert?'

'They do have tiramisu,' I point out.

'Rude not to.'

'Yeah.'

He reaches across the table and touches my hand again

before withdrawing his own – maybe scared that I don't want him to touch me – and then says, very simply, his eyes on mine, 'I love you.'

I look at his square shoulders straining his jacket the perfect amount, his squarer jaw, his lovely brown eyes with the fine lines at the corners, his beautiful lips, the slightly apprehensive expression on his face right now, and I think that what I like most about him is *him*, his kindness, his humour, just talking to him.

And suddenly I realise that my answer is easy.

'I love you too,' I say.

And then we just sit and beam at each other.

EPILOGUE
NADIA

It's the longest day of the year and I'm under the clock at Waterloo. Carole's here too, and we're waiting for Bea, Ruth and Tom.

It's exactly three years since we first met and we're going back to the tapas place as we do every year on this date.

Tom moved into my flat last year – we took things slowly for a while, until I suddenly realised that of *course* he really does long-term love me and we were just both missing out on a lot of very nice intimacy, basically, and we started dating properly.

We didn't come here together today, though. He's been watching cricket with his cousins while I had lunch with Marisa (who immediately entirely forgave me for the fake dating when I owned up after I started real-dating Tom) and then met a new client whose fiftieth I'm going to sing at (I'm now really enjoying working two days a week as a singer – weddings and other events – and three days in my accounting job).

'I see Bea and Ruth.' Carole's pointing and we stand together and watch them walking towards us holding hands. They're seventy-nine now, but are still both in very good health, thank goodness, and are planning a joint eightieth extravaganza for later in the year.

When they reach us – we stay where we are rather than going over to meet them halfway, because we have this tacit agreement that it's actually *under* the clock that we have to reconvene – we all share hugs.

It's so nice now between us – it's only been three years but it feels as though we're very old friends – but, even though it's only seven or eight hours since I last saw him, I really want Tom to be here to complete us. To complete *me*.

'Oh, there's Tom.' Bea points and we all turn to watch him hurry towards us.

'Hey.' He hugs the other three and then plants a quick kiss on my lips and gives me a very squeezy hug, not entirely letting go of me when we pull apart, which I love. 'How is everyone?'

Amidst the chat that follows, I catch Tom looking slightly oddly at me and then at the others.

'You okay?' I mouth at him.

He shakes his head, as though he's clearing it, and says, 'Yes, yes, definitely,' which makes me frown a little, because if you're completely okay aren't you actually just a bit surprised if someone seems concerned about you?

He's a bit quiet on the walk to the restaurant but finally seems back to his usual self by the time we go inside. Maybe the cricket was disappointing or something. I hope it isn't worse than that; it's very unusual for him to be like this. I hope he hasn't had bad news of any kind that he doesn't want to tell me about in front of the others.

Oddly, as soon as we're through the restaurant door, he first has a secretive word with a couple of the waiters, and then, on his way to the loo, stops for a little word with the guitar player on his platform. If it weren't for the fact that he seems kind of odd – a bit distant, like his thoughts are elsewhere – I'd think he had an anniversary surprise like a cake or something planned for us all.

As soon as he's back from the loo, Carole taps the table with her cutlery and says, 'I have news. I've met someone.'

Tom is as effusive and interested as the rest of us; whatever had him on edge (I'm guessing it *must* have been something like organising a cake) must be sorted now.

'Well,' Carole says in response to our chorus of questions, 'I went on a tennis holiday with my kids – I've always wanted to play and never had time so I had beginner's lessons – and I met him there. His name's Patrick. I've kept it quiet because I didn't want to jinx it or rush it after the Roger shit. But it's been nine months now and he seems very nice and I'm finally ready to believe that it's going to work out. So, yes, I'm just quietly happy.'

She gives a big cackle of laughter as we all laugh at the idea of Carole doing anything quietly, and then we all laugh more.

It's a lovely dinner.

Bea and Ruth fill us in on what they've been up to. (I really want to be like them when they're seventy-nine; I know the word *inspiration* is overused, and can be patronising, but they *are* an inspiration. As is Carole.)

'I love you all so much,' I tell them as we finish the champagne that Carole insisted on ordering to toast us all. 'Happy Waterloo Five meeting anniversary to all of us.'

'I think our taxi's here,' Ruth says eventually, and we all stand up.

Weirdly, no anniversary cake has materialised. Maybe it was

something to do with Bea's dairy intolerance, which interferes a lot with her pudding choices; perhaps that's why Tom seemed a little odd, maybe disappointed.

Carole's going back with Bea and Ruth to stay over at theirs for the night, as has become tradition, and Tom and I are going back to Waterloo together, as has also become tradition. Not least because we do live together now.

'Want to go for a walk by the river before we get the train?' Tom asks.

'Yes, cool.' It's a beautiful evening, not at all like the first time we met, weatherwise.

When we get down to the South Bank, Tom draws me towards him and kisses me, before moving back and holding me a little away from him and saying, 'I love you so very much.'

'I love you too.'

'I...' He looks round and a clearly drunk man bumps into us. 'Yeah, let's walk. Maybe over the bridge?'

'I like the bridge,' the drunk man says, looking worryingly like he's planning to accompany us on our walk.

Tom gathers my hand in his and says, 'Have a good evening,' to the man, and hurries me away towards the station.

When we get there, I begin to move across the concourse to where I'll be able to see the departures board without squinting, but Tom tugs me left.

And suddenly we're underneath the station clock and he's let go of my hand and, oh my goodness, he's on one knee in front of me.

My hands go to my face, before he reaches his up, and I put mine in his, in a kind of trance-like, autopilot way, because I'm basically *shocked*.

And then he says, 'Nadia, will you do me the very great honour of marrying me?'

All I can think again is *oh my goodness*.

I'm just so... so... well, there are no words.

I'm just...

'Nadia?' Tom's screwed his face up, as though he's really worried that I might say no.

'No, no,' I say quickly, to stop his worry.

'No?' He's gone completely rigid.

'Not no! I mean yes! I meant no, I won't say no!'

'So, to clarify?' he asks, sounding out each word carefully.

'My answer is yes. Yes, yes, yes please. There is nothing I would like more than to marry you.'

'Oh, thank God.' He stands up and draws me into the circle of his arms, and we remain there, just looking at each other, before, very gently, he rests his forehead against mine, and then moves his hands to cup my face, before kissing me with great care, as though I'm very, very precious.

'Were you planning this all evening?' I ask.

'Yep. I was going to do it when we met, with the others, and then I suddenly thought what an idiot I was. Like, what if you didn't want to say yes. Plus, maybe it should be more of a private moment. So then I had to cancel the celebratory song I'd arranged at the restaurant. And then I thought maybe I'd propose on the bridge but I think that man was going to follow us. So that was when I decided to do it under the clock.'

'The clock was the perfect place,' I say. 'It's *our* place.'

'Very true.' Tom kisses me again on the lips, very tenderly, and I wind my arms round his neck and pull him closer, and he deepens the kiss, and then we kiss and kiss and kiss under the clock. Our place.

* * *

MORE FROM JO LOVETT

Another book from Jo Lovett, *We Were on a Break*, is available to order now here:
   https://mybook.to/OnABreakBackAd

ACKNOWLEDGEMENTS

Thank you so much to my agent, Sarah Hornsley, for her always fabulous support and advice. Huge thanks also to the wonderful team at Boldwood. Thank you to Emily Yau, who's an amazing editor and a delight to work with. Thank you also to Helena Newton for copyedits, and Rachel Sargeant for proofreads; both of them are great! And thank you to Clare Stacey for the beautiful cover.

I have a lot of friends and family to thank, too many to name individually. Thank you, though, to all the people I've met under the clock at Waterloo over the years – it's an iconic meeting place and must have witnessed so many dramas, big and small. If only clocks could talk...

A special thank you to my family: in particular my sister Liz for her ongoing cheerleading, and my husband and children for their continued forbearance.

And thank you so much to readers!

ABOUT THE AUTHOR

Jo Lovett is the bestselling author of contemporary rom-coms including The House Swap. Shortlisted for the Comedy Women in Print Award, she lives in London.

Sign up to Jo Lovett's mailing list for news, competitions and updates on future books.

Follow Jo on social media:

- facebook.com/JoLovett-Turner
- x.com/JoLovettWrites

ALSO BY JO LOVETT

Another Time, Another Place

Can You Keep A Secret?

We Were on a Break

Meet Me Under the Clock

Boldwood
EVER AFTER

xoxo

JOIN BOLDWOOD'S ROMANCE COMMUNITY FOR SWEET AND SPICY BOOK RECS WITH ALL YOUR FAVOURITE TROPES!

SIGN UP TO OUR NEWSLETTER

HTTPS://BIT.LY/BOLDWOODEVERAFTER

Boldwood

Boldwood Books is an award-winning fiction publishing company seeking out the best stories from around the world.

Find out more at www.boldwoodbooks.com

Join our reader community for brilliant books, competitions and offers!

**Follow us
@BoldwoodBooks
@TheBoldBookClub**

Sign up to our weekly deals newsletter

https://bit.ly/BoldwoodBNewsletter